I0606617

Car wrecked, kidnapped, auctioned off, drugged, and moved five miles under the Pacific Ocean. If that wasn't enough, add amnesia to the mix. Darcey Callahan doesn't know who she is or where she's from. She doesn't remember who "the man" who purchased her is, and although her mind tells her she should not trust the man, her body betrays her. Is it possible that her body remembers what her mind cannot?

KUDOS for *Inescapable ~ Remembering~ Book 2*

In *Inescapable 2 ~ Remembering* by Madge H. Gressley, Darcey has been rescued from the human trafficking ring by Brad, but she can't remember who she is or where she comes from so she thinks Brad is just another man who has bought her. To top it all off, she discovers that she is now five miles beneath the ocean in a bio dome. There is no escape so Darcey must learn to deal with her situation and figure out who she can trust. Not an easy task when she has no memory of anything before she woke up as a captive in a human trafficking ring. Like the first book, this one is a fast-paced and intense page turner. You can't help rooting for Darcey as she struggles with her new reality. A really great read. ~ *Taylor Jones, The Review Team of Taylor Jones & Regan Murphy*

Inescapable ~ Book 2 ~ Remembering by Madge Gressley is the story of Darcey Callahan, a young woman who went from Texas to Peru to find her missing boyfriend and was abducted into a human trafficking ring. Brad, the boyfriend, discovered what had happened and rescued her, but Darcey had been in a car accident and remembers nothing before she woke up in the hands of the human traffickers. So she doesn't know who she is, she doesn't remember Brad, and she doesn't realize she has been rescued and is now free. So you can imagine her dismay when she learns that she is in a dome under the ocean off the coast of Peru, and there is no way out. Brad, on the other hand, remembers everything too clearly. He wants his lover back but knows he has to wait until she remembers him. In *Inescapable ~ Book 2 ~ Remembering*, like its predecessor *Inescapable ~ Book 1 ~ The Beginning*, Gressley's character development is superb and the story is gripping. Thought-provoking as well fast-paced and intense, this is one you won't want to put down. ~ *Regan Murphy, The Review Team of Taylor Jones & Regan Murphy*

INESCAPABLE

Remembering
Book 2

Madge H. Gressley

A Black Opal Books Publication

DEDICATION

*This book is dedicated to God who gave me the talent to write
it; to my family and friends who without their encouragement
it might never have been written;
and to my late husband,
Stu who always said,
"I taught her everything she knows."*

His touch burned my soul, and it remembered.
I searched my mind. It remembered nothing.

He knew he loved her
the first moment he laid eyes on her,
but his soul…ah, his soul remembered
the love of an eternity.

PREFACE

arcey's head throbbed, and her mouth was full of cotton balls.

I know this feeling, she thought, trying to work through the fog swirling her mind. *I've felt it before. I've been drugged. Lilly drugged me, but why? How?* Then it came to her—the pastries!

She rubbed her temples, and her arm hit something. It was a shuttle seat. She was lying on the floor of a shuttle. Using the seat for leverage, she tried to sit up and managed to look out the side of the shuttle. She didn't recognize the place. It looked as though it was still under construction. Large stacks of drywall and other building supplies lined the walls.

This must be one of the residential areas still under construction.

Darcey turned and carefully peered over the back of the seat. Across the way was a room that resembled the operations room, only on a smaller scale. Inside, Lilly frantically flipped switches and pushed buttons. Darcey could tell Lilly didn't have a clue about what she was doing.

Panic began to set in. *I have to get out of here. Now!*

She scooted out of the shuttle onto the concrete floor from the side away from the room. Crawling on her hands and knees to the back of the shuttle, she looked desperately for some way out. A short distance from the vehicle, she saw an open doorway. Glancing back over her shoulder, she saw Lilly still working on the control panel. Darcy looked back at the open doorway tentatively.

There was no cover between the shuttle and the doorway. Could she run fast enough? She still felt groggy. However, if she waited until her head stopped spinning, it might be too late.

I'm going to chance it.

Moving cautiously on her hands and knees, she inched out from behind the shuttle. She glanced back. Lilly still had her back to the windows that gave an unobstructed view of the unfinished space where Darcey was going to run through. Darcey moved out a little farther, inched herself up into a bent over position, and gave one last look at Lilly before she sprinted through the doorway. Once in the corridor, she ran as hard and as fast as she could, hoping she was going in the direction of the closest connecting corridor.

She found the connecting corridor and looked for directional signs on the wall—there were none. She guessed that she was in the center ring but had no idea which way led to the outer ring or the connecting tunnel to the main dome. She took a deep breath and ran as fast as she could, hoping she had chosen correctly.

CHAPTER 1

Awakening

Her eyes fluttered open. Just that brief motion sent shock waves through her head. It felt like a vice grip had been placed around her skull, and, with each movement, it grew tighter.

"Where am I?" she groaned. The sound of her voice echoed in her skull. She placed her hands on either side of her head. It felt like it would explode if she didn't hold it together.

How did I get here? Think. What is the last thing I remember? I was being stuffed into a car. I had been sold. Nicho—

In a flash, it all came flooding back. She rolled over, buried her face in the pillow, and screamed.

"No, no, no, no!" she screamed. Tears flowed unabated, as her clenched fists beat against the mattress. "What am I to do?" she moaned. "How am I going to live through this? How can I get out of this?" She sniffed and wiped her nose with the tail of her shirt. "If I did—no, do—where will I go? I don't know who I am. I don't know where I am. I don't have any money. I don't know anyone who will help me! Oh, God, what am I going to do?"

Panic took hold, and she began to hyperventilate. Gasping for air and struggling to sit up, she felt strong but gentle hands pull her into an upright position.

A man gently sat her up on the side of the bed. "Here, let me help you up. Put your head between your knees. That will help."

"Wh—wh—where am I?" she asked, between ragged gulps of air.

He gently rubbed her back and tried to control the urge to wrap his arms around her "You are safe," he said.

She looked up to see who that mesmerizing velvet voice belonged to and lost what little breath she had left in her lungs as she gazed into emerald green eyes.

It's him! It's the man from the gala.

She inwardly cringed and tried to move away, but there was no place to go. She was too dizzy to run. His hand on her back was doing crazy things to her heart that she couldn't explain. Finally, the stress that had been building came crashing in on her. She couldn't hold on any longer to the anger, frustration, and fear that had sustained her these past months. She hugged her middle to keep from breaking in two as the dam broke, and a flood of tears cascaded down her face.

The pain of seeing Darcey cry hurt Brad down to the bottom of his soul. He reached out, gently pulled her to his chest, and cradled her close, letting her cry herself out until there was nothing left but hiccups. Gently rocking her, he caressed her hair and kissed the top of her head, murmuring softly that everything was going to be okay, inwardly cursing Santiago for doing this to her.

I will have that bastard's head on a platter, he swore.

Slowly, she unwound her arms from her middle and wrapped them around him. He thought his heart would burst. The feel of her was ecstasy. He wanted to hold her closer, tighter, until her body melded with his, and they were one.

No matter how he longed to make that happen, for now, he couldn't do anything more than hold her. If he pushed her, he knew he would lose her. She had to learn to trust him—she had to want him.

When her crying jag subsided, it hit her. She was wrapped in the stranger's arms and hers were clinging to him like he was a life preserver that had been thrown to a drowning victim. *What am I doing? What am I thinking? This feels so right, yet so wrong. This man bought me. He paid money for me, like he would for a piece of meat. No! No! No! This is not right!*

She forced herself away from him. He let her go, and when his arms fell away, she felt cold, extremely cold.

"Just go away and leave me alone," she snuffled and picked up the tail of her shirt to wipe her nose.

He handed her a box of tissues he picked up from the bedside table. "Here, use these."

She glared at him as she jerked a tissue out of the box. It made her nervous as he watched every little move she made.

It's like he's waiting for me to do something that he doesn't like.

"Thanks," she said sarcastically and blew her nose loudly. The tissue fluttered out in front of her.

That wasn't very lady-like, she admonished herself, *Oh what the hell, he bought me and what he sees is what he's got, like it or not. Why should I care?*

A smile played around his mouth as he watched her small display of defiance. "Would you like some breakfast? It's been quite a while since you ate last."

"I don't know if I'm hungry or not," she said petulantly. "My stomach is all upset, and my head hurts, and I feel awful." She buried her face in her hands and started to cry all over again.

What's the matter with me? I don't cry, she thought angrily wiping at the tears sliding down her face with her fingers.

He reached for her again and held her tight, and it still felt right. She didn't fight him and rested her forehead on his chest.

"I will get you something for your head, and see about having some food sent in for you," he said, releasing her. "What would you like? We probably have most anything you might want," Smiling, he pulled a tissue from the box and sopped up the remaining tears from her face.

"I would like a hamburger with everything on it, fries, and a strawberry milkshake,", she immediately replied, sniffing and blowing her nose again.

Whoa! I didn't even think about that, she thought, startled at her immediate response. *I just blurted it out. Now where did that come from? Was that something from my past life?*

She stared at the crumpled tissue in her hands. In all the months, she had been held captive, she hadn't thought about what food she liked or didn't like, and no one ever asked what she liked. She just ate what was prepared and set before her, never questioning if she liked it, or if she might have liked something different.

He gave her a lopsided grin. "I think we can handle that." That had always been Darcey's favorite when they'd eaten out on Saturday's, he remembered. Maybe her memory's starting to come back.

Butterflies erupted in her stomach when her eyes met his.

What is the matter with me? She closed her eyes in order to break the connection.

"Please, where is the bathroom?" she asked, out of desperation, her eyes still closed.

She had to get away from this man. Maybe she could lock herself in the bathroom again. But that wouldn't solve anything. There would be no Nicho to come rescue her this time.

Oh, I miss Nicho. She drew her bottom lip between her teeth as she thought of him.

"The bathroom is the first door on your right," he told her. "I'll order your food."

She scooted off the edge of the bed and lost her balance, her head spinning again. He put his hand out and caught her before she even knew she was falling.

He raised one eyebrow and tried to hide the grin that was threatening to escape. "Steady. Would you like me to walk with you to the bathroom?"

"No, I think I can make it on my own," she said curtly, squirming out of his hold. "I'm just a little dizzy. Must be because I haven't eaten in a while." *What else could it be?*

She steadied herself and moved over to the bedroom door then turned back. "First door on the right?"

He nodded and watched her as she held onto the door frame for balance.

She took a deep breath, squared her shoulders, and walked out into the hall.

He called the Bajo el Mar kitchen and asked them to whip up a couple of burgers with the works, some fries, and two strawberry milkshakes. They told him it would be about twenty minutes and it would be delivered.

She closed the bathroom door and leaned against it for several minutes before deciding she had better take care of the necessities. All done, she placed her hands on the cold marble of the vanity and sighed. She raised her eyes to stare at the woman in the mirror.

Steadying herself with one hand, she pushed the shell-shaped handle down to release the flow of water into the porcelain basin. The woman in the mirror stared back at her.

She looked a mess. Her copper-colored hair was badly in need of a good brushing. She had the haunting look of sadness, accentuated by dark circles that rimmed her hazel eyes. Her face looked drawn and pale.

Will I ever know her? she wondered. She dropped her eyes and gazed absently at the water as it splashed into the basin from the dolphin shaped faucet. "Stop this. Pull yourself together." She looked up, squared her shoulders, and scolded the person in the mirror. "This is where you are now, and it isn't going to change anytime soon if ever, so you'd best get used to it."

The cold water she vigorously splashed on her face made her feel a tiny bit better.

A nice hot bath would feel even better, she thought, drying her face on an ivory-colored hand towel. She gazed longingly at the gray-green marble tub that filled half the bathroom, imagining her body immersed in a steamy tub full of fragrant bubbles.

When she walked out of the bathroom, she was startled to see the green-eyed man leaning casually against the wall waiting for her.

"Thought I'd wait for you and show you the rest of the place," he said pushing himself away from the wall. "The food just arrived and we can eat at the bar." He gently took her by the elbow and guided her into an enormous living area.

His hand on her elbow shot waves of desire and passion through her body. The place where he touched burned, the heat sped up her arm, and then there was no air for her to breathe. She jerked her arm away from his grasp, stopping the heat that was setting her body on fire.

He raised an eyebrow. A ghost of a smile touched the corners of his mouth as he let her precede him into the living room, watching as she briskly rubbed her hands up and down her arms.

The living area had a vaulted ceiling that covered the living room, the dining area, and the kitchen. A dark, marble-topped bar separated the kitchen from a formal dining area and a large, dark-brown, leather sofa and matching chairs defined the living room area. A big, flat-screen TV hung on the wall over a large stone-front fireplace. She noticed that a holographic insert stood where the logs would have been in a real fireplace and decided it wouldn't be quite the same as having a real fire burning like the ones at Vargas's. Regardless of the pretend fireplace, the entire area had a cozy, comfortable feel. The light in the room made her feel like it was a sunny day and then, she realized there were no windows.

Odd. Her eyes searched the room.

He led her over to the bar where he had placed the burgers and milkshakes. He waited until she had hiked herself up on the barstool before he also slid onto the stool next to her.

It smells awesome, she thought. Her mouth began to water as the delicious aroma assailed her nostrils.

She had her burger almost gone before she realized that he was also eating, but much slower. He seemed to be enjoying watching her wolf down her food.

"What!?" she exclaimed, glaring at him and annoyed with herself for scarfing the burger down. She took a pull from the straw in her milkshake. "I guess it's been longer than I thought since I ate last. I didn't know I was so hungry."

I know I should feel embarrassed, but I don't. What

he bought is what he's got. So he can learn to deal with it—or not!

"I'll order you another if you want. It will just take a few minutes for it to get here," he said, enjoying the un-ladylike scene she was making stuffing the last bite of the burger in her mouth. Then she sexily licked off the small dash of mustard that lingered in the corner of her perfect mouth, setting an explosion of butterflies off in Brad's stomach. It was all he could do to contain the impulse to pull her into his arms and ravish those perfect lips.

She looked at him out of the corner of her eye, notic-ing the delighted expression on his face. "No, I'll finish the fries and shake. I'll be fine," she said, stiffly, muster-ing as much dignity as she could, considering her recent lack of manners. She was not going to give him any more opportunities to laugh at her.

"When you're feeling up to it, I will show you to your quarters, they should be ready by now," he replied. He was trying to contain a laugh that threatened to escape his lips as he watched the look of indignation cross her face.

Slipping off his bar stool, he gathered up the lunch dishes and placed them on a large oval tray for the café staff to pick up later.

"Yes, that would be okay. I would like to clean up," she said, wiping her mouth with her napkin, still not look-ing at him as she placed it on the tray with the dishes. She felt dirty, her muscles hurt, and she was tired. "What time is it? I've lost all track of time," she asked, looking around.

"It's almost noon. If you're ready then?" He held out his hand for her to take. She reluctantly placed her hand in his. He felt the electric jolt he always felt when they touched. The jolt ran through his body then set off anoth-er explosion of butterflies in his stomach and a wave of desire. Startled, as she suddenly jerked her hand out of his, he searched her face. Surely that meant she had felt it, too.

A thousand tiny pulses of heat surged through her body when her hand touched his. She jerked it back and rubbed it down the side of her leg trying to dispel the inexplicable feeling his touch had created.

What was that? she questioned, looking at her hand.

He stepped aside for her to precede him out the front door. She stepped hesitantly out the door and into a wide, oval, gray tunnel. The fact that there was no defined division between the floor, walls, and ceiling, unnerved her.

What kind of place is this? She shivered as her eyes traveled over the gray expanse of the corridor. *Is this another place where I'll be locked up again? This time, is it a place with no windows? Will I ever see daylight again? At least at Vargas's, there were windows.* The questions raced through her mind. A twinge of fear crept in, and she shivered again.

She looked again at her surroundings, and the twinge became outright fear as a feeling of foreboding enveloped her. She grabbed the man's arm. "Where are we? What kind of place is this?" she demanded, her nails dug into his skin.

Brad was taken by surprise at her reaction. He had become so used to the dome, he forgot she knew nothing of this project, let alone that it was five miles down, on the ocean floor.

"I'm sorry." He winced, loosening her grip on his arm. "I should have explained to you right away where you are. You are in the bio-dome. This is the project I have been working on but was unable to tell you about." He stopped and turned to face Darcey, holding her hand as he spoke. He could feel her trembling. "Let me explain," he said, gently placing his arm around her shoulders. "A group from my senior university engineering class started this project as an experiment to create an underwater habitat capable of sustaining life over an extended period of time."

He hesitated to add the real reason for the project. A group of independent scientists had discovered that over the past three decades, the Earth's ozone layer had been depleting at a rate far faster than anyone had anticipated. Brad hadn't even told Ty and the guys who were working on fixing the damage caused by Armando's attempted sabotage. Because the ozone problem was serious, the fewer people who knew about the dome, the better chance it had of staying under wraps until it was absolutely necessary to let the public know. If that information ever leaked out, there would be worldwide panic. So, until the time was right, the rest of the billions of Earth's inhabitants were being kept in the dark.

The controlling global government, the United Federation of Nations (UFN), had been keeping a tight lid on the problem and vehemently denied any scientific research that contradicted their policy. They suggested it was being used as propaganda to cause a worldwide panic to bring down the government. Brad had heard rumors that the UFN had been researching the possibility of off-world colonization, but no hard facts had been found.

His professor at the university had been one of the scientists on the team that had discovered the rapid decline of the ozone layer. He encouraged Brad and his team to quietly develop a habitat that could sustain people when the inevitable happened. However, it was certain that if the UFN discovered the real purpose behind the Bio-Dome, they would claim it for themselves. If that happened, it was a given that any future domes built would be only for the elite of the world. There was much money to be made by selling space in the dome to high-ranking officials from around the world. That had never been part of Brad's plan. His had been, and still was purely humanitarian.

"If successful," he continued, "it would, when finished, be a complete city on the ocean floor. It would have everything a city should have. It would include businesses, theaters, restaurants, schools, hospitals, parks, farming, and would be capable of housing up to five hundred families with additional domes being added as needed. We were almost ready to take our design from the drawing board to reality when some VIPs, who had been closely watching our progress, stepped forward and made us an offer we couldn't refuse for the plans to our dome, the biosphere ecosystem, and the filtration system. Since I was the head engineer on the project, they hired me to build it. Now, here we are, five years later and five miles down on the ocean floor off the coast of Peru. The only access to the dome is by specially built submarines." He paused, noticing the blood draining from her face. "It is all perfectly safe. You have nothing to worry about. In the next few months, the dome will be ready for its grand opening."

"Fff—ff—five miles? A submarine?" she stammered, panic setting in. There was no air to breathe, her knees began to buckle, and she slipped from under the man's arm.

He has to be kidding. Doesn't he? she thought, as the floor rushed up to meet her.

Before she reached the floor, he grabbed her, putting his arm around her waist, holding her up.

"Easy," he said. "There's nothing to be afraid of. You are entirely safe," he reassured her.

"That's easy for you to say," she exclaimed, her breath coming in short gasps. "You haven't been kidnapped, locked up, and sold. How do I know you don't have something like that planned for me right now? Right here in this place, where there's no hope of escape?"

She stared at him, fear in her eyes, as she squirmed her way out of his grasp and almost fell again.

He grabbed her again. "Hey, calm down! You're going to hurt yourself." He gave her a small shake. "I promise, you are in no danger. You are safe and no one is going to lock you up ever again," He emphasized "ever again," his brows coming together as he felt her breathing hard.

She wasn't sure what he had just said. She was too busy trying to control the panic that threatened to overtake her, as well as attempting to block out what his touch was doing to her. "I have to sit down," she said, short of breath.

He kept his arm, around her waist and steered her the short distance to a strange-looking door with no doorknob. She watched as he took a card from his pocket and swiped it through a slot in a small black box attached to the wall beside the door. The door silently slid open.

He guided her through the door and into a beautiful room much like his quarters, but the décor was lighter with a feminine touch. Her shoes sank into the plush cream-colored carpet covering the floor. The soft colors of the room had a calming effect as she made her way across the room and sat down on the sofa. She put her head between her knees and breathed slowly. The man watched from across the room, worry lines creasing his brow.

This had always been Nicho's remedy when I had a panic attack, she remembered, drawing a ragged breath.

He walked into the kitchen and came back carrying a glass of water. "Here, this should help," he said, handing her the glass.

"Thanks," she said, avoiding touching him as she

took the glass. She knew she couldn't withstand another episode of the feelings that raged through her body from his touch.

He watched as she drank some of the water resisting the urge to sit down beside her and comfort her. His heart cried for her, knowing how this must be driving her crazy not knowing who she was, who he was, and being in a strange place. It couldn't be good for her sanity. His only hope was that she would start regaining some of her memory soon and that their connection to each other would be strong enough to pull her back to him from the abyss she had fallen into.

Taking the glass, he placed it on the triangle shaped, coffee table in front of the sofa. "Better?"

"Yes, thanks," she replied, trying not to look into those green eyes, which she felt could look right into her soul. It was all too unsettling.

Feeling a tiny bit better, she glanced around the room, the woman in her appreciating the beauty of it. The curved sofa she was sitting on was upholstered in a beautiful patterned fabric of muted tones of sage green and ivory. The matching chairs complemented the sofa in a solid fabric of a darker shade of sage green.

Across from the room was a formal dining area with a rectangle glass-topped chrome table and eight matching chrome chairs. The chairs should have looked hard and cold, but in the soft light of the room they glowed warmly. A light-colored, marble-topped bar separated the dining area from the kitchen area that was filled with the latest in appliances. Four chrome and leather bar stools stood like soldiers in front of the bar.

There were no windows in this space either, yet there was some sort of light that did not come from the table lamps or the wall sconces. It was a defused light, like daylight.

How can this be? Five miles under the ocean there is no daylight. How can this be? she wondered, shaking her head.

"Do you have a question?" he asked, watching the puzzled expression on her face.

"Yes." She turned and looked at him. "How come it looks like daylight in here when we are, as you say, five miles down on the ocean floor? How's that possible?"

"It's possible because of the biosphere ecosystem and filtration system designed by my friend Mike Bellington. The ecosystem controls all of the atmospheric conditions within the dome, and that includes artificial daylight. I'll explain it all to you later when you've had a chance to rest."

Her mind was in a whirl as she tried to absorb the information he had just given her. She wandered around the room, still in awe of the surroundings that he had said were to be her living space. Reaching the door on the far wall, she pushed it open slowly and peeked around it. Her eyes widened as she took in the charming bedroom before her.

The lush, cream-colored carpeting from the living room continued into the bedroom where a king-sized bed sat squarely on a six-inch high riser in the middle of the room. A cream-colored silk coverlet trimmed in sage green spread across the bed, its edges just brushing the floor of the riser. Mounds of light sage green, ivory, and dark sage green pillows were piled high against the tall ornate, whitewashed wooden headboard.

A seating area in front of the bed's footboard consisted of two matching chairs, upholstered in dark sage green brocade, and an elegant marble-topped table with a stylish cut-glass lamp sitting on it. Wandering farther into the room, she spied another seating area at the back of the bed, just behind the headboard. The tall headboard had obscured it until she walked around the bed. There, a sofa and chair, matching the ones in front, completed the furniture in the room. Also attached to the wall opposite the seating area was a flat screen TV and below, bookshelves filled with books of all sorts.

Continuing on, she opened the door opposite the right side of the bed that led into a large, over-sized marble, chrome, and glass bathroom. Sitting in the middle of the stone tiled floor was what she was sure must be the bathtub but, it looked more like a mini-marble swimming pool. She looked up at the ceiling since the lighting above the tub made it seem as though the light was streaming down from a skylight, but there was no skylight.

A glass walk-in shower with multiple showerheads occupied one corner of the bath. Elegant brushed chrome fixtures and two raised, translucent blue glass basins accented the ivory marble-topped counter that ran the length of one wall. Beveled mirrors extended from the counter top to the ceiling above it. The toilet and bidet were discretely hidden behind a blue, glass-block wall.

Another door led into a huge, walk-in closet and dressing room. Gasping, she noticed that the closet was already full of clothes.

My clothes. He brought my clothes, she thought, a smile spreading across her face as she took a closer look, running her hand down the row of dresses and across the shelves of sweaters and slacks.

Seeing her clothes seemed to make everything okay and the anxiety she had been feeling slowly began to fade away. She didn't even stop to analyze why these familiar things were so important to her.

She swung around to see him standing in the doorway. His arms were folded and he was leaning casually against the door frame, with a lopsided grin that was doing crazy things to her insides.

She took in every inch of his very male body. It wasn't just his touch that drove her crazy—it was everything about him.

He swung his arm around, encompassing the whole of the quarters, and pushed himself away from the door frame. "Well, what do you think?"

She tore her eyes away from him before answering. "It's beautiful, and this all for me?" she asked, doing a three-sixty, her arms out wide, looking at it all again. She still was unable to wrap her mind around the idea that all of what she saw was hers.

"Yes, this is yours," he said, grinning.

He resisted the overwhelming urge to pick her up and swing her around then toss her on the bed, and make love to her, but he knew he couldn't, not yet anyway. He struggled to put a damper on his growing desire as he watched her graceful body twirling around in front of him. He knew every inch, every curve and it was driving him crazy not to be able to take her in his arms.

"I'll leave you now, so you can have your bath. It's been a long thirty-six hours. You need to rest, and I have things to look after," he said, unable to stop smiling at her. "You are free to look around. Your door will never be locked unless you lock it." With that said, he turned and left her standing in the middle of the bedroom.

What did he just say? My door will never be locked? I am free to look around, she thought in amazement. *He bought me. I'm his property so I'm supposed to be his slave, aren't I? I must have missed something. Something I didn't hear correctly.*

She ran out of the bedroom, hoping to catch up with him. The concept of him giving her her freedom never entered her mind.

She reached the front door and saw it was closed. It was a sliding door but did not have the usual handhold to use in order to slide it open. She pushed and then pulled on the door, but it would not budge.

She backed up, exasperated with herself because she couldn't figure out how to open one stupid door, when it suddenly slid open. The man was standing there looking at her with that goofy, lopsided grin of his, making her stomach do summersaults once again.

"Sorry, I forgot to show you how to open the door and to give you your ID card that will let you go most everywhere," he said, stepping back into the room.

He handed her a small plastic card the size of a credit card. It had a photo of the woman in the mirror on it, with the name Darcey Callahan in big, bold letters printed underneath the picture. She stood, looking at the card and then at the man, in confusion.

"Yes, that is your name. You are Darcey Callahan from Dallas, Texas. You and I have been dating for over a year. I know this is a lot to throw at you right now, and I'm sorry. So please don't stress over it. Take it slow, give yourself time to take it all in and remember who you are. I will help you as much as I can," he told her in a rush, not knowing exactly how to handle the situation without scaring her more.

She was dumbfounded. Her legs wouldn't hold her and she collapsed on the floor. He came over and squatted down in front of her, taking her hands in his. Electric shocks radiated up her arms where her hands touched his. All of a sudden, there was no air to breathe. She had an overwhelming urge to throw her arms around him and bury her face in the curve of his neck. Instead, she struggled to let the urge pass and sat there frozen. Her mind was slipping into a numbing void as she stared at the man in front of her. She was not actually seeing him at all. Her heart beat wildly.

"It's okay," he said, drawing her into his arms to

comfort her. "You are safe now. You no longer have to worry about what will happen to you. I didn't plan on telling you this so soon, but I realized you had to have an ID card, and it would have to have your name and photo on it. I didn't have a choice." He paused, waiting for her to absorb all he had just said.

Darcey pulled back out of his arms, a million questions racing through her mind. She couldn't give voice to any of them. All she could do was stare at him, her mouth open. It became increasingly hard for her to breathe.

A small frown slid across his face as she pulled back. "It's okay. When you're ready, I will tell you everything that I know about what happened to you. But in the meantime, let me show you how to use your card."

He would leave it at that for now and hoped that changing the subject would alleviate some of the stress she was feeling right now. He took her hands and pulled her up, mesmerized by her hazel eyes as she looked into his.

Brad averted his eyes to break the connection and cleared his throat as he began explaining how the ID card worked. "You take your card and slide it like this, in this slot." He pointed to a small back box on the inside resembling the one on the outside of the door. He took the card from her hand and slid it through the slot in the small black box, and the door closed. He slid it again, and it opened. With one last pass of the card, he closed the door.

"To lock the door," he said, pointing to the button on the top of the box. "Just push this button here, and you will see a red light come on to indicate the door is locked. Push the button again, and the door will be unlocked. Do you want to try it?"

Brad looked at her bewildered expression as he handed the card back to her. Maybe he should have handled it differently, slower, but it was too late now.

"I—I—ge—ges—guess," she stammered, her mind still in a jumble, trying to make some sense of what she had heard him say.

Darcey took the card from him and stared at it, unable to comprehend how the face and name on the card could be her. The face looked like the one in the mirror, the one that had been looking back at her these past months, but she felt no connection to the name or to the face.

"Here, let me help you," he said, partially drawing her out of the stupor she had slipped into.

Blankly, she looked up as Brad took her hand holding the card and slid the card through the slot. The door opened. Then he repeated it, and the door closed. Then he took the forefinger of her hand and pushed the button, and the red light came on. He pushed it again, and the light went off.

"There, see how easy it is? There's also a slot outside beside the door. Want to try it by yourself?"

He grinned at her, but instead of his smile lifting her spirits, her face reddened in frustration that he had made her feel like a helpless child.

"No, I've got it," she said curtly, yanking her hand out of his.

She couldn't tell if her heart was beating rapidly because of his touch or because she was agitated at herself for acting like a fool.

"Well then, I'll be off," he said. He needed to leave before he made matters worse. He had to give her some space and time to set things right in her mind. "Oh yes, one more thing." He paused just inside the door. "There's a pager on the bar. Use it if you need me. It is synced with my phone. Remember to take it with you if you go exploring. This is an enormous place and, until you know it, it is easy to get lost," he cautioned, and then he was gone.

Trying to calm her irritation at his condescending manner and being treated like a child, she was still attempting to put the things she had just been told in order, but nothing stayed in place. It all kept jumping around. She looked at the card in her hand and then at the slot on the wall. Dazed, she took the card and slid it through the slot. She watched as the door opened. She slid it again, and the door closed. She had no idea how many times she numbly repeated the process before the jumbled mess in her mind settled and she could think again.

The man had said her name was Darcey Callahan and that she was from Dallas. Those names meant nothing to her. They didn't jog anything in her memory. She had thought she would feel relieved to know her real name, but it was as foreign to her as the man. She felt no connection to it. The only things real to her were these past months.

"He said don't worry about it. What good would it do anyway? What can I do about it? It is what it is. How would worry change anything?" she grumbled to herself.

It won't, but when you see him, have him tell you about this Darcey Callahan. You may be surprised what you find out about her.

Who are you? Get out of my head! Leave me alone!

I can't leave you alone, we are one and the same. You just haven't remembered me yet, but you will. I'm here to help you find your way back... The voice was fading away. *...you will remember...*

Then, it was gone.

She shook her head and looked at the card in her hand and the face on the card. Yes, it matched the one in the mirror, but she still didn't know her. She only knew who she had been for these past months—Saleem.

She took a slow turn and walked back to the bedroom. She needed to get cleaned up. She felt sticky, dirty, and was sure she didn't smell too pleasant either.

The water began to flow into the marble tub as she turned on the tap. She discovered soap, washcloth, and towels behind the rattan doors of a large, freestanding cabinet across from the tub. Slowly, inch-by-inch, she slipped into the steaming water. It felt like heaven as the bubbles engulfed her body right up to her chin.

Later and feeling much better, and dressed in a pair of jeans and a white boyfriend shirt, she walked into the kitchen and looked in the gleaming, stainless steel fridge to see what there might be to eat. It was empty. She turned to look through the cabinets. They too were empty of food, but were stocked with all types of cooking utensils, pots and pans, dinnerware, drink ware of all kinds, and silverware.

She grabbed the pager the man had left her, put it in her pocket, and opened the front door. She stepped out into the corridor, and looked left, and then right, seeing nothing, but the gray expanse of the corridor in either direction. She turned around and saw the slot for an ID card on the wall beside the door. The number 308 was stenciled in bold, black numbers above the slot. She made a mental note of the number, slid the card, and the door closed.

"That was easy," she commented to herself.

Darcey had no idea where either way led so she tossed a mental coin—heads go right, tails left. Heads it is. She started walking, noticing every so often, there would be another number with a slot beside a door. She guessed these were other living quarters.

Darcey had gone maybe fifty feet when she heard a soft humming sound coming up behind her. With a quick turn of her head, she saw a golf-cart-type vehicle heading in her direction. She jumped back and pressed herself flat against the wall to let it pass. Too late, she noticed there had been no need to move. There was plenty of room for her to keep walking and the cart to pass.

Feeling foolish, she gave a half-hearted smile to the people in the cart as they drove by. The cart turned left a short distance in front of her. She jogged to where it had turned. It was another corridor.

Interesting.

Standing in the middle of the junction of the two corridors, she looked around to find something to help her to remember her way back. She saw, on either side of the connecting corridor's walls, directional signs with arrows pointing in the direction the cart went. Bajo el Mar Café and Main Street Plaza stood out in bold, black letters. Then she turned to look at the sign on the corridor wall behind her. It had numbers 300-325 with an arrow pointing right and 399-375 pointing left.

Now that she had her bearings, Darcey took off down the corridor, following the cart. She could see farther on that the corridor she was walking down opened into a partially finished area. However, before she reached it, another corridor intersected the one she was in, running perpendicular to it.

Looking right, she saw the Bajo el Mar Café that the man had said he ordered their food from. She paused and peered through the row of large glass windows into the interior of the cafeteria. Lots of tables and chairs filled the dining area. A cafeteria-style food line ran down the side, several vending machines sat against one wall, and a beverage station with every imaginable beverage available sat next to the vending machines. She made a mental note to come back here after she finished exploring.

There were only a few people in the café, and she didn't see the man, so she continued on, toward the open area. Reaching it, she saw that it was a plaza and still under construction. Many workers were bustling about, working on what appeared to be twenty large rooms that ringed the outer edge of the circular plaza.

What had the man said? It would be like living in a city, but under water? This could be a shopping area, like a mall.

Walking on into the center of the plaza, she realized it would be a park when completed. She marveled at the workers laying sod around a stone paver sidewalk that circled a fountain. There were park benches stacked just off to the side, waiting to be installed in the grassy area.

Looking behind her, she noticed that the corridor she had just come through, continued on across to the other side of the plaza, and she headed toward it. Reaching the next intersection, she saw directional signs again. The Services & Maintenance arrows pointed in both directions. The signs with Pacific Theatre, Costal Library, Stingray Bowling Alley, Hydroponics, and Bajo el Mar Café pointed to the right. Corporate Offices, Pacific K-12 School, ORCA Medical Wing, and Bajo el Mar Café pointed to the left.

Then it hit her—the perpendicular corridors were circular.

This is strange. What kind of place is this—no windows, but yet, it's like the sun is shining, and the air feels fresh like you're outside? And, he tells me this is five miles underwater with some kind of ecosystem running it all? she wondered in amazement. *I'll have to ask him to explain all of this now that I have my wits about me again. And I'm going to have to ask his name, too. I just can't keep calling him the man. Strange, he hasn't bothered to introduce himself. Odd.*

She wandered on, turned left, and walked toward the corporate offices. That seemed to her the best place to look for him. There were more people here going about their business.

The doors to most offices were either open or had large glass windows that opened onto the corridor. Everyone she saw or met was friendly. They smiled and said "Hello" as if they knew who she was, but otherwise left her alone.

Strolling past several offices, she casually looked in each of them, smiling when she found the office happened to be occupied, still hoping she would see the man, but she didn't find him in any of the offices. She walked on. Since she didn't have a watch, she guessed it had been maybe an hour or so that had passed by the time she eventually wound up back at the Bajo el Mar Café. Darcey stood outside, debating whether to go in.

I sure could use a cup of coffee. Do I need money? she fretted. *I don't have any, but I could ask. Surely, they could afford to let me have one cup of coffee on the house.*

Her mind made up, her hand reaching for the door, she pushed it open and hesitantly walked in. Then she saw him walking across the floor toward her with that lopsided grin of his turning her knees to jelly. Her heart beat faster, and butterflies erupted in her stomach. She felt excited to see him and didn't take the time to analyze why—she just was excited to see him.

Brad saw Darcey hesitate before coming in the door and hurried across the floor to meet her. She looked lost but, seeing him, her face lit up with a big smile and Brad's heart took wings.

"Darcey, I'm so glad you found your way here. Are you hungry?" he asked, taking her hand and leading her over to a table. "Sit and I will get you something."

"All I want is a big cup of coffee, please." Darcey smiled at him still holding his hand as she sat down. The vibes she was feeling felt right and she let her hand linger in his grasp, relishing the heat from his touch as it raced through her body.

Brad looked down at their hands and then up into her eyes.

He wasn't sure what he saw there, but it wasn't fear—acceptance maybe? Was she feeling the connection as he felt it? His heart pounded.

"I'll get your coffee. Are you sure you don't want something to eat?" he asked, again.

"No, just the coffee," she replied.

Her eyes followed his tall, muscular frame as he walked away. The surge of heat from his hand raced up her arm all the way to her heart—it started doing crazy things.

She wasn't sure what had just happened, but she liked it, and she felt completely safe for the first time in months, even safer than Nicho had made her feel. At this moment, she felt like she could fly.

While Brad was getting Darcey's coffee, his phone vibrated. Pulling it out of his pocket, he saw that it was Luis Vargas, who had helped him rescue Darcey.

"Luis, I'll have to call you back. I'm not in my office. Give me about five minutes." Brad put his phone back in his pocket and took Darcey her cup of coffee. "I have an important call I need to take. Can you make it back to your quarters, or would you like to wait here for me, and we can go together?" he asked her, hoping she would wait.

"I'll wait. This is nice to just sit here, watch people, and know I'm not locked in a room. Do I need money to get another cup?" she asked, blushing, embarrassed at not knowing what the protocol was for acquiring another cup of coffee.

"No, just go get all the coffee you want and something to eat, too. I won't be long," Brad said, walking away his heart soaring.

Brad hurried down the hall to his office, a goofy smile plastered across his face. Entering, he stopped to pour himself a glass of Scotch before he sat down and picked up the phone to call Luis.

"I have excellent news," Luis said. "I have the location where you can find Carlos."

"Luis, it is good to hear your voice. Thank you for all your help," Brad responded while anger and frustration welled up inside of him at the mention of Carlos's name. It immediately squelched the euphoria he had been feeling just moments ago.

"Carlos is in Lima, along with his other two associates. They are staying at a house just outside of the city. I will email you the directions. It seems he has come into an inheritance of some sort and will be staying in Lima for a while," Luis told him. "Tell me how is Darcey? I have not told her grandmother yet. I will wait to tell her grandmother until you have had time to help her remember."

"Darcey is doing well. I believe some things are coming back to her. Her reaction to me is changing. She is more comfortable with me. I haven't had to dodge any flying objects or fists lately." Brad heard Luis laugh. "I hope to have good news for you in a few weeks." He took a drink and set the glass on the desk. "I need to go. Darcey is waiting for me," he said, a hint of anticipation in his voice. "Tonight will be our first real time together, so I want it to be special. I will call you in a few days and let you know what happens with Santiago."

"I will look forward to hearing from you." Luis hung up and emailed Brad the directions where to locate Carlos Santiago.

Brad didn't check his email before he left, deciding

that Santiago would still be there tomorrow, and he didn't want anything to distract from the evening he had planned. Earlier, he had given instructions to the Bajo kitchen staff about what he wanted delivered to his quarters for this special evening. Everything should be ready at seven.

He glanced at his watch. It was going on four-thirty.

Having emptied her cup, Darcey picked it up and walked over to the beverage station for a refill. Walking back, she chose a table closer to the windows where she could watch the busy people in the corridor. Wherever this was, it was bustling with activity, and it was wonderful to just sit and know she would never be locked up ever again. She glanced down the corridor and saw the man heading toward the café and an explosion of butterflies came back.

Brad pulled the door to the café open and was pleasantly surprised at the feeling of happiness he felt radiating from Darcey. The feeling grew the closer he moved toward her. When he reached the table, the feeling had grown to one of pure pleasure. He didn't know if she was remembering, but he certainly hoped so. An unabashed grin spread across his face as he gazed into her eyes. "Do you want to finish your coffee here or take it with you," he asked as he sat down, his eyes never leaving hers.

"If you're ready, I can take my coffee with me," Darcey told him. A smile played around the corners of her mouth and she was having a hard time controlling it. The smile wanted to spread across her face and she couldn't let that happen. It had only been a few hours since she had come to know him. It was too soon to be having such strong feelings for him.

I don't know this man, and I don't want him to get the wrong idea about me. I may be his property, but I'll be damned if I will give myself over willingly, she vowed.

However, she wasn't sure how long she could hold out. Her body responded of its own accord whenever he was close and that worried her. She willed herself to resist the onslaught of emotions that would come the next time he touched her.

Brad stood and extended his hand toward her. "Okay, let's go then."

Darcey avoided taking it, knowing she couldn't handle touching him again. Instead, she picked up her coffee cup in one hand and slid the chair back up to the table with the other.

Keeping her distance seemed the better choice for now, even though he hadn't made any untoward advances.

He's always behaved like a gentleman. Could I have misjudged him? He certainly isn't Nicho, but he seems to be just as concerned about me as Nicho was. She pondered that thought as they walked to the Café door.

"We'll take my shuttle back so you won't have to walk," he said, holding the café door open for her.

Ten minutes later, Brad parked the shuttle in the designated shuttle parking area located about twenty yards from his quarters. They walked the short distance to his door.

"I thought we would dine in tonight." Brad opened the door and motioned to her to enter. "Dinner will be delivered around seven."

"What time is it?" Darcey asked. "I don't have a watch and I haven't seen a clock anywhere," she said, looking around to see if he had one.

"Sorry, I didn't realize you did not have a watch. I will get you a clock and watch if you would like," he said making a mental to pick one up for her. "It's a little after five. Would you like to rest a while before dinner?" he asked. "You can lay down on my bed—or go back to your own quarters," he added quickly.

Oh, shit! Why did I mention my bed? Damn! He watched her reaction out of the corner of his eye.

A bit of pink tinged her cheeks. "Thank you, but I would like to change clothes before dinner, so I think I will go back to my quarters," Darcey replied, turning away from him and heading for the door.

She waited, not looking at him, for him to open the door. The circling butterflies in her stomach fluttered at the mention of 'his bed' and she knew she was blushing. She gritted her teeth in frustration as they erupted into a full-blown explosion when his arm brushed against her as he reached to slide his card through the slot.

Stupid! Stupid! Stupid! she admonished herself. *What's with you? No! Forget it. You're just hungry, that's all.*

Brad watched as Darcey walked the short distance to her quarters. He felt that she seemed much better. At least, he hadn't noticed any adverse reaction when he mentioned she could rest in his bed. Maybe her memory of him would come back sooner than anticipated—he hoped.

He didn't know how much longer he could hold out not touching her. The brief brush against her as he opened the door nearly drove him over the edge.

How can she not feel the power of our connection? And, if she does, how can she remain so calm?

❧❧

Entering her quarters, she was amazed, yet again, that this was all hers. She went over, flopped down on the sofa, swung her legs up, and marveled at her newfound freedom.

Clasping her hands together behind her head, she leaned back against the sofa's arm. *Maybe this being owned by the man might not be so bad, after all,* she speculated.

What had he said? We had been dating in my past life? Damn, I wish I could remember, but there's nothing but a blank space before I met him at the Gala.

A smile spread across her face and her eyes closed.

But when he touches me, a thousand fingers of heat surge through my body. There is something there. I can't explain it. Could it be, my mind does not remember him, but my body does? She let the thoughts roll around in her mind for bit, then sat up and placed her feet on the floor.

Kicking her shoes off and flexing her toes in the lush carpet, she stood and walked to the bedroom to change for dinner, no closer to an answer.

CHAPTER 2

Lilly Snoops

Carrying a handful of reports, Lilly opened the door to Brad's office. She planned to leave them so he would be ready to work on them first thing in the morning. She was nothing if not efficient and possibly borderline OCD. Everything about her life was completely organized, right down to her toothbrush that hung perfectly vertical in its holder. "A place for everything and everything in its place." Her mother had pounded that into her head since she'd been big enough to walk. Placing the reports on Brad's desk in a neat pile, she noticed he had left his computer on.

Wasteful, wasteful, she thought annoyed as she reached over to turn it off.

Her hand paused in midair when she noticed the contents of his email inbox were displayed on the monitor. Glancing briefly at the list, one email, in particular, caught her eye. It was from Luis Vargas. Curiosity got the better of her, even knowing she shouldn't, she opened it anyway.

The message jumped off the monitor's screen at her. *It seems that Carlos has recently inherited the ranch of one Armando Martinez in Lima. You will find him and his two friends there.*

Lilly pulled Brad's chair out from the desk, collapsed into it, and stared at the offending email displayed on the monitor's screen.

What the hell does this mean? she pondered. *Why is he staying at Armando's residence? Armando's lawyer had assured me there were no living relatives, so how did Santiago inherit Armando's ranch?* That question rattled her self-imposed, aloof exterior.

All of these months she had been successful in keeping everyone in the dark and manipulating things from behind the scenes, always careful that nothing would connect her to Armando or to Javier's plans. She did not need a wild card popping up now and ruining everything she had worked so hard to conceal. And with Brad seeking to exact his 'pound of flesh' on Santiago for what he had done to that woman, it might cause the authorities or Corporate to come snooping if Santiago suddenly turned up dead, especially now that Armando's connection to the missing woman was a matter of public record.

Then she paused and realized there was nothing that would connect her with either Armando or Santiago—no paper trail that would lead back to her.

How stupid of me to worry, she thought, relieved, a slight smile playing around her mouth. *I have been so very careful to destroy everything that could possibly connect me to Armando. And, as for Santiago, I've no dealings whatsoever with him.* She sat up straight. *This must be some of Javier's doing. Damn him!*

Lilly had been furious with Javier when he had not consulted her first before soliciting Armando.

"I could have told him just what a loser Armando really was. But, nooo, he plowed right ahead and arranged with Armando to handle the job," she fumed. Then it dawned on her that she was in Brad's office and the door was open. She quickly stepped across the office, shut the door, turned off the light, and closed the window blinds.

On her way back to Brad's desk, a smug, self-satisfied feeling slowly spread through her as she thought about the elation she had felt upon hearing about Armando's "most unfortunate accident." She had gleefully clapped her hands at the news, but that had been short lived as she knew Javier's decision to eliminate him had come too late. Things had already been screwed up. Still, it had made her day.

Now, none of that mattered since she had taken control of the situation and strongly stressed to Corporate that it was imperative for Brad to be called back to handle the situation personally. She had manipulated Corporate into letting her be the one to go to Dallas to retrieve Brad. She knew that with Brad back in the dome, he would see just how valuable she was to him. However, that too, had been short lived. Because, upon arrival, she had been slapped in the face with the news that Brad had a girl-friend.

She had been furious at the news and would have made the woman disappear then if it had not been for the fact that she had had to return to Lima the same day. Then she had been overjoyed at the news that the woman had been kidnapped. However, she had to maintain her façade of sincere sympathy, and it had galled her immensely each time she had had to pretend to really care.

Then there was the situation of hiring the tech crew to work on the virus that had been uploaded into the filtration system. She knew that the Eastern Alliance had been behind it, and when Brad came asking her opinion about hiring some experts, she had been thrilled. She then had contacted Javier for his recommendation, and he had assured her that Ty Horton was nothing but a hack and could not handle the job. Time would run out before Horton could even find out what was happening.

Hiring the new technical crew had been another stupid move on Javier's part, Lilly fumed as she sat tapping her fingers furiously on the arm of Brad's chair, stress building at the thought of her perfect plan being derailed right before her eyes. *How could he not have known who they were?*

She should have trusted her own instincts and researched them herself. If she had, she would not be in this situation now. The virus would have done its job and ORCA would now be scrambling to try and fix the problem. Too late, she had realized that someone in the Eastern Alliance must have been feeding Javier false information, manipulating him to their own agenda.

"Javier never had the backbone to do what was needed for this job in the first place," Lilly growled. "But it is still not too late for me to keep things on track."

Chatting up Matt and gaining his trust had been a priority in her plan. It was imperative that she acquire knowledge about everything pertaining to the operation of the new hydroponics system. In just the few short weeks that she had been working with Matt, she now knew more than enough to do what was necessary.

However, it would have been so much better if they had just listened and let me handle the whole damn thing from the beginning.

Slowly, a plan was forming in Lilly's mind on how to handle this new situation. First, she would find out just what the connection was between Santiago and Armando. Then she would anonymously contact Santiago and inform him that the boyfriend of the woman he kidnapped would be paying him a little visit. A sinister snicker escaped her lips as she thought about the possibility of each man eliminating the other. If the Gods smiled favorably, her problem would solve itself. She smirked as she picked up the phone and called Armando's lawyer's number. She checked her watch, it was a little after four. He should still be there.

"*¡Hola!*" the receptionist answered.

"Yes, I would like to speak to Eduardo, *por favor*," Lilly said.

"*Uno momento, por favor.*" The receptionist put her on hold and the on-hold music grated in her ear. Drumming her fingers in frustration, she gritted her teeth and endured the noise.

"Eduardo, here," he answered, annoyed at the lateness of the call. He had just been ready to walk out the door for home.

"I need to know how Carlos Santiago is connected to Armando. You said he had no living relatives," Lilly accused him.

"We did not know about Santiago until three weeks ago." Eduardo rubbed his forehead, cringing from what he knew was coming. *How did she find out?* he wondered. He purposely had not called her about this information, because he knew she would overreact, just like this. "Carlos is not a relative of Armando's, but he is the stepson of Maria, the housekeeper, and, as you know—" He let out an aggravated sigh. "—Maria has inherited all of Armando's property and money," he finished, clenching his jaw in agitation.

"I do not know if this will cause complications or not," Lilly ventured. "I have found out that Daniels is determined to seek revenge on Santiago for what he did to that American woman. However, I think I can arrange it so that they will eliminate each other," she said thoughtfully, more to herself than to Eduardo.

"Are you sure that is a wise thing to do? Is there any chance it could lead back to us? We are cutting it close as it is. We cannot afford for anything to go wrong now," Eduardo worried, his fingers paused drumming in midair. He was beginning to worry what would happen if his connection in all of this were found out. *The only reason I have hung on this long was for the money*, he reflected.

"Nothing will go wrong," Lilly growled at Eduardo, "I have what I need to stop the dome from opening. We just need to make everyone believe that Javier is the sole mastermind behind all of this and then get that woman out of the way," she said, irritation evident in her voice. Lilly had refused to call Darcey by name ever since Brad had brought her back to the dome. Lilly would take pleasure in seeing to the removal of that woman herself.

Everything had been working out just fine. It had taken Lilly most of the five years she had been with OR-CA, to connive and lie her way to a position in the dome. The last position she had acquired had been under mysterious circumstances. Nonetheless, once there, she had made herself indispensable. Then, gaining Brad's trust, she had wormed her way into being second in command next to Brad. Quickly, she had earned his complete trust. She now had far-reaching run of the dome, which included everything pertaining to its operation. It would have been only a matter of time before Brad saw her for what she was—a full partner to him in running the dome. To her, the dome was her life—their life. Then Corporate had sent him to the Dallas office, he met that woman, and it had ruined everything. Brad did not see anyone but her. He could not talk about anything but her. Lilly had been ecstatic at the news that Darcey was missing.

It was her, her, her! Lilly's mind screamed.

Frustrated after Javier and Armando's botched attempt to get the plans, Lilly had gone directly to Corporate seeking permission to let her go to Dallas to bring Brad back to the dome. The only thing she had not counted on was meeting Darcey. Lilly had hated her the minute she laid eyes on her that day at Mike Bellington's. It took all of her strength to sit there, watch as Brad fawned over her, and not jump up and scratch her eyes out.

"If you are sure," Eduardo said hesitantly. "I will leave all of the final details in your capable hands."

With that, Eduardo hung up swiftly. She had already given him too much information for his own good. He did not want to know any of the gory details. The less he knew, the safer he felt. Besides, by the time he reached home now, his wife would have dinner on the table and he would have no time for his nightly cocktail before dinner. He hated having his routine interrupted.

Lilly decided she would not call Santiago tonight but would wait until Brad left on the sub in the morning. She wanted to give Santiago just enough time to prepare for Brad's visit. She smiled at the thought of Brad walking into an ambush. It would be over quickly. It would serve him right for hooking up with that woman. Lilly changed the email back to "unread," and left Brad's office as she had found it, humming to herself, satisfied with her plan.

CHAPTER 3

Some Questions Answered

The food arrived right on schedule, and Brad set to work making everything perfect. He stepped back to admire the table he had just carefully set before lighting the candles. Replacing the ARC electric lighter in its charger base, he turned on the music and lowered the lights. Nervously rubbing his hands together, he gave everything one final look. He was ready to go get Darcey. He slid his card through the slot, triggering the door to open and there she stood, her delicate hand raised, ready to knock. For a moment, there was no air to breathe. His heart was pounding, his palms sweating, just like the first night he saw her.

"You look beautiful," he said finally, smiling, letting his eyes roam over her graceful figure in the black, form-fitting jumpsuit. The plunging neckline, accentuated by a single diamond pendant that rested just above the valley where the graceful curves of her breasts met. "Please, come in," he said, swallowing hard. *I'll never make it through this evening,* he thought.

"Thank you, sir." She gave him a cheeky grin, noticing his eyes had missed her face entirely, and walked in. "Wow, everything looks wonderful."

"A glass of wine?" Brad held up the bottle.

"Yes, please." She smiled at him, inhaling the delicious aroma floating in the air. "What's that wonderful smell?"

"I thought maybe you would like to have a juicy Texas sirloin, done to perfection," Brad grinned, handing her a glass of wine. "Salad, baked potato, and, of course, Texas toast. That was your favorite back home."

"I'm sorry. I don't remember," she said and sighed sadly. "I wish I could." She wanted more than anything to remember who she was, to put a name to the face in the mirror that looked back at her each morning, and have it mean something—anything.

"Don't worry about it. It will come if you don't force it," Brad assured her. "You probably won't remember everything at once, so don't expect it."

"Thanks, I'll try to remember that." She half-smiled at him, taking a drink from her glass. Inhaling, she turned away from him so he couldn't see the sadness in her eyes.

But I do expect it, she thought bitterly. *I want to know it all—right now. I don't like this feeling of being the middle, between who I was before on the right, who I am now on the left...and...me in the middle, belonging to neither side.*

"Dinner is served, madam." He bent at the waist and made a wide sweeping gesture with his hand toward the dining table.

She turned and laughed at his over-exaggerated maître d' impersonation and followed him, where he made a major production of seating her at the table.

She watched him over the fresh bouquet of white roses in the center of the table, as he refilled their glasses with wine, glad for his comic performance. It lightened her mood. She began to relax. As hard as she tried, she couldn't take her eyes off of him. Drinking in every inch of him, she believed he truly was the most handsome man she had met in this new life, maybe in her old life as well if she ever remembered.

She thought about Quin—handsome in a rugged exotic way with the scar down the side of his face, and Nicho—roguish, with a hint of dark mystery in those amber eyes. But this man—this man was one hundred percent all male—perfect in every way. It was something she couldn't define in words, but he had an essence that neither Quin nor Nicho possessed. That something was reaching deep down inside of her, pulling her toward him. He caught her staring and smiled that lopsided grin of his. Her heart jumped into overdrive and butterflies erupted in her stomach. Blushing, she diverted her eyes to stare at the bouquet.

Why does he do this to me? she wondered, annoyed at herself that he could stir such feelings in her with just a grin that made her hot and cold all at the same time.

Brad forgot what he was doing, as he watched the soft glow of the candlelight caressing Darcey's face, and almost overfilled the glasses. Catching himself in time, he laughed. He was acting like a schoolboy on his first date. He hadn't felt like this since the first time he saw Darcey—hot and cold all at the same time, butterflies in the pit of his stomach, heart racing, and sweaty palms. He couldn't tell if she was feeling the same way, but she was feeling something. He was sure of it. She was blushing.

"Tell me about me, please," she asked, clearing her throat, moving on from the awkward moment. "But first, you must tell me your name. I need to know what to call you. Somehow 'hey you' just doesn't fit," she said with a nervous giggle, and neither did 'the man' that she had been calling him in her thoughts.

He grinned sheepishly. "Sorry, I should have introduced myself first thing. I don't know what I was thinking. It's Brad—Brad Daniels." *You dope! Yeah, I wasn't thinking*, he chastised himself. He had been so thankful to have her safe and back with him, he had blanked out the fact that she had no idea who he was.

Darcey's mind remained a blank. His name stirred nothing inside of her. He could have easily been called John Smith and it would have had the same effect.

No, his name means nothing to me, but the physical stuff—the touching, that grin, those eyes—now that's something else, she reflected, as the corner of her mouth turned slightly upward. *My body remembers something. I just wish it would pass the information on to my brain.*

"Let's eat and I'll tell you all of what I know happened to you," Brad said, vigorously slathering his baked potato with butter to hide his nervousness.

During dinner, Brad told her everything he knew that had happened to her since they had started dating. He told her how they met, about his job and why he couldn't tell her about it, and then why he had to come back to Peru. He told her about Armando and the car crash, about his search for her leading him to Morocco. He conveniently left out the part Vargas had played in him being able to buy her at the auction, the DNA test, and her grandmother. However, he did tell her he had found Carlos and he had plans to take care of him personally. He didn't trust the authorities to do the job.

The meal finished, Brad and Darcey settled themselves on the sofa. Darcey curled up in the corner on one end and Brad, not wanting to be too far away, settled for somewhere in the middle of the sofa—close, but not too close.

"Tell me, did I have friends? What was my life like? Did I have a job, parents, brothers, sisters?" she asked, excited at last to have some questions answered about her life before she was kidnapped. Hoping against hope, that something he would tell her would trigger a memory.

"Yes, you have lots of friends," he said, adjusting himself into a more comfortable position. "Your best friend is Marti Campbell. You have been friends since grade school. You have a job, you're a graphic designer at one of the largest firms in Dallas. You've been working for them since you graduated college—"

"My parents? Who are they?" she interrupted.

"I'm sorry," he said softly, reaching for her hand, "but your parents were killed in a car accident when you were thirteen." He didn't know how else to break it to her other than to come right out and say it. He didn't want to hurt her, but maybe the jolt of hearing that her parents were dead would trigger something. He gently squeezed her hand. "Your Uncle Jack, who is your father's brother, raised you after your parents died," he told her.

She listened to the words, but she had not memory of any of those things. She had thought that once she knew, she would remember, but instead, she was more lost than ever. She had all of the information at her fingertips but couldn't grab it—the pieces were all there, floating, just beyond her reach. It was like the nightmare she'd had on the boat, and then that first night at Vargas's.

Brad watched her face as he told her about her parents. He could see she had no memory of them, and could only imagine what she was feeling now—lost, maybe.

"Tell me about my best friend, Marti," she suggested wanting to change the subject. "Tell me everything about her."

She needed to think about something else besides her parents. It was bad enough that they were gone but worse, she couldn't even remember them. She was sure she had grieved over her loss at the time, but now, it felt right that she needed to do so again even though she couldn't remember them. She settled herself farther back into the corner of the sofa, drawing her legs up beside her.

"Well, where to begin?" Brad paused, noticing she had pulled her legs up beside her, creating a barrier between them. "You and Marti have been best friends since grade school. In college, you majored in Art and Graphic Design. Marti majored in Phys Ed and played catcher for the girls' softball team. After you both had graduated, Marti and her father went into business together and own Campbell's Sporting Goods in Dallas. You were hired by one of the biggest design agencies in the Dallas/Fort Worth area. You have been, twice, awarded 'Graphic Designer of the Year.'" He paused again, catching the look of anticipation on her face, hoping something would trigger a memory.

"The two of you never do anything without the other. It's like you two are two halves of the same whole. I have to tell you, sometimes it's a little creepy the way you two mesh together." He chuckled. "The first night I met you at the Sweetwater was when you and Marti and some of your girlfriends, all came together for your weekly girls' night out." He turned and looked into her eyes. "I knew you were 'the one' the moment I laid eyes on you, and I knew you felt it too. When we danced, the rest of the world melted away. There was just you, me, and the music. I wanted to take you home after the bar closed, but you gals have some sort of a girl thing—if you come together, you go home together sort of pact." He shrugged and grinned. "Try as hard as I could, I couldn't talk you into letting me take you home. You had to go with Marti," he told her, shaking his head. And, then, like a bolt of lightning, it hit him—he would contact Marti and fly her here to help Darcey restore her memory. He would have Lilly arrange that in the morning. A rush of adrenaline coursed through his veins.

Yes! That's the answer, he thought excited. If it hadn't been so late, he would have jumped right up and called Lilly right then.

Brad poured the last of the wine in her glass. It was getting late, and Darcey needed to get some rest. These past forty-eight hours had been exhausting for him. He could only guess how they had affected Darcey. She looked tired, and the wine was making her sleepy. He smiled, as she tried to keep her eyes open.

"Would you like me to walk you back to your quarters?" Brad asked, smiling as she yawned.

The temptation, to pull her into his arms, almost pushed him to the breaking point. He wanted to ask her to stay, but he knew it was too soon, and he had given her a lot to think about. She needed some alone time to absorb everything. No, he wouldn't push her. She had to come of her own accord. Besides, she was half asleep now. He would be lucky to get her back to her quarters before she completely passed out.

"Yes, that would be nice," Darcey said through a yawn, forcing herself to stand up. Through half-closed eyes, she made her way to the kitchen with her glass and set it on the counter.

She covered her mouth to hide a very unlady-like yawn. "Would you like me to help clean up?" she asked, hoping he would say no. She didn't think she could stay awake long enough to walk the few yards to her door, anyway. She yawned again.

"No, the Bajo staff will take care of this in the morning, but thanks anyway." Brad chuckled watching her yawn again. He put his arm around her shoulders and guided her out into the corridor. He noticed she didn't flinch as his arm settled softly on her shoulders. He could have pulled her closer but didn't, not yet.

Baby steps.

They stopped in front of Darcey's door. Brad waited, amused while she missed the slot with her card and tried twice more before she succeeded.

Brad grinned at her. "Well, good night. See you in the morning," he said, watching her sway in the doorway. "You can call the Bajo and have your breakfast delivered. I know you haven't had time to do any shopping."

"Yes, I suppose that would be nice if I had a way to call them," she mumbled through a yawn, rubbing her eyes.

"Oh, that. Yes, I suppose it would help to know how to do that." Brad grinned. "Please step inside." He took hold of her shoulders and turned her toward the living room, gently pushing her along. "Over there on the desk—" He pointed. "—you will find the phone system for the entire dome. Right now, only the occupied quarters and offices are in the system. It works just like a cell phone, but you cannot place long distance calls yet. When completed we will have our own phone system, much like any other cell phone system." He showed her the electronic address book.

Through bleary eyes, she looked at what he was showing her. The names and numbers wouldn't hold still so she could read them.

Oh well, maybe they will have settled down by morning, she thought, stifling another yawn. She was tired and she needed him to go. "Thank you. You've given me lots to think about," she said politely, maneuvering him toward the door. She didn't want to think about anything else. All she wanted right now was to curl up in that big bed in her new bedroom and go to sleep. She put her hand on his chest and gently pushed him out the door.

"I'll see you in the morning," she said, yawning again, as the door slid shut.

Darcey stood staring at the door. Her mind refused to think about any of the things he had told her. It was screaming "sleep" at her. She kicked off her shoes as she walked toward the bedroom, took off her clothes, let them lay where they fell, and snuggled naked under the coverlet. Before she fell asleep a thought occurred to her.

Did he have his arm around me? It felt like he did. Maybe I just dreamed it. I'm sooo sleepy. The fog of dreamland descended on her.

ↁↁↁ

Brad watched Darcey's door slide shut, smiling at the image of her standing there half awake, beautiful, and so vulnerable. A surge of love enveloped his heart.

Turning, he jogged off down the corridor toward his office. He needed to check on the email from Luis. It was too important to wait until morning.

Flipping on the overhead lights, he crossed to his desk and sat down. The screen saver rotated through images of Darcey. He moved the mouse, and the computer sprung to life. The images of Darcey blinked away and Brad's inbox displayed on the screen.

He scrolled down the list looking for the one from Luis, double clicked on the email, and it opened up. Brad scanned the email and fell back in his chair like he'd been punched. Luis had written that Santiago was at Armando's ranch.

What the hell is Santiago's connection to Armando?

Lilly had said his lawyer told her Armando had no living relatives. Well regardless, he was going to take care of the son-of-a-bitch tomorrow. Contemplating the situation, Brad decided he would not tell anyone, including Lilly, that he was going. There still might be someone here, who could tip Santiago off. Corporate had not come up with anyone besides Armando, but that didn't mean there couldn't be someone else, too.

Brad decided on his course of action. First, he would leave Lilly instructions to arrange for Marti Campbell to be flown down to Lima. Next, he would call Luis and see if his man was still in Lima. After much thought about the situation, he decided he was going to need backup when he went after Santiago. It wasn't just Santiago he would have to take care of, now, there were the other two, also. He looked at his watch. Luis should be finished with lunch by now. Brad punched in Luis's number on his cell. He didn't want a record of the call showing up on the office's call logs—just in case.

Luis heard his phone ring and pulled it out of his jacket pocket. It slipped and dropped to the floor. Picking it up, he checked for damage.

"Yes, what do you want?" Luis growled into the phone.

"Howdy." Brad laughed. "Sorry. Have I caught you at a bad time?"

"My apologies, Brad. I just dropped my new phone, but it appears to be okay." Luis sat down on the edge of the sofa. "What can I do for you?"

"I'll be quick, so you can get back to whatever you were doing." Brad laughed again. "Is your man still in Lima? I am going to deal with Santiago and I'm going to need backup since his other two friends are here with him. I'd like the playing field to be somewhat level."

"Yes, he is. I will give him a call and have him contact you. Do not do anything until you hear from my man, Angelo."

"Thanks, but have him call me on my cell. I don't want anything showing up on the office call logs. We still haven't found out who is behind the sabotage," Brad told him.

"Nicho will be back today, would you like me to send him over, too?" Luis asked as he walked over to his desk to look for Angelo's cell number.

"No, I think Angelo and I can take care of things." One thing Brad didn't want or need was to have Nicho show up and muddy the waters. He had avoided talking to Darcey about her relationship with Nicho—or anything that had happened at Luis's, for that matter. It brought out his green-eyed monster every time he thought about Nicho.

Brad hung up, turned off the computer and lights, put the instructions for Lilly about contacting Marti on her desk, and jogged back to his quarters. It was just past one.

This would be a short night.

CHAPTER 4

Looking for Santiago

Brad fumbled around, trying to find the button to shut off the shrill buzzer that was ripping through a dream about Darcey. Finally, he found it, silenced it, then fell back onto the pillow, and stared at the ceiling. He wasn't exactly sure how he was going to handle Santiago. Perhaps when Angelo called, they could work out a plan, since that was Angelo's kind of business.

He flipped the covers back, sat up on the side of the bed. The thought of Santiago touching Darcey pumped anger and adrenaline through his body. Brad knew he needed a plan. The thought of killing someone was unsettling, to say the least, but his only other option was to have him arrested, and he knew from Santiago's rap sheet, he had never been prosecuted. Brad just couldn't take the chance that the son-of-a-bitch would get off, yet again. He would reserve making any final decision until he had talked with Angelo.

While the coffee brewed, he dressed and called the

sub captain, telling him to have the sub ready by seven thirty.

Brad filled two mugs with coffee and carried them down to Darcey's quarters. She opened the door in her baby blue silk robe that clung gracefully to the curves of her body, leaving no doubt in his mind she had nothing on underneath. Her hair was tousled but even with no makeup on, she was breathtakingly beautiful to him. His heart turned over and the butterflies erupted in his stomach. He knew he was crazy in love with this woman and had been from the first moment he saw her, but his soul—his soul had been in love with her for an eternity.

He flashed her a toothy grin. "Coffee, madam?"

What a pleasant surprise. Darcey was elated and gave him a sly, sideways grin, stepping aside for him to enter. Excitement stirred in the pit of her stomach as she watched him carry in the mugs and place them on the bar. *Where are all these wonderful feelings coming from? Why can't I remember this man? I so desperately want to remember him, to remember everything. My body remembers, why won't my mind?*

"Here, better drink it while it's hot," Brad said, taking a drink of his. "I don't have much time this morning. I talked to Luis last night, and one of his guys is here in Lima and is going to help me with Santiago. I am going topside as soon as I leave here, but I wanted to see you before I go. Lilly will be available if you need anything," he said, watching her as she took her coffee and curled up on the sofa.

"Lilly?" she questioned, frowning faintly.

"Yes. Lilly Montego. She is my executive assistant." *Another slip on my part,* he thought. "Sorry, I forgot you have not officially met her yet. However, you did briefly meet her once at Mike's stables in Dallas. She will be available if you need anything. I have asked her to show you around and introduce you to our people."

"Oh, thank you," she said absently. She was more worried about what might happen to Brad than she was about being escorted around. "Do you think there will be trouble?" she asked thoughtfully. She wasn't sure who this Santiago person was. Brad had told her he was the one who kidnapped her, but the only one she could think of was the Creepy Man. She had never heard Creep Man's name. Quin had called him a broker, so unless she saw him, she wouldn't know for sure. A little shiver of apprehension crept up her spine.

"I don't know. I hope not. I think it should be okay with Luis's man there," Brad told her, even though he didn't know for sure how this was going to play out. He didn't want to worry her.

"Why don't you just turn him over to the authorities?" she asked, watching him over the rim of her cup. That seemed the simplest solution to her. And, a lot safer.

"I've checked his rap sheet, and he has been arrested numerous times for trafficking but never prosecuted. Best I can determine, he has always had an alibi or been able to bribe his way out. As I said, he's never been prosecuted, and I can't take the chance it will happen this time, too. There's nothing for you to worry about," Brad said, his smile fading as he watched the frown deepen on her face.

He walked over and sat on the coffee table in front of her. He took her coffee mug, set it on the table beside him, then gathered her hands in his and kissed them, avoiding the palms. That can wait till later. "I told you, everything is going to be okay. You don't need to worry about anything. You are safe here. No one can hurt you here." Brad squeezed her hands. "Now, I have a surprise for you. I am going to bring Marti down so you can talk with her. Marti can fill in the blanks that I can't. She will be here in the morning."

"I will look forward to meeting her—again." Darcey gave a weak laugh. *Will she be the key to unlocking my memory? I hope so.*

Brad stood up, dropped her hands, and kissed her on the forehead—a sheer reflex. He cleared his throat and stepped away from her. "I've got to go. The sub will be waiting for me. I'll call you later and let you know how things went." He turned and walked toward the door.

Darcey was still sitting on the sofa. He couldn't tell what she was thinking. That had been a stupid thing to do. He had promised himself he wouldn't do anything to upset her.

It didn't even register that he had gotten up or kissed her or left until she heard the door slide shut. Darcey sat there trying to figure exactly what she was feeling. *Do I really want to know who I was? Will knowing my name be enough? Do I really want to know all of the rest? I thought I did.*

She had been worrying about it for months. It had been on her mind twenty-four/seven since she had woken up in that dirty little room. But, now, she knew her name, and it meant nothing. Would knowing the rest make any difference?

Over the past several months, she had grown used to her new life, although she had never admitted it to herself, until now. Even though she had been kidnapped and kept locked up in a gilded prison, she found herself enjoying being pampered and catered to. She had grown used to the designer clothes, the jewels, and the finer things that had been given to her. She had enjoyed a different kind of freedom—one with no responsibilities and no decisions to make. Was that something she really wanted to give up?

Will you just listen to yourself? A tiny faint voice echoed from somewhere in her past. *Darcey Callahan, you can't say you like what has happened to you so much that you want to continue being someone else's property.* The voice was getting louder. *Think about it—you want to know about your life, past and future. They can both exist for you. You don't have to give up one for the other. Think about it.*

She didn't know where the voice in her head was coming from, but it was like a long-lost friend coming to visit.

You know who I am, Darcey. I'm your inner voice, your conscience, your intuition, your voice of reason. Listen to me. Let me help you through this. I will lead you in the right direction. Trust me.

How can I trust you, I don't even trust myself to make sound decisions anymore, she questioned the voice.

You can trust me. I will not let you down. You need to listen to Brad. He is the right one for you.

How can I do that? I don't remember him. Was I in love with him? What did he mean to me? Can you answer those questions? Darcey demanded of the voice.

You will know the answers to all of your questions when the time is right. I will help you find the right time. Trust me.

"This is ridiculous. I'm talking to myself. Someone is going to come and lock me up," she said out loud and tuned the voice out.

Darcey looked at the clock Brad had brought her and saw it was seven fifteen. What had Brad said? He was leaving at seven thirty? He was going to go find Santiago. She worried that something terrible was going to happen, but couldn't do anything about it. She would just have to wait till she heard from Brad. She stood up and headed for the bedroom to get dressed, and then she was going to have breakfast.

As she passed the desk, she decided to call for breakfast like Brad had suggested. The lady taking her order said it would be delivered in half an hour, plenty of time to get dressed before it arrived.

ↄ৲ↄ৲

Brad dashed back to his quarters, pulled his Glock out of its hiding place, shrugged into his jacket, and put three extra clips in his jacket pockets. He slipped the gun into the waistband of his jeans at the small of his back and adjusted his jacket so it covered the gun. Checking his watch, he saw it was going on seven fifteen. There was plenty of time to get to the sub's bay.

The sub's captain welcomed Brad aboard, closed the hatch, and started the ascent up to the top.

"There's fresh coffee in the galley," the captain said to Brad's back as he headed in that direction.

Brad laughed. "Thanks! That's just what I had in mind."

Some of the sub's crew was still in the galley when Brad walked in. Raising his hand in greeting as he walked by the table where they sat, he went straight for the coffee pot.

It wasn't the best idea to have more caffeine since he was already wired to the hilt in anticipation of the confrontation with Santiago. He felt the gun in his waistband as it was pushed against his back when he leaned against the back of the chair he sat down on—an unsettling reminder he might have to use it before the day was over. Thank goodness, his jacket covered it up. The captain would not have been pleased to know he had a gun onboard. Although it wasn't loaded, firearms were forbidden on the subs.

His phone vibrated and he pulled it out of his pocket. The caller ID indicated it was from Luis. He wondered what Luis wanted.

"Luis, what a surprise," Brad greeted him. "What's up?"

"Morning, Brad," Luis said. "I just wanted to let you know that Nicho will be arriving this morning. I checked out Carlos and his two compatriots. They are nothing to be messed with. So, I am sending Nicho to help out. I do not want to lose you. My men are trained in this sort of thing. It is their job. Let them handle the bad stuff."

"Thanks, Luis, but I think Angelo and I can handle the situation," Brad said, as his stomach sank. The one person he didn't want to show up was on his way here. But there was no use in trying to talk Luis out of it—his mind was made up.

"Nonsense, my boy. This will be a good thing and make, as you said, the playing field more level." Luis laughed. "You will need to pick Nicho up. His flight will arrive at eight-thirty. Call me when it is over."

"Yes, I will pick up Nicho and give you a call when it's over." Brad hung up staring at his coffee cup.

Now, why did I say I would pick Nicho up? he wondered, questioning his own sanity. He wasn't going to surface before ten. Maybe Angelo would call before then and he could pawn picking up Nicho off on him.

Keeping Nicho and Darcey apart might not be so hard, after all, he thought. I will just make sure Darcey stays five miles under the Pacific in the dome.

His phone vibrated again and he saw it was Angelo.

What timing, he thought. *The universe is smiling this morning.* Brad let it ring two more times before he answered.

"Hello," Brad said.

"Hello, Angelo here," he said. "Where do you want to meet?" Straight, and direct to the point. No useless chatter was how Angelo liked it.

Following suit, Brad replied, "I just heard from Luis. He is sending Nicho. I have to pick him up at the airport. His flight arrives at eight-thirty, but, I won't be topside until ten. Can you pick him up?" Brad asked.

"Sure thing. Where do you want us to meet you?" Angelo asked again.

"Let's meet at the Starbucks near the airport. I'll be there as soon as we dock. Say by eleven? No later than eleven-thirty," Brad told him.

"Right. We'll see you there," Angelo said and hung up.

CHAPTER 5

The Quiet Surface Ripples

Lilly was up early. She hadn't slept well. She had tossed and turned, worrying about Santiago and Brad.

Might as well go on into the office, she thought, brushing her hair. She knew Brad wouldn't be in before eight so she would not have to worry about calling Santiago just yet. Brad would be leaving sometime before noon, she figured. It was a two and a half hour journey to the surface so, it was possible he might leave before ten.

Lilly rinsed out the teapot, filled the kettle with water, set it on the stove to heat, and reached for the tea canister. The canister was empty. Lilly slammed the lid down on the tea canister, switched off the burner with force, and walked out the door.

"The morning is getting off to a poor start," she grumbled.

Walking into the Bajo el Mar Café, Lilly stopped at the beverage station, filled the large size disposable cup with hot tea, and added three sugars. She then carefully placed the plastic lid on top, selected a pineapple pastry from the food line, and told the cashier to put it on her tab. The cashier glared at Lilly's back as she walked away.

Lilly could feel the hostile daggers in her back, but it didn't bother her in the least. All of these people will be gone in a few weeks, she thought smugly. She could afford to ignore them now.

Lilly took the opposite way around the service ring so she could walk past Brad's office before entering hers. She had guessed right, he had not come in yet.

Opening the cabinet doors above her credenza, Lilly took out her favorite tea mug, carefully removed the plastic lid from the disposable cup, and poured the hot tea into the special mug. Placing the lid and cup in the waste bin, Lilly pulled her chair out to sit down and noticed a note from Brad on her desk. Setting her mug on the stone Thirsty Coaster, she picked up the note and sat down as she read what Brad wanted her to do—contact a friend of Darcey's, a Marti Campbell in Dallas, and make arrangements to fly her down on the corporate jet.

Lilly's frowned as she glared at the note.

"What the hell is he thinking?" she fumed. "This is not a corporate related job—the corporate jet should not be used for this," she muttered. "It is a waste of money to bring this person here and for what? To keep that damn woman company while he goes off to look for Santiago?"

She crushed the note in her hand and threw it on the desk. If it were actually possible for steam to shoot from someone's ears, then straight shots of steam would be blasting from Lilly's.

Drumming her fingers in frustration on the desktop, Lilly knew she couldn't do anything about it now. She had no choice but to follow his instructions and arrange for this woman, no matter how much it irked her, to be flown to Lima. Lilly picked up the note and ran her hand angrily across the paper to press out the wrinkles in order to read the number for Marti Campbell. Lilly heard a woman answer.

"Hello?"

"Hello. Is this Marti Campbell?" Lilly switched from anger to business in a split second, speaking in a pleasant tone as she wadded up the note again and threw it in the trash.

"Yes," Marti answered. She had looked at the caller ID before she answered and saw it was coming from the ORCA Corporation. Her heart skipped a beat. Maybe they had news of Brad or Darcey.

"This is Lilly Montego, I am Señor Brad Daniels's Executive Assistant Director of the Bio Dome Project. Señor Daniels has requested me to ask you to come to Lima, Peru. It is in regards to Señorita Darcey Callahan. I believe it has something to do with her loss of memory, but he will explain it all when you arrive. The corporate jet will be ready to leave from the Dallas International Airport at eight this evening. Can you be ready by then?" Lilly quipped.

"This is about Darcey? How is she? Where is she? Can I talk to her—" Marti was bombarding Lilly with questions when Lilly interrupted her.

"I do not know. This is all of the information I have. Can you be ready to leave at eight?" Lilly cut her off. It irked her having to do this and she was not going to spend another second answering this stupid woman's questions.

"Well, yes I can. But can't you tell me something about Darcey now?" Marti asked, bewildered as to why this person couldn't give her some information about Darcey.

"No, I cannot give you more information about Señorita Callahan because I do not have any more information to give you. It is not my job to give you information on Señorita Callahan. My job is to give you information about your trip," Lilly ground out. She was losing it. She had to get herself under control. The woman on the other end was not going to get under her skin. Lilly gritted her teeth in frustration. "Please, be at the airport at seven and go to ORCA's private entrance gate. There will be a shuttle waiting for you. Be sure to bring your passport. The shuttle will take you to the ORCA hangar where you will board the corporate jet. Do you have any questions?" Lilly finished giving her the instructions through clenched teeth. Her knuckles on the hand gripping the receiver were turning white. She hoped the woman did not ask any more questions. Lilly had reached the end of her politeness.

"No, I don't think so." Marti could hear the change in the woman's voice and wondered what her problem was. "I will be at the private gate at seven. Thank you." *Strange woman,* Marti thought. *Wonder how she got to be Brad's assistant.*

Lilly slammed the phone down, all of her calm reserve gone. She had reached the boiling point. This is not good, she thought.

She took a drink of her tea. It was lukewarm. Disgusted she slammed the cup down. Tea sloshed over the rim, forming amber puddles on a stack of weekly reports.

That was it! Lilly gritted her teeth and looked around for something to throw.

Then, like a switch that had been pushed to 'off,' her reserve kicked in and the tantrum was over. Lilly concentrated on cleaning up the spilled tea and straightening her desk.

Glancing at her watch, she saw it was already ten minutes till nine. Lilly stepped out into the corridor and walked the short distance to Brad's office. It was still dark.

CHAPTER 6

Exploring

Darcey ate breakfast and left the dishes on a tray outside her door for someone from the Bajo to pick up later. She checked the clock. It was almost nine, so Lilly should be in the office by now. She shoved her feet into a pair of sandals, put the pager in her pocket, and left, heading for the corporate office area. Brad said she had met Lilly at Mike's, but Darcey had no memory of her—or of Mike, for that matter.

Passing Brad's office, she saw that it was dark, like the feeling she had in the pit of her stomach about this thing Brad was doing. She didn't like the idea of Brad going off on his own in search of this Santiago person, even if he did have someone else to help him. She was sure he had no idea how dangerous these people could be. She had heard stories from the other women about the men Vargas dealt with. They did not give a second thought to killing someone—man or woman—if they got in their way.

She guessed she had been lucky to have not experienced anything like that while she was in Creepy Man's custody. But, she remembered Quin had said that if Creepy Man had ever found out what they had done, he would be hunted down and killed. She shuddered at the thought.

Looking up, she saw a woman walking toward her. The woman had a strange look on her face. Darcey wasn't sure if it was disgust or hate. Whichever it was, she felt an immediate cold chill cover her entire body. As the woman got closer, her expression changed, and Darcey could read nothing on her face. *Maybe I just imagined it because I had been thinking about the Creepy Man*, she thought.

"Hello, you must be Señorita Callahan," Lilly said, keeping her hands by her side while a cold smile played around the corners of her mouth. "I am Lilly Montego, Señor Daniels's Executive Assistant. I am sure he has already told you that I will be glad to help you with anything you might need or want to know." The words tasted like battery acid in her mouth. The last thing she wanted to do was help this woman with anything—except to help her die.

"Hi, I was just coming to find you to see if you have heard from Brad, yet," Darcey said, forcing a smile as she watched Lilly closely. Darcey was getting bad vibes from this woman and felt a prickly sensation at the base of her neck.

Good. Your intuition is beginning to kick in.

There's that voice again, Darcey thought.

Yes, I'm back and you'd better listen to me on this. This woman is up to no good.

You may be right. I feel horrible, evil vibes radiating from her, Darcey agreed.

Go with it then. Follow your instincts on this.

Lilly's eyes narrowed at the question. *What did she*

mean about "hearing from Brad?" she asked herself. *Has he gone and left without telling me?*

Lilly, clinched her teeth. "I am sorry…have I heard from Brad?" she asked, trying to control her voice.

"Yes, Brad left early this morning for some meeting in Lima," Darcey told her. If Lilly didn't know about Brad's meeting with Santiago, he must have had some reason for not telling her, so Darcey wasn't going to give her any more information.

"Oh, that." Lilly gave the impression that she knew all about it. "No, I've not heard from him, but I will let you know when I do." She smiled a cold smile that never made it past her lips. "If you will excuse me, I have some reports to file before ten. I will be in my office if you need me." She turned sharply on her heel and marched back in the direction she had come from, leaving Darcey bewildered, standing in the middle of the corridor, staring at her retreating back.

Fuming, Lilly slammed her office door. The 'bang' echoed down the corridor.

Well, this is just fine, Lilly seethed. *What else can go wrong?* Now, she had no way of knowing how soon Brad would try to get to Santiago. If she didn't hear from him soon, she would try calling his cell. She could not risk calling Santiago until she knew for sure what Brad's plan would be. She sat down, put her elbows on the desk, and her forehead in her hands. *What was I thinking letting that woman get under my skin? I am letting my emotions run unchecked and that is not good.*

Lilly's normal controlled exterior was beginning to crack. It was time for another dose. She got up, shut the window blinds, and locked her office door.

With her hands shaking, she pulled the gold chain from around her neck and selected one of the two keys dangling from it. Bending over she unlocked and opened her bottom desk drawer and lifted out a small, silver, metal box from its hiding place. Taking the other key, she unlocked the box. Lifting the lid, she set out two small glass vials, a syringe, a small rubber hose, and a package of sterile needles. She sat and stared at the objects on her desk, shaking her head.

This is too soon.

Sighing, she turned around to the credenza and grabbed a small bottle of rubbing alcohol and a couple of sterile cotton balls from the first aid kit. She fastened the needle in the syringe, and pushed the air out, then reached for the first vial. Swiping the top with the alcohol soaked cotton ball, she plunged the needle into the vial and drew out two ccs, then repeated the procedure with the second vial. Eyeing the syringe, she laid it on the desk, wrapped the rubber hose around her arm just above the elbow, and tied it snugly. Stretching her arm out, she rubbed the bend of her arm with the soaked cotton ball. The needle slid easily into the raised vein. As soon as the dose hit the bloodstream, a calming effect washed over her. Closing her eyes, she sighed and relaxed against the back of her chair, relishing in the euphoria as the drug raced through her body.

That was way overdue, she thought. Promising herself now, she would be more careful in the future—no more mistakes. The stakes were too high. "The In-Charge Lilly" was back in control.

⸙

Well, that certainly wasn't what I had been expecting, Darcey thought. *I wonder what got her upset so much that she slammed her office door. Maybe she isn't as friendly as Brad thinks. Guess I'll just do some more exploring on my own.*

Darcey shrugged and walked on in the direction she had been going when she ran into Lilly. She passed the corporate offices. Glancing in the direction of Lilly's office, she saw the door was closed and the blinds pulled shut.

Odd.

Passing the service area, she stared through the windows of one room marveling at all of the equipment lining the walls and wondered what all of it had to do with maintaining the dome. Just as she turned to walk on, she collided with someone in jeans and cowboy boots.

"Oh, excuse me!" Darcey said, blushing. "I'm sorry I wasn't paying attention to where I was going. I hope I didn't hurt you."

"Not at all, ma'am," the man said, touching his old, battered Stetson. "I shouldn't have been barrelin' out the door like that. Didn't hurt you, did I?" *Where have you been all my life, beautiful lady?* he thought and grinned wider.

Darcey laughed. "No harm done. I'm new and was looking at all of the equipment in there." She turned and indicated over her shoulder the room he had just left.

He grinned as he touched his hat again. "Ty Horton, ma'am. It'd be my pleasure to show you what all that does. I'm through with my shift, so how about right now?" *Yes, indeed!* he thought.

She extended her hand. "Hi. I'm Darcey Callahan, pleased to meet you, and yes, that would be wonderful if you would like do that," she said, returning his smile. "I think Brad had scheduled Lilly to show me around, but she seems a bit busy at the moment." She laughed to herself, remembering the door slamming.

Taking Darcey's hand in his, Ty pumped it up and down. "You must be Brad's Darcey. He said he was bringin' you here. Glad to meet ya, ma'am," Ty said. He released her hand. "Where ya wanna start?" he asked, his spirits slightly dampened now. *Brad, you lucky dog*, he thought. *You didn't tell me she was a real looker. Some guys have all the luck.*

"I don't know. This is all so new to me. Exactly what is this place? she asked, as they turned and started to walk on. "Brad has not had time to explain all of it to me in detail, yet. He has just given me the basics. Why don't we just start here and see where we wind up?"

"Shall we?" Ty indicated that they should begin walking. "Well, this is a bio dome, designed and built by Brad. We're five miles under the surface of the Pacific Ocean, just off the coast of Peru. When this is finished, the dome will support up to five hundred families. It will be a small city on the floor of the ocean," he told her.

"Yes, that's what Brad has told me, but I would like to know more. What is all this equipment for? Darcey asked, pointing at the equipment that lined the walls of the room they were passing.

"That's the reactor and air-filtration system room, better known as the operations room. It holds the heart and soul of the dome," he said.

"This is all so amazing," she said, trying to take it all in. "How long has it taken to build this?"

"This is the sixth year. Official opening of the dome will be sometime next month. However, it will take another couple of years for everything to be completed," Ty told her, as they walked on around the service ring to the entertainment area.

Ty explained all of the things that would be available when the dome was completed as he escorted her around. It was a little past noon when they wound up back at the Bajo el Mar Café and Ty asked her to join him for lunch.

"Thanks, I would enjoy that," she told him.

CHAPTER 7

The Plan

It was ten-fifteen when the sub docked and Brad hailed a taxi. He gave the driver the address and hit the callback button for Angelo.

"Brad here. I'm on my way. Should be there in twenty minutes or so. Did you have any trouble picking up Nicho?" he asked.

"No, the flight was on time. See you in twenty," Angelo said and hung up.

The taxi pulled up in front of the Starbucks. Brad tossed a couple of bills over the seat toward the driver and got out. Checking the tables on the patio, having never met Angelo, he looked for Nicho. He spied them seated at a table farthest away from the street. Brad walked toward the table and gave a small recognition nod.

Nicho stood and extended his hand. That caught Brad off guard. The last time they had seen each other it had not been on the best of terms.

"It is good to see you again," he said, shaking Brad's hand, but he never smiled. It was not good, but Luis said he must work with this man. It was in the best interests of everyone. "I trust all is well."

"Yes, all is well and it's good to see you again," Brad said, also not smiling. *This is a switch*, he thought. *Back in Morocco, he had wanted my head on a platter. What's with the change in attitude?*

Angelo sat there, watching the sparring match, and wondered just what these two had in common besides their dislike for each other. *This should be interesting*, he thought. He just hoped, if push came to shove, he did not get caught in the crossfire.

"You must be Angelo," Brad said, extending his hand in the direction of the man still seated. Angelo appeared to be about Brad's age with shoulder length sandy colored hair. His blue eyes stood out in his darkly tanned face. The five o'clock shadow added to his unkempt, sinister look. Brad was glad Angelo was on his side.

Angelo shook Brad's hand but did not stand up. "Yes, glad to meet you."

Nicho and Brad sat down. Brad casually looked around, checking to see if anyone might be within hearing distance before speaking. "Okay, I presume that Luis has filled you in on what's going on?" He looked from Nicho to Angelo, who both nodded. "Short and simple— we need a plan," he said, leaning forward looking from Nicho to Angelo again. "I can design and build a bio dome to exist five miles down on the ocean floor, but this sort of thing is way out of my league."

"Yes, Vargas explained the situation when he contacted me and asked me to do some scouting," Angelo said. "I have checked out the location where Santiago and his friends are. They are on a ranch that was owned by Armando Martinez, who recently departed this earth." Angelo smiled at his reference to Armando's demise. He did not exactly know the guy but had heard the rumors going around about Armando. It appeared that his death was not a great loss to anyone. "The main house is surrounded by a security wall. There are only two entrances—the main gate, and the delivery entrance. Both have electric gates."

"Are the gates locked all the time?" Nicho asked.

"As far as I can tell, the delivery gate is only opened when a delivery is made. The main gate, however, is left open when one of them leaves and is closed when they return. If the gate is closed, it is a pretty sure bet they are all inside." Angelo leaned forward as he talked, drawing a layout of the gates on a napkin. "I have been watching pretty much twenty-four-seven since Luis called. The pattern has never changed." He tapped the napkin with the pen.

"What times do they leave the ranch?" Brad asked, pulling the napkin over and studying the drawing.

"It depends. There does not seem to be any regular schedule for coming or going," Angelo said. "However, I have only been able to watch for the past two days. In that time, they have left the ranch four different times. Best that I can determine Santiago has never left. It has always been the other two. Sometimes together, sometimes alone. That's the best I can tell you."

"So there is no easy way in if the gates are closed," Nicho surmised, speaking more to himself, than the other two. "Is there any way to open the service entrance from the outside?" he asked, thinking that particular gate would be less conspicuous than storming the front one.

"Short of cutting the power, I would say no," Angelo stated, leaning back in his chair and tapping his pen on the table. "Let me ask this—are we planning on having a discussion with these guys, or are we going to eliminate them?"

"My plan is to take 'em out—period," Brad said,

emphatically stabbing the napkin with his finger and sending it sliding across the table toward Angelo. He looked over at Nicho. "What's your assessment of Santiago? You've had dealings with him."

"Yes, regrettably, he is the one I dealt with when I picked up Saleem. I am sorry—Darcey," he corrected himself. "He is not to be trusted. I have no qualms about taking him out, permanently." Nicho looked at Brad as he spoke, and their eyes met in mutual agreement.

"Angelo, you and Nicho have had more experience in dealing with this sort of thing, what do you suggest?" Brad asked, looking from one to the other.

Angelo had been sitting there thinking about that very thing. A plan was what was called for—a delaying plan, like Vargas asked him to put together. Vargas had told him to do whatever it took to keep Brad out of the mix until his elite forces got there and could take care of Carlos. Angelo was not sure why Vargas wanted this, but he was being paid to work, not to ask questions. However, he did hate that he would be missing out on the action. "If it's the decision that we eliminate them, then I suggest a surprise attack." Angelo looked from Brad to Nicho. He could tell that Brad was anxious to have it over with, but Nicho, on the other hand, gave nothing away. Angelo had no way of knowing if Nicho was in on Vargas's plan or not. He gave no indication he knew anything about it in the conversation from the airport. Angelo could read him in later if necessary.

"As much as I want this finished, I can understand doing it the right way. We need something that the authorities will not question when it's over. I don't want anything reflecting back on ORCA," Brad said, looking at Angelo. "What do you have in mind?"

Angelo nodded. "Agreed. I propose we watch for a couple of days and see what deliveries they get and when.

It will be easy to stop one of the deliveries and take it in ourselves. The delivery most likely will be met by the kitchen or house staff. They will be easy to deal with. I have asked questions of people who knew Armando, and they have told me he only had an elderly housekeeper and one maid. There was a groundskeeper, but Armando had let him go shortly before he was murdered."

Brad and Nicho listened as Angelo talked on.

"Since I have the only car and a residence here, we will go there and finish our conversation," Angelo said, standing up, noticing that the patio was filling up with lunch diners. He waded up the napkin and stuffed it in his jeans pocket.

They trailed out, following Angelo to his car in the parking lot. The hot, noonday sun bounced off the silver BMW M6 Coupe, as Angelo opened the driver's side door. It was a tight fit for Brad to fold his six-foot-seven-inch frame into the backseat.

Angelo slipped in behind the steering wheel and started the engine. Nicho was the last in. He handed his briefcase to Brad then shut his door.

Angelo punched the accelerator to the floor, squealing the tires as he left the lot. The thrust pushed Nicho and Brad into the back of their seats. Nearby pedestrians stopped and gawked as they barreled down the street, tires smoking.

"Man! This baby can move," Brad said, admiringly, thinking he outta check into buying one of these.

"How long have you had this?" Nicho wanted to know. "The last time I was here, you had an Audi. This is a big step up."

"Yes, I suddenly found myself single again and decided it was time to live a little while I still could." Angelo laughed. Next to dumping that damn witch he'd been living with, the BMW had been the best freaking decision he had made in years. Twenty minutes later, they pulled into a parking lot beside Angelo's apartment building. They took the stairs two at a time instead of the elevator to the third floor. It was quicker and no one noticed them.

Angelo's apartment was modest compared to the vehicle parked outside, but comfortable. Two bedrooms meant someone would have to bunk on the couch unless they wanted to sleep together. Angelo smiled at the idea. They could flip for the bed. He laughed to himself as he pulled three cold beers from the fridge. Angelo tossed a bottle of beer to Brad, who had stepped out on to the balcony, barely missing the sliding glass door. He then handed one to Nicho, who had made himself at home, lounging in Angelo's favorite chair.

"Gentlemen, gather round the table so we can map out our strategy." Angelo motioned for them to move to the table. Reaching under the counter, he pulled out a gun. "First, we need to see what kind of fire power we have. We do not know what we may be up against. So, it is best we are prepared," he said, laying his MAC-10 on the table.

"I brought my Glock," Brad said, pulling the gun from his waistband and laying it on the table.

Nicho got up and picked up his briefcase. He laid it on the table and popped it open. Inside, the newest carbon fiber body AR-15 lay nestled snugly in a bed of black foam rubber. Nicho pulled out the pieces and assembled it in a matter of seconds. He held up the gun for them to see. "Gentlemen, meet the new carbon fiber TRITech AR-15. Totally undetectable when passing through metal detectors and X-ray machines."

Angelo reached for it and passed the gun back and forth between his hands. "What does it weigh? It is almost like holding nothing."

"It weighs less than a pound without the clip. With

the clip, somewhere around two pounds." Nicho tossed Angelo an empty clip. "That one holds forty rounds. I never carry bullets with me. I can always pick some up wherever I'm going."

"Well, it seems we are ready in the firepower department," Brad said, reaching for the AR-15. "Nice gun. What's this baby cost?" he asked, running his hand over the gun, enjoying the feel of its texture.

"Around forty-five hundred," Nicho told him, as Brad handed the gun back to him.

"The first item of business is to get a van, something we can disguise as a service vehicle of some sort," Angelo said. "Nicho, will you call around and see what's available?"

"Okay, I have a connection that can get us what we want, no questions asked. I will call him when we are done here," Nicho said, breaking the gun down and putting it back in the briefcase. He was hoping there would be some action where he could see what this baby could do. It performed like a dream on the firing range, but that was not like using it under pressure.

"We will also need a car, something less noticeable than my BMW." Angelo laughed. "Have your contact get us one."

Nicho pulled out his phone and called his contact. Brad stepped out on the balcony and called Lilly.

"Hello, Lilly here. How may I help you?" she asked, in her now-calm business voice.

"Hey, Lilly, Brad here," he said. "Just wanted to check in to see how Darcey is."

Lilly gripped the handset hard, till her knuckles turned white. *Of course, that woman would be his first concern, not the dome or me,* she thought angrily. "She's just fine. I believe I saw Ty escorting her around just before lunch," she said curtly, her free hand clenching and unclenching rapidly.

"That's great. If he's showing her around, you won't have to disrupt your day to do it," Brad told her. "Sounds like everything's under control. I'll call you later."

Brad hung up before Lilly could respond, leaving her fuming because he had not asked one question about the dome, or her, plus, she had not been able to question him about Santiago.

Brad immediately called Ty's cell. He wanted to tell him 'thanks' for taking Darcey around.

Ty looked at the caller ID before answering. "Ty here. What's up boss?"

"Hey, just talked to Lilly and she said you were giving Darcey the grand tour." Brad laughed. "And I wanted to tell you thanks for doing that. I haven't had time yet.'

"Not a problem. My pleasure to help out where I can." Ty chuckled. "We're getting' a bite to eat right now." Looking at Darcey, a brief stab of envy hit him. "You want to talk to her? She's right here."

"Sure, if you don't mind," Brad said.

Ty handed the phone to Darcey. *I'm going to have to get out more. It's been too long since I've had female company.*

She took the phone. Butterflies began in the pit of her stomach in anticipation of hearing his voice. "Hi," she said.

"Hey, how's it going? Has Ty been showing you around the dome?" Brad asked, her voice setting off the butterflies that exploded in his stomach. He closed his eyes and enjoyed the moment.

"Yes, we've been all over the place. I can't believe all of the wonderful things that are happening here," she told him, her heart rate increasing as she listened to the velvet tones of his voice. *What's the matter with me? All*

I have to do is hear his voice, and I have no control over my emotions.

"I'm glad you are having a wonderful time. I'll be gone for a few days. This thing is going to take longer than expected. I told you to check with Lilly if you needed anything, but since Ty has been showing you around, I'm going to ask him to keep an eye on you. That way Lilly can keep her mind on running the dome till I get back," Brad explained to her. "I miss you. I will be back in a few days. Let me talk to Ty, so I can tell him to watch out for you."

"I miss you, too," Darcey said. "Please be safe." She handed Ty the phone. She was amazed at her instant response. She didn't hesitate to say she missed him because she really did. It had just come naturally—like it had been a part of her for a long time. *Just go with that feeling. It's leading you in the right direction,* that little voice whispered to her.

Ty put the phone to his ear. "Yeah, boss man?"

"Ty, will you keep an eye on her for me. This trip is going to take longer than I expected, and I'm not comfortable leaving her all alone. So, if you would do that, I'd be forever grateful," Brad explained. He knew she would be safe, but just knowing there was someone she could turn to, if necessary, gave him peace of mind, and he could put his full attention on, Santiago.

"Sure, man. No problem. I'll be glad to watch your little lady." Ty laughed and winked at Darcey. Yeah, I definitely have to get out more.

"Thanks, I'll see you in a few days then. I guess everything else is running okay?" Brad asked. He still had that nagging feeling that something else was going to happen.

"Yeah, so far everythin's runnin' as smooth as a new baby's bottom. I don't think we'll have any more problems," Ty assured him. "Don't worry. My guys are on top of things. See ya when ya get back."

"Yeah, see ya." Brad hung up and walked back inside.

Darcey and Ty finished lunch and walked back to the operations room where Ty had promised to show her the equipment that made the dome work.

There was a low hum that she assumed was the reactor running. An electrical smell hung in the air. The room had a chill, and she guessed that was because of all of the computers and various complicated-looking control panels that lined the walls.

In the middle of the room was a rectangular opening with a railing on three sides protecting the public from falling down a stairway leading to subterranean depths below the floor.

"This first room, here, has the desks for the tech guys who make sure everything runs smoothly." Ty motioned to the area with several unoccupied desks.

"How many tech guys work here?" she asked, noticing all the empty desks.

"Right now, there are two who look after the reactor, and the four of us, who handle the bio-filtration system. All of these desks will be full when the whole thing is up and running full force," Ty said. He looked around to see where the other guys were. "If I can find them, I'll introduce you to them." He walked over to the railing and leaned over. "Hey! Are y'all hidin' out down there?"

"Yeah!" someone shouted from the depths below the floor. "Be right up."

Boots thudded on the stairs as someone approached.

"Well, hellooo!" the lanky young man said as he took the last two steps up the stairs in one big leap. "Who have we here?" he asked, grinning.

Ty glared at him a silent warning to behave himself.

"Hey, take it easy. This is Darcey Callahan, the boss man's lady."

"Well, mighty pleased to meet ya, ma'am." He grinned, touching his well-worn cowboy hat and giving a slight bow. He was bumped from behind, almost sending him face down on the floor by two other men, who had bounded up the stairs just a few seconds behind him.

Darcey blushed and laughed at the antics of the men. *Who are these guys? They remind me of the Three Stooges. But who are the Three Stooges? Did I know who they were in my past life? Was part of my memory coming back? Somehow, I knew they were three goofy guys that did crazy things. That much I am sure of.*

"Darcey, here are the other two who are in charge of the filtration system. This is Matt Wilkins, Scott Taylor, and you've just met Steve 'Hot Dog' Nelson. Gentlemen, let me introduce you to the boss man's lady, Darcey Callahan." Ty beamed, making a wide arc with his arm encompassing the three men, who were looking like the kid who had been caught with his hand in the cookie jar.

"Ahem, pleased to meet you, ma'am," they said, almost in unison, touching their hats.

"However," Scott said, stepping forward, "I believe we've already met. I'm Marti's stepbrother. We met several years ago at the wedding of my father and Marti's mother."

"I'm sorry, but I don't remember you. I was in a car crash and I've lost my memory," she told him. "But I'm glad to meet you anyway—again." She laughed. "I'm glad to meet all of you."

"Come on, guys, I want to show Darcey how this thing works, and how indispensable we are to the dome." Ty laughed, steering Darcey toward the stairway that led down to the filtration system. "Careful, watch your step," he cautioned.

The guys moved over to let them pass and followed as soon as Ty and Darcey had reached the bottom. They weren't going to let Ty take all of the credit. Falling over each other racing to the bottom, they all arrived almost at the same time.

Darcey laughed to herself. *Yes, definitely the Three Stooges.*

They showed her around and told her all about the sabotage, how Matt had written the program that 'saved the day', and how the other guys had implemented it and cleared out the virus. All four of them were proud of their work, and not the least bit modest about it, either. She liked these guys and hoped they would be friends.

❧

Lilly hung up the phone, fuming, after talking to Brad. She did not get a chance to question him about his plans. That left her at loose ends on when, or if, she even wanted to contact Santiago now. She had a meeting with Matt in a few minutes and had to calm down. That was going to be difficult, as she was still angry about Brad's concern over that damn woman. Lilly closed her eyes and took several deep breaths, willing herself to relax.

She had been working on Matt for weeks, gaining his trust, taking it slow in order to learn how the hydroponics worked without causing suspicion. Now, she had all the information she needed to complete what Armando and the Eastern Alliance had messed up in their feeble attempt to delay the opening of the dome.

One of the major things that the Bio Dome Project boasted was its experimental hydroponics system that not only shortened the growing process, but increased production. The experimental integrated system allowed for a new cycle to come online when the previous cycle was halfway through its completed cycle. It made the Bio Dome completely self-sufficient for fruits, vegetables, and grains with no lapse in the growing cycles. The variety of fruits and vegetables that was growing in the gardens was astounding. The seed and sprout stores had every known fruit or vegetable variety available either in seed form or sprouts.

Matt walked into Lilly's office with a big grin on his face. "Afternoon, Miss Lilly," he said, sitting down in one of the chairs in front of her desk. "Ready to go over to the gardens?" he asked, twirling his hat in his hands. "They will be finishing up installing the growing units and getting the solution tanks connected."

"Yes," Lilly said, as she stood up and turned off her computer. "Let's go."

It's a little early to be working on the tanks, she thought. Javier had told her the tanks would not be ready until the week before completion. Apparently, he was not as privy to the workings of the hydroponic section as he'd led her to believe. *When am I going to quit listening to him?* she scolded herself.

They walked over to the hydroponics area next to the Bajo el Mar Café. Matt used his ID card to enter. That was something else she was going to have to get. Her card would not let her in the hydro area, and what she needed to do could not be done from the outside. She would have to requisition herself an ID card for the hydro area. That was something she should have done months ago but had neglected to do it since Javier had assured her his plan would work. However, no one would be suspicious of the request coming from her.

Stepping inside, the warm, moist air felt like a tropical rainforest. It smelled fresh and clean. They walked past the workers who were putting up the remaining units, where the actual plants would be introduced.

"These will all be ready next week to put the seedlings in." Matt smiled, as they walked from one section to another.

"But isn't that a little soon?" Lilly asked. "The actual completion date isn't until the end of next month." This was the first she had heard about planting early. Her plan relied on the planting not happening until the week before the scheduled completion and opening date, leaving them no time to replant after her plan went into action.

"Just a little precaution because of the attempted sabotage earlier," Matt said, as he got down on one knee to check the connections to a solution tank. "We'll have plenty of time to work out the bugs before the opening." Getting up, he brushed off the knee of his jeans and walked on. "Plus, corporate wants to use the first harvest to prepare the food that will be served at the opening." Matt didn't notice the scowl that crossed Lilly's face.

A change of plans may be in order, she thought.

❧❧

Bam! Bam! Bam! Sounded on the apartment door. Angelo had called for pizza.

"Get that! It's the pizza," Angelo shouted from the bathroom to whoever was closest to the door.

Brad jumped up off the couch and headed for the door. Just out of curiosity, he looked through the peephole first. The guy on the other side of the door did not look like a pizza deliveryman. Brad backed away from the door and motioned to Nicho to come over, pointing to the door.

Bam! Bam! Bam! Again on the door.

Nicho looked through the peephole and started laughing. "That is my contact with the van." He opened the door. "Hey, man. What took you so long?"

The contact laughed, punching Nicho on the shoulder. "This place is hard to find. Next time send me GPS coordinates."

Nicho walked over to the couch and sat down, motioning to him to sit down. Nicho knew this guy well enough to know he would try to gouge them on the price, so some firm negotiating was going to be needed. "What do you have for us?"

"I have got what you want for the van and the car," the contact said, his eyes jumping between Brad and Angelo and back to Nicho. "But it is gonna run double this time. Overhead has gone up—you understand." He paused and chuckled nervously.

Nicho was not smiling. "Okay, what is your double-figure?"

"The van and car are both untraceable, should they need to be—you understand?" He gave another nervous chuckle, looking from Nicho to Brad and Angelo. His tongue ran across his thin lips. "But for you, I have a special deal, both for ten grand." A nervous smiled played around his mouth.

"A special deal, eh?'" Nicho slapped him on the shoulder. "Well, how did we get so lucky? And only ten grand?" he said, sarcastically with a hint of a threat underlying the remark. He turned and winked at Brad and Angelo.

"Ummm, Yeah. Well, I could go a little lower, take a little less on my end, you know," the contact said, running his finger around the inside of the neck of his shirt collar.

Nicho smiled big, showing his teeth. "Well, that is real nice of you. Just how much less?"

"I could go as low as eight." The contact waited, his eyes flipping from one to the other. A droplet of sweat trickled down the side of his face.

Nicho's eyes narrowed and the friendly pretense disappeared. "Well, that is mighty nice of you. Why don't we call it four, and we have a deal?"

"Aw, come on, man. I have to make something out of this. You are leaving me no room for profit here," the contact wheedled. He fidgeted, adjusting his position on the sofa several times.

Nicho laughed. "Hey, that sounds like a personal problem to me. Tell your man to take less. You will get your money when we pick them up. Where are the vehicles?" He stood up and offered him his hand.

"I will call you with the address," the contact said, reluctantly taking Nicho's hand. *Shit, I will have to pay Joe the agreed price for the two vehicles and just eat the damn loss,* he grumbled inwardly.

Angelo opened the door just as the pizza deliveryman was ready to knock. Nicho slapped his contact on the back and pushed him out the door. The deliveryman stepped aside to let him stumble past, looking at Angelo in confusion.

"You ordered a pizza?" the pizza delivery guy asked, looking at the receipt taped to the box's lid, checking the address.

"Yeah. How much?" Angelo pulled his wallet out and handed the man the money.

CHAPTER 8

Darcey Meets Marti—Again

Marti fumed about the phone conversation she'd had with Lilly as she packed her small case. That woman had a real problem. For the life of her, Marti couldn't see why Brad had ever made her his executive assistant. She would suggest to Brad that he pay for a course in people skills for her.

Sorting through her closet, Marti picked out several outfits before she finally settled on four. She neatly folded the outfits and put them in the case on top of her shoe bag, beside her makeup bag. Marti zipped the case shut and set it by the front door.

Earlier, Marti had called and left messages for all of the girls and then called her dad. He was excited that Darcey had been found and that she was okay in spite of her memory loss. He volunteered to drive Marti to the airport and told her not to worry about how long she might be gone. He had everything under control at the store.

Ashley called back around four. She had been at the

jewelry market all day and was exhausted, but with the news about Darcey, she felt revitalized. She would have to plan a party to celebrate as soon as they could get Darcey home.

"Are you sure about it? They've actually found Darcey?" Ashley asked, enthusiastically.

"Yes, Brad's executive assistant called and said she's fine, but has lost her memory. They are flying me down to see her. I leave tonight," Marti told her.

"This is wonderful news. Have you called everyone else?" Ashley asked. "If you haven't I can do it."

"Yes, I've called everyone, but so far you are the only one to return my call," Marti told her. "But, it's just a little after four so they're probably not off work yet. Would you mind checking to make sure everyone knows, just in case they don't return my call before I leave?"

"Sure, no problem. What time are you leaving?" Ashley asked.

"They are flying me down on the corporate jet. I have to be there by seven, but won't take off until eight," Marti explained. "It's an eight-hour flight, so I should be getting there in time for breakfast."

"Wow! The corporate jet! How cool is that?" Ashley said. "I sure wish I was going with you. Be sure to tell Darcey 'Hi!' for me."

"Yes, I'll tell her all of you have been worried and that you're all glad she's okay," Marti said. "I'll call you when I get there." She hung up and called her dad. "Dad, I've got everything ready. Do you want me to meet you at the store?" Since her dad was taking her to the airport, it didn't matter where she left her car.

"Come on down to the store. It's closer to the airport from here, and you can put your car in the warehouse."

The drive to the store took a little longer than she expected because of the road construction on the freeway.

Pulling into her parking space at the store, she looked at her watch. They still had time to grab something to eat before she had to be at the airport.

Marti grabbed her purse and went inside to get her dad. He was with a customer, so she waited behind the counter, thumbing through the latest sportswear catalogs that had arrived, trying not to worry about her best friend who probably wouldn't know her at all. What would she do if she couldn't help Darcey remember? *Silly girl! Think positive. I will help her remember—no doubt about it,* Marty thought optimistically.

Her dad rang up the purchase, thanked the customer for their business, turned around, and leaned against the counter with his arms folded. He smiled at her. "You all packed and ready?"

"Yeah." Marti smiled back. "Come on. We have time to grab a bite before we have to leave for the airport," she said, walking toward the automatic doors. "You can drive. I'll pull mine around to the warehouse. Have someone open the door for me," she yelled over her shoulder, as the doors slid closed.

They arrived at the airport around six-thirty but had difficulty in locating ORCA's private gate. After asking several of the airport personnel, they found a security guard who directed them to ORCA's entrance. They drove to the end of the terminal and found the road. Once they turned on the road, Marti could see the gate with a sign *ORCA Corp. Authorized Personnel Only* on the fence.

Marti's dad stopped the car in front the gate since the man on the other side showed no indication that he was going to open it for him to drive through. He helped Marti with her bag, gave her a hug, and kissed her forehead. "Take care and you call me as soon as you get there. You hear?"

"Yes, I'll call as soon as the plane lands," Marti told him. "Don't worry. Everything's going to be okay." She gave him a final hug and walked up to the gate. The man opened it just enough for her to walk through.

"¡*Hola*! Señorita Campbell, I presume?" the man asked. "I am your flight attendant. If you will follow me, *por favor*?"

Marti smiled, looking around for the shuttle that was supposed to be there. "Yes, that's me."

"It's just a short walk to the plane." The attendant took her bag from her hand and started down the tarmac.

Marti turned back one more time to wave at her dad before she took off hurrying after the man.

The attendant, who was several steps in front of Marti, glanced back over his shoulder to make sure she was following. He slowed his pace so she could catch up.

"I am sorry," he apologized. "I have a tendency to walk faster than most people."

"Not a problem," Marti said with a laugh, falling into step beside him. "It's been a long day for me and I'm running a little slow."

They boarded the plane and were in the air by eight-o-one. Marti was the only passenger. The crew consisted of the pilot, co-pilot, and the attendant who had collected her at the gate.

"*Señorita*, the galley is open if you are hungry or thirsty," the attendant said as he paused by her seat before continuing on his way to the front of the plane.

"No, thank you," Marti said, "I've already eaten." She smiled, unbuckling her seat belt to get more comfortable. "I would like some magazines if you have any, I forgot to pack something."

"Certainly," the attendant said and continued down the aisle to the front of the plane.

He disappeared behind the curtain at the end of the

aisle. Several minutes later he reappeared carrying a stack of magazines.

"I did not know what you would like, so I brought several." He placed them on the table in front of her. "Let me know if you need anything else, *por favor*."

"Thank you. These will be plenty." Marti picked up the *People Magazine* and started thumbing through it. She really didn't want anything to read, but just something to keep her hands busy, and maybe occupy her thoughts. She worried about Darcey. What if she couldn't help her to remember? Could they still be friends? Would Darcey still want to be friends? It was all so unpredictable. It would break Marti's heart if she couldn't pull this off.

Somewhere around midnight, Marti turned off her overhead light, reclined her seat, and drifted off still worried about Darcey. It was what she did best—worry.

The smell of freshly brewed coffee pulled Marti back from dreamland. When she opened her eyes, it was still dark outside the plane's window. The only light was the sliver of light that shown between the curtain and the wall at the end of the aisle. Marti put her seat in its upright position and reached up to turn on her overhead light.

"Hello?" Marti called, watching the curtain. "I sure could use some of that coffee."

A few minutes later, the attendant pushed the curtain aside, and Marti could see there was a small galley behind him. He came toward her carrying a tray with a cup of coffee, several packets of sugar, three small plastic containers of creamer, and two fresh-baked scones.

"This is super!" Marti said, moving the magazines aside so he could place the tray on the table. "The scones smell wonderful. Thank you." She looked up at the attendant, but he had already started back toward the galley.

Certainly doesn't talk much. She took a sip of the coffee. It was hot and rich. She looked at her watch. It was three twenty-nine. *We should be landing in about thirty minutes.* Finishing her coffee and a scone, Marti stood up and stretched. Wondering where the attendant was, she walked toward the galley just as he emerged from the cockpit area carrying a large mug.

"I'm looking for the restroom. I would like to freshen up before we land," Marti inquired.

"The restroom is in the rear of the plane." He pointed toward the back of the plane and turned to fill the mug with coffee. He didn't say any more, just opened the door and re-entered the cockpit.

Marti barely made it back to her seat before the pilot turned on the seatbelt sign. She pulled the seatbelt across her lap and slipped the buckle in place, locking it as the landing gear's motor whirred into action and the wheels locked in place, vibrating the cabin floor.

From the plane's window, Marti watched as the plane came to a standstill in front of a large hangar, wondering if Darcey would be there to meet her. *No, probably not,* she thought. *Why would she come to meet someone she didn't know?*

Emerging from the cockpit the attendant opened the plane's door, motioning to Marti that she could deplane when she had collected her things.

"There is a limo waiting below that will take you to the dock where you will board the submarine. The sub will then take you to the dome to meet your friend," he said as a matter of fact. He looked at Marti with raised eyebrows as her eyes flew open wide and her mouth dropped open.

"Submarine?" she squeaked. "What submarine? Submarine? Like ocean type submarine?" Her voice was getting louder.

"Yes. That's how you get to the dome where your friend is. I presumed you had been told about this." He sounded aggravated.

"No!" she practically shouted. "No one said anything about a submarine or a dome or anything even close to that."

"*Por favor*. Do not stress over this. It is a simple matter of taking the sub to the dome It is perfectly safe," he said, exasperated. Reaching down he took her case from her clenched, white-knuckled fist. In that moment, he made a split-second decision to accompany her. They couldn't have a hysterical female on board the sub. "I will be going with you. It is all completely safe, I assure you." He motioned again for a shocked Marti to precede him down the stairs to the waiting limo.

Forty minutes later, Marti looked out the limo's window and saw the top of a submarine as they pulled up to the dock. She was surprised at the size. What she had in mind was a small two-man sub used for exploring the ocean, not this full-sized, military looking submarine. Two men were standing on the dock beside the gangplank. One stood perfectly still while the other kept checking his watch every few seconds. She guessed he was the one in charge.

Marti and the attendant emerged from the limo to be greeted by a very impatient sub captain.

"You are running behind time," the captain said, sternly looking at the attendant. "Let's get her on board." The captain motioned to the other man to gather the two pieces of luggage the limo driver had set at the end of the gangplank and follow them into the sub.

The attendant just nodded and took Marti's arm, escorting her up the gangplank and to the open hatch on the top of the sub.

Thank goodness, I wore slacks, Marti thought as she

peered down the hatch, seeing a ladder disappearing in the interior of the sub.

"I will go first," the attendant said. "I will help you down the ladder. It is very easy." He was smiling to himself as a wayward thought drifted through his mind—*too bad she is wearing slacks.*

The attendant reached the bottom of the ladder. "Okay, you can start down," he hollered up.

The captain assisted her until she had her feet firmly on the top rung. The rungs were wider than she had expected and it was easy to step down from one to the next until she reached the bottom. The first mate with the luggage descended next, followed by the captain who secured the hatch before he completed his trip down the ladder.

"Please take our guest to the galley where breakfast is being served," the captain instructed the attendant. The captain turned to address Marti. "Our trip to the dome will take approximately two and a half hours. Ask Thomas here if you need anything, *por favor.*" With that, the captain turned and walked away.

"So you are Thomas?" Marti asked, wondering why he hadn't introduced himself before this.

"Yes," he said simply and motioned for her to follow him.

Strange man, Marti thought as she followed him down the narrow passageway. She had never been claustrophobic, but too much time spent in this could change all of that. She took a deep breath, just to make sure there was enough air, and inhaled the delicious aroma of sausage and eggs floating out of the galley doorway.

∽∾∽

Refilling her mug from the coffee urn, Marti sat back

down at the table where Thomas was finishing his third cup of coffee.

She had tried several times to engage him in conversation, but only succeeded in getting single syllable answers or grunts. This was very frustrating for someone who loved to talk.

"Is there a restroom on this thing?" she asked, slightly aggravated at the cold shoulder she was getting from Thomas.

"Yes, it is called 'the head.' I will show you the way."

He got up and walked to the door. He waited, stone-faced, for Marti to set her cup down and follow. He could do without this chatty female and was beginning to have second thoughts about having had accompanied her. Thomas preferred the quiet and avoided people whenever possible. Unfortunately, it was unavoidable this time.

Two and a half hours later, the horn sounded, signaling the sub had reached the dome. Marti quickly ascended the ladder into fresh air and what looked like sunlight, but soon realized it wasn't. She had taken three deep breaths before she stepped out onto the gangway. The air tasted fresh and sweet with a little salty tang mixed in.

Thomas followed her down the gangway with her cases. "This way, *por favor*," he said, indicating the corridor leading away from the docking area. "We will go this way to find your friend." Walking a few yards down the corridor, he stopped and motioned for her to get in a golf-cart like vehicle. "We will take the shuttle to your friend's quarters. It is too far to walk," he said, flipping the switch. The electric motor jerked to life and they drove off.

Marti wasn't sure, but she felt they were traveling up an incline the farther they went along the corridor, as if it was spiraling upward. Everything was monotone gray, so it was hard to distinguish floor from walls or from ceiling.

Spooky.

Some twenty minutes later, Thomas stopped the shuttle in front of what he told Marti was her friend's quarters. Marti jumped out and picked up her cases from the back. Thomas had already knocked once on the door when she stopped beside him. He waited a couple of minutes and knocked again.

From somewhere behind the door, came a faint muffled, "Just a minute, I'm coming."

The door slid open, and Darcey stared, bewildered, at the two people standing there. She didn't know either one.

"Darcey!" Marti let out a joyous yell and bounded into Darcey, wrapping her arms around her, and hugging her tight. Darcey staggered backward a few steps from the force of Marti's overly exuberant greeting.

"Oof!" Darcey expelled her breath as the woman slammed into her. "I'm sorry, but who are you?" she asked, pulling the woman's arms from around her and trying to regain her balance.

"Oh, Darcey, it's me, Marti!" she said and reached to hug her again.

Darcey took a step backward. "I'm sorry, you'll have to excuse me. But I don't know you." She looked past Marti to the man still standing outside the door. "Am I supposed to know you, too?" she asked, not sure what to expect now.

"No, I just transported your friend here. If everything is all right, I will go now," Thomas said. He turned abruptly, jumped into the shuttle, flipped the switch, and took off down the corridor.

Darcey turned and looked at the woman who said she was Marti—the Marti who Brad had said was her best friend. *I have no idea who this woman is, but that's no reason to be rude*, she thought. "Please, come in," she said. "I am truly sorry, but I don't know you. You will have to tell me how we know each other."

Marti turned and smiled at Darcey as she walked past her. Darcey closed and locked the door. She didn't know why she locked it. It was just a feeling she'd had ever since her run in with Lilly yesterday.

"Sure thing, girlfriend. Where do you want me to start?" Upbeat and smiling, as always, Marti looked around the room for the best place to sit. She decided on the sofa. Sitting down, she patted the seat next to her, indicating that Darcey should sit beside her, but Darcey had already headed for the kitchen.

"How about some breakfast? Coffee maybe?" Darcey walked into the kitchen, opened the fridge, and pulled out some ham and a couple of eggs. "I can fix us an omelet. Do you like omelets?" she asked, looking around the fridge's door at Marti.

"Yes, but don't bother on my account. I had breakfast on the sub, but I could do with another cup of coffee," Marty told her, leaving the sofa to walk over and sit on one of the bar stools. "Please, don't go to any trouble for me."

"No trouble, I haven't had breakfast, so making extra won't be a problem." Darcey smiled, set a cup in front of Marti, and placed the coffee pot on a trivet within Marti's reach. "Now tell me all about you and me," she said, as she started preparing her breakfast.

Marti proceeded to tell Darcey all about their relationship from the beginning. About grade school, college, graduation, jobs, friends, and family. Marti told her about how her parents had died in a head-on crash on their way back from Abilene. How her dad's family had shuffled her from family member to family member until her dad's brother, Jack, had taken her in and raised her. Marti told her that there wasn't any family left on her mother's side, and she had no brothers or sisters. But Marti and her dad thought of Darcey as family and that Marti loved her like the sister she always wanted.

Marti then elaborated on how Darcey had met Brad and how much they had meant to each other. How they spent every moment together when he was back in Dallas from the job in Peru, about what happened when Brad left, and how she had almost gone to pieces trying to find him. And, last, how much trouble she had caused by going off without telling anyone what she had planned. The minutes flew as they talked, Darcey asking questions—Marti providing the answers. It was mid-morning before Darcey looked at the clock.

"Oh, crap! I forgot about the time." She just realized she was still in her pajamas and was supposed to meet Ty at eleven for another sightseeing venture. "Excuse me while I get dressed. I'll be right back." She smiled, jumping off the barstool and jogging to the bedroom. *Marti has given me so much to think about. I just wish I could remember anything, just one little thing that will make sense.*

I told you, don't worry about it. Things will come back when you least expect it, that tiny voice told her. *Just let it happen.*

She threw on her slacks and a tee, then, grabbed her sandals, slipping them on as she walked back into the living room. Marti was still sitting at the counter.

"Here, I'll put your case in the bedroom," Darcey said, picking it up. "I don't have a spare bedroom, but I believe the sofa makes into a bed." She laughed, something about this reminded her of a distant memory of a slumber party.

You see? I told you things would start coming back. Just give it time, the little voice said.

"I'm supposed to meet a friend of Brad's who is going to show me more of the dome," she told Marti. "Slip your shoes back on and let's go. I'm sure you're curious about this place, too."

Marti cocked her head and looked at Darcey with questioning eyes. "Yes, just precisely where are we? And that sub. It's just crazy!"

"We're five miles below the Pacific Ocean, off the coast of Peru." Darcey laughed at Marti's expression. She could only imagine that she must have looked a lot like Marti when Brad had explained to her about the dome and sub.

Marti blinked then stared. "You-have-got-to-be-kidding—five miles?"

"Yes, five miles, can you believe it?" Darcey started for the door. "Come on, let's go." She was feeling elated for the first time in months.

They talked as they walked over to meet Ty, who had been pacing in front of the Bajo el Mar Café, waiting. Ty spotted them as they rounded the corner from the corridor.

Who have we here? he wondered, smiling as Darcey and Marti approached.

Ty touched his hat and gave them a sideways grin. "Well, well, well! Two beautiful ladies. How did this old cowboy get so lucky?"

"Ty, this is Marti Campbell, Marti this is Ty Horton," Darcey said, introducing them.

She could see Ty was already smitten with Marti and had a feeling that it was mutual. *We will have to have some "girl talk" later*, she mused, making a mental note to herself. *Girl talk? Where had that come from? Is it possible that was something we had shared before? I'll think about this later…*

Darcey made a wide arc with her arm to indicate the entire dome. "Ty and his buddies keep all of this going."

Ty laughed. He turned and indicated for them to walk with him to the shuttle parking lot. "Well, come on, ladies. I'll get us a shuttle, and we'll go sightseeing."

They climbed in. Darcey let Marti sit in the front seat with Ty and noticed that neither one objected.

"Want to stop by the operations room again? Marti might like to see where I work," Ty asked, but he was already heading in that direction and had almost reached the front of the operations room before he finished the question. "Well, since we're already here, why don't we take a look around inside?" he drawled, laughing.

Marti smiled sweetly at him. "I'd love to see where you work."

"Well, right this way, ladies." Ty jumped out of the shuttle and helped them down. Stepping over to the operations doom door, he opened it to allow the women to enter first.

CHAPTER 9

Matt's ID Goes Missing

The message light on Lilly's phone was blinking when she set the Styrofoam cup of tea down on the desk. Reaching up in the cupboard, she took her favorite tea mug out and sat it on the stone Thirsty Coaster on her desk before punching the message play-back button. As the message played back, she removed the plastic lid from the Styrofoam cup and poured the steaming tea into her mug.

The voice on the message started, "Lilly, I am sorry but, due to the recent attempts at sabotage, plus Armando's murder, Corporate will no longer issue new ID cards until after the official opening of the dome. I suggest if you need access to the hydroponic section, that you have Matt assist you. I am sorry, but there will not be any new cards issued until after the opening."

Lilly still had the foam cup in her hand. She crushed it and flung it as hard as she could. Little drops of tea immediately went spinning out as it flew silently through the air and landed on the seat of the chair in front of the desk. Her jaw tightened. That was not at all what she had expected to hear. Lilly knew that security had been tightened but had not expected to have the ID cards curtailed as well. She had not been topside since Armando's murder, and Brad had not mentioned anything about it. Of course, his head had been up his butt since he brought that damn woman here. Now, she had no choice but to try to get Matt's ID card. Lilly stood there, hands clenched into tight little fists, grinding her teeth.

Taking several deep breaths and relaxing her hands, she looked up just as the shuttle with Ty and a couple of women went by her office window. She recognized the one in the back—it was that damn woman. Her jaw tightened. The other must be the stupid woman from Dallas. Lilly stepped to the door to see where they were headed. The shuttle stopped in front of the operations room. Ty, and the two women got out and went inside.

Wondering what they were up to, Lilly casually strolled from her office to the operations room and peered through the window before entering. "Hello everyone," she called, as pleasant as was possible, considering what she was thinking at the moment.

"Well, hello there!" Ty touched the brim of his hat and gave her a big Texas grin. "You're just in time for the grand tour. I'm going to show these two beautiful ladies what goes on around here."

"Thank you, but I've already seen it all many times." Lilly looked at Ty and then at the women, "I'm sure you will find this all very interesting. Will Matt be joining you?" she asked, casually, looking back at Ty.

"I imagine he will and probably Scott and Hot Dog as well." Ty grinned again. "It's been quite a while since these old cowboys have had two such lovely ladies to escort around. Would you like to join us for lunch? We'll probably wind up back there around one or so," he asked, out of politeness. He knew Lilly was Brad's second in command, but, for the life of him, he couldn't understand why. Lilly grated on his nerves.

"Thank you, but no. I have reports to get out," Lilly said, barely able to restrain herself from grinning over her exceptionally good luck. She knew exactly where Matt kept his hydroponics ID card. And, now, learning that Matt would be out for the morning, she knew exactly what she would do. "Well, enjoy your tour, I have work to do." She actually smiled as she turned and walked out into the corridor. In fact, she smiled all the way back to her office.

Darcey watched as Lilly left. *That is one weird woman. I'll have to mention to Brad about how she has been acting,* she thought. Turning around, Darcey saw Ty take Marti by the arm and lead her over to the control panels, where he started explaining how and what part of the reactor it controlled. Then he explained how it was his job to make sure everything ran smoothly. She smiled to herself at how he conveniently left out mentioning Matt, Scott, or Hot Dog.

She watched Marti's eyes glaze over, trying to take in all he was saying. She knew what Marti was feeling, having experienced the tour just yesterday, but under the watchful eyes of all the guys who made sure she knew just how important each one's job was.

Thudding footsteps raced up the stairs from down below and two cowboy hats appeared simultaneously at the top of the stairs.

"See, I told you Darcey was here." Hot Dog punched Matt in the arm. "And look, she's brought a friend."

"Howdy, ma'am," Hot Dog said, touching the brim of his hat and turning to Ty. "How 'bout an introduction, man?"

"Sure thing," Ty said, clearing his throat. "This is

Marti Campbell, Darcey's friend from Dallas." He made a big sweeping gesture in Marti's direction. "Marti, these two crazy dudes here, are Matt Wilkins and Steve 'Hot Dog' Nelson. Along with me, and Scott Taylor, who should be here shortly, we are the resident geeks," he said smugly.

Marti smiled at them. "Nice meeting you guys." *It's a regular smorgasbord of hunks here,* she thought as she looked over at Darcey and winked. She was definitely going to call the girls back home and tell them all about this.

Another shuttle pulled up outside the operations room door. Scott jumped out and swaggered in, reading the papers on the clipboard in his hand.

"I've finished the inventory in the—" He looked up to see everyone looking at him, and then he noticed the new face and grinned from ear to ear. "Well, aren't you a sight for sore eyes?" he said, taking his hat off and looking at Marti, who was looking at him, astonished.

"Oh my gosh!" Marti exclaimed, her eyes wide in amazement. "Scotty! I didn't make the connection when Ty mentioned your name. Oh my gosh! This is great!" She ran over and threw her arms around him.

Everyone else stood staring at them with wide eyes.

His arms around her waist, Scott picked her up and swung her around, laughing. Putting her down, they hugged again and turned to look at four astonished and questioning faces.

"This is my step-brother," Marti said, smiling, still holding onto Scott's hand. "We haven't seen each other for over six years. Not since my mom and his father got married and moved to Wyoming."

"Well, I'll be," Ty said. "I forgot you mentioned that when you first met Darcey. Talk about a small world."

Darcey stood there, watching it all unfold, and

couldn't remember having ever met either Marti or Scott. She was envious of the easy camaraderie between them. She barely had someone she could remember from two months ago, let alone someone from six years ago.

Will this nightmare ever be over? Salty tears stung behind her eyelids.

You're stressing again—stop it! And, quit feeling sorry for yourself. You can handle this, you know you can. Her little voice floated to the front, poked her, and reminded her this was no time for a pity party.

Stuffing her disappointment down, she inhaled and put on a brave face. "Okay, guys, let's get this show on the road," she said, walking over and poking Ty on the arm. "At this rate, it will be noon before we get out of here." She laughed, heading for the door.

ɔ৲ɛ৲ɔ

Lilly entered her office, smiling. Yes, this is going to work out all right, after all, she thought.

She would watch from her doorway to see when they left and then slip in the operations room and take Matt's ID for the hydroponic area. Lilly stepped over to the door and leaned out, just enough, to be able to see when they left.

Gleefully, she watched as they all piled into the shuttle. Laughing and talking, they drove off. Quickly she stepped out into the corridor and looked around. No one took notice of her, so she started walking, with measured steps, in the direction of the operations room. She kept reminding herself to walk in her normal manner, even though she wanted to run as fast as she could to get there, as the thrill of what she was about to do pumped through her body.

She carefully stepped into the operations room, surveying the area and checking for anyone who might still be there. Seeing no one, she headed straight for Matt's desk. Sitting down in his chair, she slowly pulled out the drawer where Matt kept all things relating to the hydroponic systems, including his hydroponic ID card. It slid open easily. Inside were several bulging file folders, manuals on the solution tanks and planting stands, several hydro related magazines, and numerous reports.

Lilly grunted at the weight of the file folders and magazines as she lifted them out of the drawer and placed them on the desktop. Peering back into the drawer, she saw Matt's well-worn, black leather wallet and picked it up. It fell open, revealing several ID cards, allowing access to various parts of the dome.

Matt is such a creature of habit. She chuckled as she lifted his Hydroponic ID card out of its pocket. *Pity, he thought he was so clever not to carry his wallet around. Thank you, Matt, for being so cautious.*

She replaced the wallet exactly where it had been, then the magazines and file folders in the position she had found them, and pushed the drawer shut. Picking up the card, she gave it a small kiss before putting it in her pocket. Lilly's step was light. She smiled all the way back to her office.

Upon reaching her office, Lilly took the card out of her pocket and placed it in the drawer with her little metal box. The drawer was a safe hiding place.

Lilly sat at her desk feeling quite smug about her little adventure that had gone so well. Then she spied the daily reports sitting in a neat pile on the corner of her desk and decided she had better call Brad and give him the report to keep up appearances. She was sure he would be worrying why she hadn't called. She picked up the phone and called his cell.

CHAPTER 10

The Plan—Phase Two

Carlos watched Quin and Ricardo as they neared the gate. He pushed the button. The gate swung open. They were going to the bank to withdraw the money Vargas had finally put into his account for that American woman.

Carlos had been afraid he was never going to see it, since Vargas had cut all ties and told him to never darken his door again. Then this morning out of the blue, his bank had notified him the money had been deposited into his account.

After arranging with the bank, Carlos had sent Quin to withdraw part of the money. He needed a little folding money in his pocket. His funds were running low, and he still had not found another buyer for his merchandise. Not that he had any at the moment, but looking for new merchandise had been unexpectedly curtailed when he had had a run-in with some of Vargas's men last week. Several broken ribs and a concussion had laid Carlos up for the past week, so he had left it up to Quin and Ricardo to do the scouting. So far, they had not found anything that was worth his time.

Carlos was getting restless and needed some fun. Pulling out his little black book, he thumbed through the pages, stopping at the one with a big cherry red lipstick kiss.

Ah, yes Crystal. He sighed, remembering her sweet, innocent little sister who had garnered him a handsome penny. He chuckled, thinking how easy it had been to take her right from under Crystal's nose. Crystal had been frantic when she found her sister missing and had come to him for help in looking for her.

Stupid woman. If Crystal hadn't been such a tyrant, her sister would not have run off, making is so easy for me.

Crystal was a transplant from Los Angeles, and her business had been doing very well here. Well enough that she had brought her little sister here after their parents had died in a skiing accident in Colorado. Pulling his phone out of his pocket, Carlos punched in Crystal's number.

"Crystal, Carlos here. I need a party…" Carlos arranged with Crystal for a catered affair for Friday evening.

෨෨෨

Brad lost the toss for the bed and stretched out on the couch as best he could, with the arm of the couch hitting him mid-calf. His fully extended six-foot-seven-inch frame was not meant to fit between the arms of a five-foot couch. Finally, he pulled the cushions off, placed them on the floor, and fell asleep.

It was a little after seven in the morning when Nicho's contact called back with information on where to

pick up the van and the car. Angelo happened to be familiar with the area but he wasn't comfortable going without
some protection. Holding open a black leather bag, he
dropped the loaded MAC-10 in, along with a couple of
extra clips. Brad slipped his Glock into his waistband and
an extra clip in his pocket.

Angelo had handed the bag to Brad in the backseat
before he slid in behind the wheel. He estimated it was an
hour drive to the address Nicho's friend had given them.

An hour and a half later, Angelo found the address.
Slowing down and looking for the entrance, they drove
past a dilapidated wooden privacy fence. It stood maybe
ten feet high and had once been painted a brilliant blue,
but the paint had peeled and faded by the sun to a dusty
gray blue. A rusted *Keep Out* sign hung lopsided from the
heavy rusty chain that had been strung across an opening
in the fence. Angelo pulled the car up to the chain. Nicho
hopped out, unhooked the chain from a nail that had been
bent upward to hold it, and let it fall to the ground. Angelo slowly drove the BMW through the opening, the tires
crunching the cinders covering the lane as it moved forward in the middle of a graveyard of discarded vehicles.
Coming to a halt in front of a shack with boarded up windows and rusted tin corrugated siding, Angelo decided it
must be what served as the office for the yard.

The men looked around cautiously. In the distance,
they could hear dogs barking and the sound was getting
louder as the dogs moved closer. Angelo reached his arm
across the back of the seat, and Brad placed the bag's
strap in his open hand. Angelo slipped the strap over his
shoulder, put his hand inside the bag, and took the MAC-
10 off safety before slowly opening his door. Nicho
stepped out on the other side, moving so Brad could unfold himself from the backseat. Brad moved the Glock
from his waistband to his jacket pocket as he stood up,

but stayed behind the door—just in case.

Three enormous Rottweiler's, with ears laid back and teeth bared, came barreling out from between two stacks of flattened and rusting vehicles. They were barking viciously and were headed straight for the BMW, their big paws kicking up loose cinders, sending them flying out behind them.

"*¡Parada!*" Nicho's contact came running from the shack, yelling at the dogs. "*¡Parada!*"

The dogs slid to a halt in the loose cinders, changed directions, and, with their tongues lolling out, loped over to the shack where Nicho's contact reached down and playfully rubbed them behind the ears. "Sorry about that." The contact grinned, but he really wasn't sorry. He was still pissed off about losing money on the deal and would have been damn glad if he could have let them loose to tear them a new asshole. He grinned bigger. "I had intended to have them penned up before you got here."

"Just keep them out of the way," Brad said, his hand still in his jacket pocket, "and it will be fine."

Nicho walked out from behind the BMW's door and headed toward the shack. Brad and Angelo followed— Angelo's hand still inside the bag. He wouldn't think twice about putting the shittin' dogs down.

"Where are the vehicles?" Nicho asked, looking around.

"They are back here." The contact motioned for them to follow and started walking around to the back of the shack.

Nicho followed right behind him, Brad hung back, watching over his shoulder, and Angelo's finger moved to the trigger. The dogs sat on their haunches at the edge of the shack, watching as the men made their way to the back area.

Rounding the corner, they saw an older model, white GMC cargo van, and a more recent black Volvo sedan. Both vehicles appeared to be in decent shape on the outside.

Nicho opened the driver's door of the van and looked inside. Stale beer, cigarette smoke, old pine air freshener, and an odor he couldn't quite name, hit him in the face. The driver's seat was pretty well worn, some springs showed through the faded and worn gray cloth on the side closest to the door, but the seat itself was still serviceable. The passenger's seat was in slightly better condition.

Nicho opened the back doors, letting fresh air flow through. He could see the original carpet had been replaced with pieces of now dirty and stained orange shag carpet. The same carpet pieces had been glued to the sidewalls and ceiling as well. In spite of the fresh air flow, the smells were stronger here and mixed with other unidentifiable odors, causing his eyes to burn.

He walked around to the driver's side and held out his hand for the key. The engine turned over on the first try and purred quietly. "This will do," he said, turning off the engine, and wondered how long it would take to fumigate it.

Brad stuck his head in and wrinkled his nose. "We'll have to do something about the smell. I'm not sitting eight hours in there with that smell." He walked away rubbing his eyes and coughing.

"Not to worry," Angelo remarked, and followed Nicho over to the Volvo. "I have a friend who knows how to take care of that kind of thing."

The Volvo was in decent shape on the inside as well as the outside. The leather seats were cracked and worn from use and age, but otherwise okay. The interior smelled of old carpet, dust, stale cigarette smoke, and sweat.

Nicho opened the door to the Volvo and extended his hand for the key. The leather seat crackled, as he sat down and put the key in the ignition. It turned over. The engine of the Volvo ran as smoothly as the van. "These will do fine," He turned and smiled at his contact, who looked relieved. "I will get you the money."

They turned and headed back to the front of the shack. Angelo still had his finger on the trigger as he watched the dogs stand and wag their tails as the contact approached. Nicho caught Brad's eye and motioned for him to open the BMW's trunk. Inside, he found a brief-case. Brad carried the case over and set it down in front of Nicho's contact. The dogs growled, watching Brad walk away, then turned and immediately began sniffing out the briefcase.

"It is all there—the amount we agreed on." Nicho pointed to the briefcase then turned to Brad. "Flip you for the van?" He laughed, as he tossed the Volvo's keys to Brad.

"Thanks, man." Brad gave him a sideways grin. "I don't think I could have made it in there."

Both men laughed.

Maybe Nicho isn't such a bad guy, after all, Brad thought.

Angelo waited till both men had started the vehicles before he placed the leather bag on the passenger seat and slid in behind the BMW's wheel, but keeping the safety off.

They dropped the vehicles off at Angelo's friend who assured them he could make the van smell like new.

CHAPTER 11

Crystal's Place

The red message light blinked, repeatedly, as the men walked into Angelo's apartment. Angelo punched the play button.

"Hey there, baby," the voice on the answering machine purred. "You said to call if I heard anything about Carlos. Well, I'm calling. Call me back and I'll give you the details. Better yet, why not drop by and get it in person?"

Angelo turned and grinned at Nicho then Brad, who nodded knowingly.

"That was Crystal one of my contacts. I reached out to her about Carlos," Angelo said, plopping down in his favorite chair before Nicho could. "Want to go for a drink?"

Brad opened his mouth to say that sounded like a plan just as the phone in his pocket buzzed. It was Lilly. He frowned. "Excuse me, I've gotta take this," Brad said, walking out on the balcony. "Brad here," he said hesitatingly. "Is everything okay?"

"Everything is fine," Lilly said, a little taken aback by Brad's voice. "I am calling with the daily report. I did not get to give it to you yesterday before you left. I have yesterday's as well as today's. Where would you like me to start?" she asked, straightening the reports spread out on the desk in front of her for the third time.

"Is there anything in the reports that needs my immediate attention?" Brad asked with a scowl, pacing back and forth on the balcony. Brad knew Lilly was efficient, sometimes too efficient to the point it made him look like a slacker. Still, she was the cog that kept everything running in the dome, and, for that, he was glad.

"No, I don't believe there is any emergency at the moment. Everything seems to be running smoothly and on schedule. The hydroponic system will be ready by the end of the week for planting." Lilly paused to give Brad an opportunity to say something. When he didn't, she continued, her jaw tightening. "Miss Callahan's friend from Dallas has arrived and they are being shown around by Ty and his friends."

"That's great. I'm glad her friend has arrived. I'm sure it will help her remember her past. Thanks for taking care of that for me," Brad responded, looking out over the balcony railing and watching the traffic speeding by below.

"It was my pleasure." Her fingers tightened around the receiver as she said the words. "How much longer do you think your meeting will take," Lilly asked, hoping he had forgotten he had left without telling her all the particulars of his trip. Maybe he would reveal some information as to what his plans for Santiago might be.

"I'm sorry. I don't know. It will probably be two or three more days, at least," Brad said, turning and leaning against the railing. "I'll give you a call when I'm coming back. In the meantime, just keep everything on schedule.

You're doing a super job and I do appreciate it. Also, you won't have to worry with Darcey. She has Marti and Ty looking after her."

Lilly became concerned when Brad didn't mention Santiago. That left her in a quandary about whether to call Santiago or not. But, then again, she could just let nature take its course. If Brad came out on top, she could still take care of him just like she had planned to do for Darcey.

"Thank you," she said stiffly. "I will keep everything, as you say, on schedule until you return. If there is nothing else, I will file these reports and let you get back to your meeting." She paused, waiting for Brad to say good-bye.

"Yes, thanks, Lilly. I'll let you know if you need to do anything else. Bye for now."

Brad slipped the phone back in his pocket. It had been at least five minutes since Brad had last thought about Darcey. He felt a twinge of jealousy, thinking about Ty and Marti watching over her, but it couldn't be helped. He needed to take care of the Santiago situation. Santiago stole something from him and Darcey, something that they might never get back. The man had to pay.

⋰⋱

Angelo stopped the BMW in front of a classy-looking nightclub. The valet opened the passenger side door for Nicho and Brad to get out, then stepped smartly around to Angelo, his hand held out to receive the keys.

Angelo watched through narrowed eyes as the valet drove off in the BMW. *There'd better not be a scratch on that when I come back.*

The doorman held the door open for them. It was semi-dark inside, and it took a few minutes for their eyes to adjust. It was obvious from the furnishings that the club catered to an up-scale clientele. This was not a dirty hole-in-the-wall, that Brad had anticipated.

Since, it was early afternoon, there were not many people in the club. Most of the stools at the bar were empty. Angelo motioned for Brad and Nicho to go on over to the bar while he turned and walked toward the back. Nicho and Brad both ordered a draft beer. The bartender set two foam-topped, frosted mugs in front of them and waited for someone to pay.

"Flip you for it." Brad laughed. "You call it."

"Okay…heads," Nicho said, pulling out a coin.

"Naw, man, we'll use mine." Brad laughed again, flipping his coin in the air. "I think your damn coin has two heads." Brad caught the coin in his hand, turning the hand palm down as he slapped it on the back of the other hand, "Still want heads?"

"Yeah, sure." Nicho laughed, putting his coin back in his pocket. "Cannot blame a guy for trying."

"Well, you're a lucky dog. It's heads." Brad showed him the coin. "But there's no flipping for the bed tonight. It's mine."

Brad pulled out some bills and tossed them toward the bartender who snatched them up as if he was afraid Brad would pull them back. Brad turned and looked at Nicho. They both laughed.

Brad looked up to see Angelo reflected in the mirror that ran the length of the back bar, walking toward them with a sultry brunette hanging on his arm.

"Gentlemen, this is Crystal," Angelo introduced them, smiling at both men. "Crystal tells me that Carlos is planning a party Friday out at the ranch, and it is a catered affair. I think we have our in."

Brad raised an eyebrow and looked at Angelo then at the woman leaning heavily against him, his arm protectively wrapped around her waist. Brad didn't like the idea of discussing their plans with this woman. They couldn't afford for anything to go wrong. He wanted to make sure Carlos and the other two pieces of shit were taken care of with the least amount of chaos possible.

Angelo caught Brad's questioning expression and placed his hand on Brad's arm. "There is nothing to worry about. Crystal has a score to settle with Carlos, too. She is with us. She knows it was Carlos who kidnapped her sister two years ago, but has no way of proving it. Crystal wants Carlos out of the way as much as you do." He smiled down at Crystal and gave her a squeeze. "Crystal has offered to help us with our plans. If you will follow us…" He turned with Crystal, his arm still around her waist, and headed back toward her office.

Brad and Nicho shrugged, picked up their beers, and followed. Brad still had doubts about including this woman in their plans. It wasn't wise to have so many people involved—that's when things always went wrong.

Several hours and much discussion later, they came to an agreement on a plan of action. Crystal would provide the necessary catering company logos for the van and uniforms for the men. As part owner of the business, she could arrange things without suspicion. She would also arrange for their van to carry the food that needed to arrive first, making it easy to get them inside. After that, they were on their own.

The men piled into Angelo's BMW and drove over to Angelo's friend who had been fumigating the two vehicles. They had the last few hours left of Wednesday, all day Thursday, and Friday morning to get things ready.

Angelo silently thanked the powers that be. This is the perfect foil that Luis has been hoping for to delay Brad just enough for his elite forces to handle Santiago and his two friends. He couldn't have planned it better.

He would report to Luis later after everyone had gone to bed.

Picking up the van and Volvo from Angelo's friend, they drove them over to Crystal's warehouse for the van to be outfitted and for them to select the uniforms to wear on Friday. The van would be picked up Friday morning. Brad followed the BMW in the Volvo back to Angelo's. It would be used for surveillance until Friday morning.

CHAPTER 12

Close of Day, Wednesday

Brad pulled into the parking spot next to the BMW and shut the engine off. He felt an adrenaline rush, mixed with anger and a twinge of fear, as he thought about what would be happening Friday. He gripped the steering wheel, locking his elbows, and pushed himself back into the seat, shutting his eyes. He had no idea what the outcome of all of this would be. Hell, he could wind up going to jail or, worse, getting himself killed. But there was no way he would let Santiago get away with what he had done to Darcey.

Brad had never given much thought to the seamier side of life, but this had opened his eyes to a whole other world. A world where people didn't give a second thought about killing one another. A world where women were treated as sub-humans and worthless, their only value a commodity to be bought and sold, forced into slavery or prostitution. Then when the women were used up, they were discarded like pieces of trash—a world he had only read about or watched on the ten o'clock news. A world that now touched him in ways he'd never imagined.

Brad had never thought himself a vindictive person, but things change, people change. He would have his pound of flesh with no regrets.

The sound of car doors shutting invaded Brad's thoughts. Turning his head, he saw the other two disappearing through the front door of the apartment house.

Better get a move on, he thought and climbed out of the car.

When he entered the apartment several minutes after the other two, Angelo had his head in the fridge, taking stock of their beer supply. He pulled out the last two beers and placed them on the counter. Shutting the fridge door, Angelo looked at the guys and announced he was going to the market to pick up more beer and steaks. Nicho grabbed the two bottles off the counter and tossed one to Brad as he plopped down in Angelo's favorite chair and popped the top off the beer. Angelo glared at him before he pulled the door closed behind him.

Brad strolled out on the balcony and called Darcey. He hadn't heard the soft melodic tones of her voice for at least eight hours, and he needed to hear it, to assure himself that she was all right and safe. He missed her and could never get enough of her when they were together in Dallas. It had been heaven. In contrast, these last weeks had been pure torture—wanting to touch her, hold her, feeling her warm flesh against his, all the while knowing he still had to give her time to remember. He wanted this thing with Santiago over and done with.

Contemplating the hot orange globe silhouetting the landscape, Brad waited for the phone to ring. It rang once, twice, three times, and she had not picked up. Brad let it ring three more times and waited for the voicemail to kick in. The green finger of jealousy poked him as he thought about her being out with Marti and Ty. The past three days without her had been worse than the three months she had been missing. He sighed and left a message, saying he missed her and would call back later.

ↄﻭↄ

Darcey said goodnight to the guys as Ty stopped in front of the operations room to drop them off for the final check of the night, before driving Darcey and Marti over to her quarters. They had enjoyed a delicious dinner in the Bajo el Mar Café, and she thought it had been the end to a perfect day.

By the time, Ty stopped the shuttle in front of Darcey's quarters, it was just a little after ten. They'd had a full afternoon of sightseeing and she was worn out and ready to fall into bed, but Marti and Ty were still deep in conversation. Darcey had the distinct feeling that neither one of them was conscious of her presence.

"Would you like to come in for coffee or a nightcap?" Darcey asked out of politeness but really hoping that Ty would say he was ready to call it an evening.

"Why that's mighty kind of you," Ty said, briefly glancing in Darcey's direction before turning his attention back to Marti. "I'd love some coffee. How about you Marti?"

Darcey could see that Marti had fallen under Ty's spell. She had hardly taken her eyes off of him all day. Scott had elbowed Darcey several times when it seemed like Marti and Ty were off in a world of their own. Darcey remembered Marti had told her that that was how Brad and she had been, so wrapped up in each other that the rest of the world did not exist. Try as she might, Darcey couldn't remember, and it hurt. Tears stung the corner of her eyes.

Blinking back the tears, Darcey set about putting the coffee pot on while Ty and Marti made themselves comfy on the sofa. So wrapped up in each other, neither glanced in Darcey's direction when she placed the cups on the coffee table. Darcey took that as her cue to make herself scarce. "If you all will excuse me, I'm calling it a night," she said, yawning for effect. "You can show yourself out Ty and Marti knows how to lock up. See you all tomorrow."

Passing the desk on her way to the bedroom, she saw the red light on the voice mail flashing persistently. She picked up the handset and put it to her ear. The soft velvet tones of Brad's voice caressed her ear and butterflies soared in her stomach. She hadn't realized just how much she missed his voice, how much she truly missed him. She played the message through again just to listen to his voice.

Sometime later, she thought she heard Marti come into the bedroom to retrieve her bag. Darcey had laid out sheets and a pillow beside the bag with a note telling Marti where the towels and things were in the bathroom. Darcey heard the door to the bathroom close softly as she drifted off.

∾∾∾

Lilly checked her special desk drawer before turning off the office light. It was locked up tight. Securing her office door, she noticed a shuttle pull up in front of the operations room. She stepped back into the shadow of the doorway, watching Matt, Scott, and Hot Dog leave the shuttle and enter the operations room. The shuttle drove off with what appeared to be Ty and the two women.

Slinking cautiously down the corridor toward the operations room, Lilly stopped when she reached the edge of the window and peeked in, watching as the men checked the control panels, entering data in their handheld palmtops. She was especially interested in watching Matt as he moved from one panel to the next, plugging the palmtop into the port from which data was transferred to his palmtop before moving to the next panel.

Finished, Matt placed his palmtop in its holder and strolled over to his desk. Lilly froze, holding her breath as she watched Matt sit down and pull out the hydroponic drawer. Reaching in, he pulled out one of the file folders and spread its contents out on the desk. Shuffling through the papers, he pulled out two, put the rest back, and closed the folder, leaving it out on the desk. Standing up, he walked over to Scott, talking to him while pointing to something specific on the papers. Scott nodded his head in agreement with something Matt said. Lilly couldn't hear their conversation and she was too far away to see what the papers were.

Both men walked back over to Matt's desk, still talking. Matt sat down and pulled out the drawer. Lilly felt a chill in the pit of her stomach. This time Matt pulled out all of the file folders and then the wallet. He flipped it open, sorted through the cards, and frowned. Matt looked up at Scott, said something, then shuffled through the cards again.

Lilly watched as he emptied the contents of the drawer on the desktop, her heart pounding in her chest. Oh, quit worrying she told herself. He will have no way knowing I took the card. He will never suspect me, so I will just play dumb if he says anything about it. Her heart rate slowing, she decided she would be pressing her luck if she stayed much longer. Slowly she edged away from the window and went back toward her office.

Matt was at a complete loss as to what might have

happened to his hydroponic ID card. He distinctly re-membered putting the card back after he had taken Lilly with him to view the progress of the installation of the solution tanks.

"Can't you just request a new one?" Scott asked as he helped look through the contents of the drawer.

"Yeah, I guess I'll have to," Matt said, frowning. "This is really strange."

℘℘℘

Carlos was fidgeting again, pacing the floor while he downed his fifth bourbon. His head throbbed and his ribs still would not let him inhale, except in short, shallow breaths.

Quin and Ricardo had been gone longer than expected. Carlos had called the bank and found out that they had picked up the money around one. Carlos had expected them back no later than three that afternoon, so, when they had not shown up by four, he had been calling Quin's cell every few minutes since then. But it went directly to voice mail each time. Now it was going on eight, and, besides being worried, he was really pissed off. Carlos did not like thinking that Quin and Ricardo would make off with his money, but that's what it was beginning to look like. He could not go to the police. There would be too many questions about the money, and he could not call Vargas. The man had kicked him out. And, now, he was in no shape to take care of it himself.

℘℘℘

Running and out of breath, Quin pushed Ricardo through an open doorway in the alley. Quin paused long enough to make sure they hadn't been followed before he felt they could stop to catch their breath. They had been running since late afternoon after picking up the money from the bank. A black SUV started following them as soon as they left the bank's parking lot, although Quin did not notice them until he made a wrong turn and wound up in a residential neighborhood. That was when he noticed the SUV. It stayed a block or two behind but made every turn Quin made.

Who are these people? he wondered. *What do they want? Could they be after the money?*

Carlos had been plenty jumpy after the run in with Vargas's guy. He went from anxious to paranoid, making sure that either Quin or Ricardo called or texted him every hour on the hour whenever they went out. Quin had thought it was a little ridiculous at the time, but now, maybe not.

Even after weaving his way through the residential area, trying to find his way back to the freeway, he had still not shaken off the SUV. Finally seeing a directional sign pointing to the freeway, Quin made a sharp U-turn up and over the grassy median of the boulevard and floored it, heading in the opposite direction. Ricardo grabbed his seatbelt and locked it in place. It had taken the SUV two more blocks before it made the same U-turn across the median in hot pursuit.

By the time the SUV was following, Quin had made it onto the freeway and was weaving in and out of traffic, cutting in between cars and initiating angry honking horns. Ricardo was thinking he was doubly thankful he had his seatbelt on as he looked over and saw the speedometer climbing close to the red zone.

Quin could see the SUV in his side mirror as it gained on him. He knew he had no hope of outrunning the SUV in their current vehicle. He spied an exit ramp and swerved, cutting off the car next to him causing it to spin out of control as he sped down the ramp. The SUV barely missed the spinning car but followed Quin's exit.

Quin had no idea where he was and at this point did not care. His only thought was to lose that damn SUV. Not slowing as he reached the bottom of the ramp, he turned the car hard to the right on the connecting street, fishtailing as he accelerated. Seeing no other vehicles, he floored it, blowing through intersections and praying that there was nothing coming. Quin saw a parking garage up ahead on the left and made a sharp turn into the garage. Traveling far too fast, he slammed on the breaks and yanked the steering wheel hard to the left to avoid hitting the wall in front of them head-on. The car slid sideways skimming the passenger's side down the concrete wall. Ricardo's eyes bugged out as he saw the wall coming too quick and too close. He grabbed the crucifix around his neck and kissed it in desperation, silently praying to God to let him live.

Quickly checking the rearview mirror, Quin did not see the SUV behind them and hope that it had not seen them turn into the garage. He quickly maneuvered the car into a spot where he could see the street outside. He and Ricardo crouched down in the seat. Quin adjusted the side mirror so he could watch the street. They had made it just in time as the SUV sped on down the street past the garage.

Popping back up and throwing the car into reverse, Quin backed out of the spot slamming into a car across from them in his haste. Pulling out slowly, looking for the SUV and not seeing it, he floored it, squealing tires and heading back in the direction they had come. He had to get rid of this car and get something faster if he wanted to get away from the SUV. Quin and Ricardo glanced at each other as they sped down the street. Ricardo craned his neck, looking out the back window to keep an eye out for the SUV while Quin concentrated on driving.

"We need a faster car," Quin shouted at Ricardo. "Keep your eye out for something we can grab quickly," he grunted swinging into another parking garage. "There might be something in here we can hotwire."

"Over there!" Ricardo shouted, pointing to a sleek black Jaguar in the last parking space.

Quin slammed on the brakes, screeching to a stop. The sound echoed through the garage. They scrambled out and checked the doors. Finding them unlocked, they grinned at each other at their unbelievable luck. Quin reached up under the dash, pulled out the appropriate wires. He wiped the sweat from his brow before it trickled into his eyes and made the connection. The engine sprang to life. Quin shifted into reverse and backed out. Shifting into first, he slammed down on the accelerator, tires squealing and leaving a significant amount of rubber on the concrete floor. Quin felt a rush as the Jaguar sprang into motion.

Tearing down the street, heading for the freeway, the SUV passed them going the opposite direction. Having spotted Quin and Ricardo in the Jaguar, the SUV pulled a big U-turn and bore down on them. Quin mashed the accelerator to the floor. The speedometer hit eighty, ninety, one-hundred-ten, and still the SUV remained right on the Jaguar's bumper. Quin wondered just what the hell they had under the hood. They should have been walking away from the SUV in the Jag, but it was still right there on their tail. Quin pushed the Jaguar harder and the SUV kept up. He watched the grill of the SUV come closer, and then it rammed the Jaguar in the rear bumper, making it leap forward, fishtailing. Quin grunted as he worked the steering wheel, getting the car back under control.

"*¡Dios mío!* Make sure you have your seatbelt fastened," he shouted at Ricardo as the SUV rammed them again. This time Quin was ready for it. He saw the on ramp to the freeway up ahead and floored it again. The Jaguar hit the ramp at one-hundred-twenty. The wheels lifted off the ground, and the car flew several yards before it bounced down and fishtailed as the tires gripped the roadway again.

Quin had not taken the time to see if anyone was coming before he shot up the ramp, not taking into consideration his or Ricardo's safety—let alone anyone else's, for that matter. If someone were there, they could get the hell out of his way. All he wanted was to ditch that damn SUV.

He swerved, cutting off a semi-truck full of cattle. The semi slammed on its brakes. The trailer, tires squealing, swung wildly around, blocking the ramp and oncoming traffic. The cattle, forced against the sides of the trailer as it swung around, busted through the wooden slats, spilling scared, injured, and bawling cattle onto the freeway. A chain reaction pile-up, involving numerous vehicles, stretched out behind the overturned cattle hauler.

The SUV took to the berm, skirting most of the chaos on the roadway and sped after the Jaguar. Quin kept one eye on the rearview mirror watching for the SUV, and the other watching out for the traffic as he zig-zagged around cars. He spotted an exit ramp and headed for it across three lanes of traffic, sending vehicles spinning out of control, crashing into each other, as he cut them off. He sped down the ramp into an industrial area where warehouses stretched out on both sides the street.

"Keep your eye out for some place we can pull in and maybe lose them," he told Ricardo, who had already started scouting.

"There!" Ricardo shouted. "There! On the right!"

Quin gave the steering wheel a sharp turn to the right and shot up the incline, through the open bay doors. He slammed on the brakes and screeched to a halt, just inches away from pallets full of shrink-wrapped cases of coconut cooking oil. Looking quickly around, he saw no way out other than the way they came in.

Quin looked in the rearview mirror and the SUV was barreling up the incline behind the Jaguar. Ricardo and Quin popped their seat belt buckle releases. They swung open the car doors, and rolled out onto the concrete floor at the same time the SUV slammed to a stop, missing the Jaguar's rear bumper by inches.

Quin and Ricardo scrambled up and raced to the rear of the closest pallet of cooking oil. Ducking behind it just as a hail of bullets pierced the containers, releasing hundreds of streams of cooking oil pouring out onto the floor. They looked at each other, and then sprinted for the door they had both noticed at the same time.

The men from the SUV, yelling at each other to watch out, were having trouble negotiating the slippery floor. Slipping and sliding in the golden liquid slowed them down and gave Quin and Ricardo time to bolt through the door. It was an office. Ricardo grabbed a chair and shoved it to Quin who blocked the door with it, ramming the back up under the doorknob and giving it a hard kick to lodge it tight.

They looked around for an exit because it wouldn't be long before the men from the SUV would be breaking the door down. The only other door in the office led to a supply room. That left the windows. Ricardo looked out and judged the distance to the ground to be less than fifteen feet. Ricardo motioned to Quin to grab a chair and, together, they threw the chairs, sending a shower of clattering glass shards to the ground. Clearing the broken pieces away, they climbed out the window and landed on the ground below.

As they ran, they could hear the gunfire and shouting

as the men from the SUV broke through the door.

Quin and Ricardo rounded the corner of a nearby building and were out of sight by the time the men looked out the window. Sprinting down the alley that ran between the buildings, Quin looked for any open door where they could hide to catch their breath. They ran past two more buildings, trying each door they came to. Quin tried the door on the next building over and was rewarded when it opened. He shoved Ricardo in, checking to make sure they had not been followed, before shutting and locking the door. The quiet room found them bent over and resting their hands on their knees, both men breathing hard.

"We can't stay here," Quin said, looking around to see exactly where they were. From what he could see in the dim light, it looked to be a business office of some sort.

Several cubicles with desks and chairs filled most of the room. On the far side, he could make out several doors. Checking to see where the doors led, they found all but one opened into other private offices, but the one that didn't, opened into a dark hallway. They started down the hallway keeping close to the wall.

Quin could see a soft glow of light filtering out from under a door farther down the hallway. He cautioned Ricardo and they crept slowly toward the light, quietly pulling their guns out as they went. Soft music was playing somewhere, probably from behind the door.

The music was louder just outside the door. Quin reached for the doorknob and slowly turned it. Ricardo moved out from behind Quin, his gun off safety, ready to spring, as Quin pulled the door open.

In one swift move, Ricardo was through the door and making a wide sweep of the room, holding the gun out in front of him. The room was empty.

Quin followed Ricardo in cautiously, surveying what appeared to be a reception area. Quin could see the street through the double glass doors and noticed a man walking up the sidewalk toward them. Quickly crouching down behind the counter, Quin grabbed Ricardo's arm and pulled him down, too.

"Someone is coming," he whispered. "We've got to move." He motioned to the door of the hallway. Still crouching they slipped back into the hallway and pushed the door closed, leaving only a small crack for observation.

Several minutes later, the man pushed the glass door open with force and strode across the floor to the counter. Quin could hear him grumbling, but could not make out what he was saying. The man pulled his cell phone out of his pocket and looked at the screen before hitting a button.

"Yeah, I am still here," he told someone on the other end with disgust. "Yeah, I am upset. I just stepped out the back for a smoke and somehow the damn door got locked," the man said, running his hand through his hair. "No, I did not lock it! Why the hell would I lock it? I had to walk the whole way around this stinking building to get back in," he said, exasperated and pacing back and forth in front of the counter. "You're right, I am damn mad. It's not enough I have to stay till eight just so some stupid suit can drop off his report. I had to walk half a mile just to get back in the damn building. It's after eight, and he still has not shown up." The man pounded his fist on the counter. "Yeah, well, I'm giving him fifteen more minutes, and then I'm leaving," he said, stopping and looking at the glass doors. "I will see you in a few." The man put the phone back in his pocket and walked over to stare out the glass doors.

Muttering again to himself, he flopped down in one

of the chairs, grabbed a magazine off the table, and started flipping through it.

Quin and Ricardo were still huddled in the dark hallway. Quin motioned to Ricardo to back up a bit to give him more room.

"What time do you think it is?" Ricardo whispered.

"No idea," Quin whispered back, "but it must be after eight from what I heard of his conversation."

This was the first time Quin had had an opportunity to think about something other than staying alive. He was beginning to worry about Carlos. Quin had no way of contacting him since he had lost his phone. By now, Carlos probably thought they had run off with the money. Quin adjusted his position to get a better look out the crack to see if there were any phones. Hopefully, the man would leave soon and he could call Carlos, to let him know what was going on, and then figure a way to get out of here.

Quin heard a noise from the outer room and looked up in time to see the man stand, throw the magazine in his hand down on the floor, and stride toward the glass doors.

"Well, it is about damn time you showed up," the man said through clenched teeth. "I have a life, too, you know."

"Sorry," the suit said, unconcerned. "If you will drop these on Mason's desk, then you are dismissed." The suit looked the man up and down, held his arm out and picked a non-existent piece of lint off the sleeve, gave the man a nasty grin, and walked out.

The man was furious as he headed for the hallway door. Quin elbowed Ricardo and they both stood up, ready to attack the man as he came through the door. The man hit the door with the heel of his hand, sending it slamming into the wall as he stalked through it. Quin made the first move, grabbing the man's arm and pulling him forward off balance. Ricardo came up behind the man and gave him a hard whack on the head with the butt of his gun. The man groaned and slumped to the floor.

Moving quickly, Quin picked up the phone on the desk and called Carlos.

"Carlos, it is Quin," he said out of breath. "I lost my phone and could not call you. We have been chased by some men who have been trying to kill us, and, no, I do not know who they are. We had to ditch the car." Quin paused, as Carlos interrupted. "What?"

"I said, do you have the money?" Carlos screamed into the phone's receiver. It never occurred to him that Quin and Ricardo had been in mortal danger. All that was important was the money.

"Yes, we have the money. We will be there as soon as we can get a ride," he said, beginning to get aggravated that Carlos was prattling on, more worried about his money than Quin and Ricardo's safety.

While Quin was on the phone, Ricardo had dragged the man into the first office off the hallway.

"He is all nice and cozy in there," Ricardo said, grinning as he walked back to the counter.

"Okay, time to go," Quin and Ricardo headed toward the glass doors and moved cautiously out into the night.

Seeing no one around, they started walking down the sidewalk, their footsteps making soft thuds on the concrete. The street lamps cast a cold golden glow over the street and sidewalk. Reaching the end of the block, they saw a parking lot across the street that held some likely possibilities. Quin would have preferred a parking garage to do this, but they did not have much choice this time. Boosting a car, out in the open made him nervous.

Slowly creeping down the row of cars looking for a likely prospect, Ricardo tried several doors with no luck.

Headlights from an oncoming vehicle played across the hood of the car they were standing by. They ducked down between the two cars, waiting for the other vehicle to pass. It slowed as it neared the parking lot. Quin thought it was going to turn in, but instead it drove by very slow shining a high-beam searchlight over the cars and casting eerie shadows as it went by. As the light neared, they crept toward the back of the car, and by the time the light reached where they had been crouched, they were directly behind the car, out of sight. The car moved on down the street, turning off the light after it passed the lot. Quin and Ricardo stood up slowly.

"We have got to get out of here!" Quin whispered hoarsely, turning to look at the car they were standing behind. It was a Land Rover.

"Give this one a try," he said to Ricardo, who had already walked to the driver's door and gave the door handle a slight tug. It opened. "Quick go around and open the other door and put your hand on the button to turn off the overhead light," Quin whispered nervously to Ricardo. He hated doing this out in the open—too much of a chance someone might see you. A small wave of panic swept over him as he pulled the wires from under the dashboard.

Working his magic, Quin had the Land Rover humming in just a few seconds. He backed out of the parking space and moved slowly down the lot to the exit, not turning on the headlights until he was out of the lot and a fair distance down the street. The SUV was nowhere in sight. Relief flooded his body.

೧೨೧೨

It was after nine-thirty in the morning when Luis's phone rang.

"Si, Luis here," he said.

"We lost them," the voice on the other end said in disgust. "They spotted us and just outmaneuvered us." He was not about to tell him what had really happened.

"What do you mean you lost them?" Luis sat up straighter in his chair. "I want them taken care of before Brad has a chance to do something he will regret. Angelo has stalled as long as he can and has the hit set for Friday night, but I want them taken care of before then. Understand?"

"You got it, boss," the voice said. "It will be done before Friday."

"Good. See that it is and nothing traces back to Brad or ORCA," Luis said and hung up.

Luis leaned back in his chair, thinking how he had wanted to let Brad have the satisfaction of taking his revenge on Carlos. But, on reflection, he was glad now he had decided not to let Brad take the risk of getting himself arrested or killed. Luis wanted Brad and Darcey to start their life together without anything hanging over their heads. In light of that, he had dispatched three of his men to take care of the problem. Last week his men had found Carlos in one of his favorite nightspots and roughed him up. They would have finished the job but had to leave in a hurry when someone had called the authorities.

Angelo was keeping Luis up to date on their plans and was prepared to see that Brad did not get into trouble, but Luis did not want it to go that far. He was too fond of Brad to let him do something he would regret. His men would take care of the job.

CHAPTER 13

Thursday Morning

It was going on three a.m. when Quin and Ricardo pulled up the driveway to the ranch. Most of the lights were on. They could see Carlos pacing back and forth, silhouetted in the light from the doorway as Quin parked the car.

Quin was still pissed that Carlos had been more concerned about his damn money than he had with Ricardo's and his safety. Scowling, he followed Ricardo up the steps placing each foot squarely on each tread, the money belt around his waist chaffing with each step he took.

Carlos grinned, slapping Ricardo on the back as he passed. "Glad to see you all made it,"

Ricardo grunted and walked on into the house, never looking at Carlos.

Quin ignored Carlos's outstretched hand and walked on by, the scowl still in place.

Oh, well, Carlos thought, *he will get over it. Quin never stays angry long. It is not in his nature.*

Quin fell into one of the overstuffed chairs in the

study waiting for Carlos to show. Drumming his fingers on the arm of the chair, he decided he had had it. He was still angry with himself when he thought about the day he had handed the woman off to those thugs at the dock. He knew it had been foolish to let her get under his skin, but she had, and there had not been a damn thing he could have done about it. The woman had taken a piece of him with her when she left, even though she probably never knew, but he did and it hurt.

Guilt swept over Quin again when he thought that he had not done anything to save her. Thoughts of what he could have done—should have done—weighed down on him. He had had plenty of opportunity and time to sneak her off the boat after they had docked. Carlos and Ricardo had left to arrange for the transport, leaving him alone with her for over an hour. He could have saved her then, but, he had not. He had been a coward, and that knowledge pierced his soul, as if he had a soul. He was not sure anymore.

Before her, he had no compassion for any of the women he had sent into oblivion. They were a job. A paycheck. He did not see them. They had no names. No faces. But she had changed all of that. Her spirit had touched something deep inside of him. Something he thought was long dead. She made him feel alive again. She had opened his eyes to what he was a part of and made him feel guilty, but not guilty enough then to have saved her, and that hurt worst of all.

Quin cursed himself for being the coward he had become, afraid to cross Carlos. Laying his head back, his eyes closed, and, for a split second, he smiled at the memory of her. Her smell as he had breathed in the fragrance that was uniquely her. The taste of her as he kissed her and their tongues met, her unbridled passion that equaled his, the soft curves of her body, and her skin soft to the touch like stroking velvet—that had been his undoing. Mentally kicking himself in the butt, he opened his eyes and scowled again, gripping the arms of the chair, his knuckles turning white.

Carlos stopped and watched Quin from the doorway. Quin had worn that look several weeks after they unloaded that American woman. Carlos had never asked him about it. He had been paid—finally—and that was all he was concerned with.

Carlos strode over to the bar watching Quin out of the corner of his eye as he dropped ice cubes into a glass. "How about a drink? I am sure you can use one right about now."

Quin eyed Carlos pouring the amber liquid in the glass. "Sure, make it a double, straight up."

Carlos handed him the drink and poured one for himself. The ice clinked on the side of the glass as he tipped it up and almost drained it in one gulp. Still holding the decanter, he refilled the glass.

Quin studied the glass in his hand before placing it on the table in front of him. Standing up, he unbuckled the money belt from around his waist and pitched it on the table. The whiskey in his glass rippled as the belt hit the table with a thud and slid half way to the edge.

Carlos watched, surprised.

"There it is—all of it." Quin looked at Carlos, his lips curled into a sneer. "I have had it. I want my pay. You and Ricardo can handle it from here. I am going back to El Salvador," he said and, picking up his drink, settled back into the chair.

Carlos blinked and shook his head. *I had not expected this.* His eyes opened wide and he stared at Quin. "You cannot mean that. Surely you jest. What am I going to do without you? I depend on you, you know that, for sure," he whined, his spirits falling as he sank down into the chair behind him. *I do not want to deal with this right now.*

Carlos took a large swallow from his glass. He couldn't afford for Quin to leave. He depended on him to take care of the less desirable aspects of handling the women. It kept Carlos's hands clean should anything happen. That had been one of the reasons he had never been prosecuted—nothing ever linked back to him. Although he had been sorry to lose some excellent job managers over the years, he had always reassured himself that that was the risk they took when they agreed to the job.

"Yeah, I mean it." Quin swirled the amber liquid in the glass before he took a drink. "I want a change of scenery. You have Ricardo. He knows how to handle things, and he likes the job."

Quin could see Carlos hedging on letting him leave, but his mind was made up—he was leaving. What he planned to do afterward was still up in the air. His first instinct was to find the woman and make things right. He knew who picked her up and where they had taken her, but he had no idea what happened to her afterward.

Quin left Carlos brooding in the study. He was tired and, right now, all he wanted was to go to bed. He did not want to argue anymore. He was leaving as soon as he had his money. Carlos could plead all he wanted, for all the good it would do him.

Coming out of the bathroom with just a towel wrapped around him, Quin emptied out the chest of drawers and closet, packing everything, except what he planned to wear in the morning. Zipping the case shut, he set it on the floor and gave it a swift kick, sending it sliding across the polished wood floor. It hit the wall and bounced, coming to rest a few inches from the door. Whipping the towel off, he tossed it through the bathroom door and lay down naked, spread eagle on the bed. Where would he start looking for her? He didn't have any connection to Vargas, but he would try to call and see if he would talk with him. Quin drifted off with a partial plan still swirling around in his mind.

⁓∾⁓

The alarm blared, jolting Lilly out of her dream. Frowning, she reached over and hit the snooze button, hoping to recapture the dream before it evaporated. It had been magnificent. She mentally hugged herself.

Snuggling back under the covers, she drifted back…

⁓∾⁓

She was pouring the deadly solution she had so carefully prepared for the tanks that fed the plant racks. In a matter of minutes, the seedlings turned yellow, withered, and died. With each plant that fell, her heart skipped a beat. Then the scene faded and changed. Javier and Eduardo came into focus as they wrapped chains around Darcey's wrists, laughing and sneering. They looped the chain over a hook floating above a tank of bubbling acid, the bitter fumes rising in a deadly putrid cloud, circling Darcey's kicking feet. Blood dripped from the sharp edges of the chain's links as it cut into her soft flesh. Lilly watched gleefully as Darcey squirmed and kicked, pleading for her life. Then Lilly's face contorted into a menacing evil smirk. She grabbed the chain from Javier and slowly lowered Darcey into the vat of acid…

⁓∾⁓

The alarm blared again, cheating her of the final satisfaction of seeing Darcey's flesh eaten away, hearing her screams fade as her body disappeared into the stinking liquid.

Swinging her legs over the side of the bed, Lilly stretched and yawned. She felt revitalized. Even though the dream had been interrupted, the satisfaction it gave her would sustain her through the day. She quickly dressed and headed to the office, stopping at the Bajo for her morning cup of tea. Grinning, she practically danced out of the Bajo. The cashier watched her leave, her eyebrows raised in speculation.

Sitting down at her desk, Lilly stared off into space. Adrenaline surged through her body each time she re-played the dream, especially the part with Darcey and the acid. Lilly savored each moment, leisurely sipping her tea. *The time is almost here,* she thought.

∽∾∽∾

Matt had spent a restless night, worrying about his lost ID card. Bleary eyed, he padded to the bathroom to shower, hoping the hot water would relax some of the knotted muscles in his neck and back. He squinted at his reflection in the mirror and turned his head side to side with his chin gripped between his thumb and forefinger.

I look like hell, he thought. *Even a shave won't improve my mug this morning.*

It was weird how the card went missing. He knew he had put it back in its pocket in the wallet when he finished the inspection of the tanks with Lilly. He knew that because he had replaced his storage bay card at the same time, and that card was still safely tucked away in its pocket. That would mean the card would have to had disappeared sometime yesterday while they were taking the girls around.

When they left the operations room, they hadn't bothered to lock it because the day shift would have arrived just minutes after they left. Matt would check with them this morning to see if they saw anything suspicious. He thought about calling Brad but thought it better to talk with Ty first. No need to bother Brad if they could handle the situation themselves.

Matt finished shaving, shrugged into his shirt, buttoned it up and stuffed the tail inside the waistband on his Wranglers, filled his coffee mug, grabbed his hat, and left. He didn't take the time for breakfast. He needed to talk with Ty as soon as he could locate him.

☙☙☙

Darcey rolled over and stared at the ceiling as the shadows in the room softened and ebbed, debating on getting up or lying in bed for another fifteen minutes. The artificial daylight was just coming up, so it must be somewhere around six. The dome would be in full daylight in another hour.

Throwing the comforter back fanned the aroma of freshly brewed coffee that had drifted in from the kitchen, making her decision easy. Marti was already up. Darcey put her feet on the floor, enjoying the feel of the carpet, and wiggled her toes in the deep pile.

Last night she had tossed her robe carelessly on the chair at the foot of the bed. It had slipped to the floor and now lay in a baby blue silk puddle in front of the chair. Yawning, she picked it up and let the soft silk settle around her body, tying the sash as she walked to the kitchen.

Marti greeted her with a sunny, "Morning!" and poured a cup of the delicious-smelling coffee for her. "Take a seat, breakfast will be ready in a few," she said, dropping slices of whole wheat bread in the toaster. "Where's your spatula? I've looked in all the drawers," Marti asked turning around, looking at Darcey, her hand on her hip.

"I don't have one, sorry," Darcey said, shrugging her shoulders. She picked up her cup and moved around the bar to the stools, making a mental note to pick one up later.

"Well, scrambled it is, then." Marti laughed, setting the skillet on the stove. She scooped out a healthy spoon full of butter and plopped it in the skillet. It sizzled as it hit the hot surface.

Darcey settled herself on one of the bar stools. Sipping her coffee and thinking how much Marti reminded her of a mother hen, Darcey watched Marti over the rim of the cup as she bustled around the kitchen.

"Well, what's on the agenda for today?" Darcey asked, guessing she and Ty might have planned something.

"Nothing this morning. Ty has reports to get ready. So, it's a 'whatever you want to do' morning. We can talk some more," Marti said, taking the container of OJ out of the fridge, giving it a shake. "You're about out," she noted.

Only Marti would mention the juice was low. Darcey blinked. *Why did I think that?* "Talking sounds okay to me. You can tell me about you and Ty." Darcey giggled and watched as a deep crimson color crept up Marti's neck and flushed her face. "I believe we are due for some girl talk. Hmmmm?"

A vague memory drifted through the swirling fog in a faraway corner of Darcey's mind. It floated near the surface, she could almost see it. Then grayness settled back in again, but lighter and less opaque.

The phone rang…

ↄ�ↄ

The sound of the city coming to life crept in through the crack between dream sleep and waking, pushing the festering dream to the edge of Brad's subconscious. A horn blasted right under the bedroom window, adding sharp barbs to the migraine developing behind his eyes. Rubbing his temples, he lay on the sweat-soaked sheet, trying not to think about the nightmare that still invaded his sleep.

The nightmare that had led him down a dimly lit, twisted road. An eerie glow filtered through skeleton like fingers that reached up and plucked at his feet, slowing his steps as he ran after Darcey—always just out of reach. A dark cloud circled her, disembodied hands clutched her, chains, pulled her into a dark abyss.

Brad's pulse raced and cold beads of sweat formed and rolled down his forehead as the nightmare played out in his migraine-wrapped mind once more. This nightmare worried him. It reminded him of the nightmare that had haunted him when he'd first arrived back at the dome. It started just before he found out Darcey had been kidnapped.

Brad hadn't connected the dots then, but he was sure now it had been a warning from the thread that connected them, that she was in some kind of danger. He felt sure the thread was again trying to warn him. He had to make sure she was safe, or he would never forgive himself if anything happened to her. Darcey was his life.

He rolled over and reached for his cell on the bedside table. It was still early, but he couldn't wait. The phone rang once, twice…

"Hello," Darcey squeaked, her voice still husky from sleep and just one sip of coffee.

"Mornin', sleepyhead." Brad let out a soft sigh of relief when he heard her voice. He could feel the connecting thread pulsing in his veins. "Just couldn't wait any longer. I had to hear your voice," he told her. "I miss you so much." He held his breath, waiting for her to reply.

"Mornin' to you, too," her smiling voice said into the receiver. "I've missed you, too."

She felt a tingling pulse through her body as his velvet voice caressed her ear. She was amazed at her response to his voice last night when she listened to the message he had left. But, now, it was a powerful sensation, pulsing through her whole body that wouldn't stop. *How could he affect me in such a way? Was it true what Marti had said about our relationship?* Frustration tweaked her. *Will I ever remember?*

"Just wanted to check on you, make sure everything is going okay," Brad told her, still massaging his temple with his free hand. The jackhammer in his head increased.

"Yes, Marti and I are just getting some breakfast and then we're going to have some girl talk about her and Ty," she told him. Darcey was giggling, as she watched Marti fill her plate with scrambled eggs.

Blushing again, Marti ignored her.

"Wow!" Brad said. "Marti and Ty, huh? That's great." He grinned, in spite of the throbbing in his head. He never thought about anything like that happening. He had only been concerned with Marti helping Darcey regain her memory. Now this development was a pleasant surprise. He liked both and thought they would fit well together.

Bam! Bam! Bam! Angelo pounded on the bedroom door. "Get a move on," he shouted through the door. "Breakfast is ready."

Brad reluctantly said goodbye to Darcey. He slowly swung his feet over the edge of the bed and sat up with as little movement as possible. Even the hairs on his head hurt. He squinted at the light that flooded the bedroom, as the migraine pounded away inside his skull. Last night he had been too out of it to pull the shades. Now he was paying the price.

"Yeah, okay, I'll be there," he tried to yell back, holding his head with both hands to calm the shock waves his voice sent vibrating behind his eyes.

Slowly standing, he made his way out the bedroom door, shuffling his feet to minimize the effect that walking had, down the hall to the bathroom. The door was locked. Slowly raising his fist, he gave a halfhearted thump on the door.

"Any aspirin in there?" Brad asked, leaning his forehead on the door. The cool surface felt reviving. He heard the lock and lifted his head as the door opened. Nicho handed him a half full bottle of Tylenol.

"Thanks, man," Brad said, as he headed for the kitchen and some water.

His leg draped over the arm of his favorite chair, Angelo watched Brad, a smile playing on his lips.

Holding his head between his hands with the Tylenol bottled pressed to the side of his head with one hand, Brad shuffled into the kitchen.

Angelo snickered at Brad's discomfort. "You do know you have to swallow those things to make 'em work, don't ya?"

"Go to hell." Brad managed an audible whisper, filling a glass with water. He shook out four tablets and washed them down with the water. It even hurt to swallow.

Angelo choked back a laugh as he watched Brad shuffle toward the couch, holding his head with both hands.

"Sit down and I will get some ice for your head."

Angelo swung his leg off the arm and walked to the kitchen, chuckling as he filled a plastic bag with ice cubes.

Brad grunted an acknowledgment and slowly sank down on the couch. He'd never had his head hurt so damn much. Angelo came back with the ice, and Brad placed it on the back of his neck, deadening the throbbing.

Nicho sauntered over to the counter and poured a cup of coffee. Taking it to the table, he sat down. "I thought you said breakfast was ready," he said, looking at Angelo and then at the kitchen.

"Well, I had to get you all up somehow." Angelo gave him a toothy grin. "Now that you're up, I can throw some eggs and ham together. If you want anything else, you'll have to go get it."

Nicho took another drink, "Okay by me," he said.

Brad groaned.

✍✍✍

Standing in the doorway to her office, tea mug in hand, Lilly watched Matt drive by in the shuttle. Preoccupied, he never noticed her. She wondered if he was still worrying about the ID card. Probably was. Matt was so meticulous about things she was sure he would not rest until he knew what had happened. This worried Lilly a little, but she was confident she had left no trace that could connect back to her.

Strolling toward the operations room, tea mug in hand, she planned to casually drop by to see if she could learn anything.

The shuttle was sitting outside the operations room, so Lilly was sure Matt had already entered, but she decided to glance through the window before entering anyway. She saw Matt and some of the day shift guys huddled by the stairway.

They looked up as Lilly entered. Matt frowned and turned to the other men. "We'll talk later." He moved toward Lilly, meeting her halfway. "Miss Lilly, what can I do for you?" he asked, forcing a smile.

The day shift guys had been telling him they had seen Lilly leaving the operations room right before they came on duty yesterday morning. They guessed she had not noticed them as they had walked over from the Bajo instead of driving a shuttle.

"Just wanted to see if you were going over to the gardens today. I would like to go if you are," she said, her business face in place, just a trace of a smile touched her lips.

"No, not today," Matt said curtly.

He wasn't going to volunteer anymore, just in case she was involved. He hardly thought so, but you never knew. Better safe than sorry, he thought.

Lilly sensed a wall going up so she didn't push the issue. "Well, if you change your mind, please let me know. I find the gardens so very interesting," she said, smiling her best business smile now. "I'll talk to you later." She walked out.

Matt watched her leave, hoping he was wrong about her. He would finish his conversation with the day shift guys before he made a decision. In the meantime, he could use one of his workers' IDs when he needed to.

Lilly walked slowly back to her office, contemplating what had just happened. She felt that Matt had been a little cold toward her, but maybe it was her imagination. After all, he could have no way of connecting her to the loss of his ID card.

CHAPTER 14

Justice Handed Out

The black SUV drove slowly by the entrance of Armando's ranch. The gate was closed. According to the information they had received from Luis, Carlos and the other two should be inside. The men talked amongst themselves and decided to wait until someone left. The gate would be open and they could make their move—much easier and quieter than busting through the gate.

The SUV pulled onto a small dirt road a short distance from the front gate. The road wound around and went up a small hill, giving them a perfect vantage point to watch the gate and still be out of sight. Parking in a small grove of trees, they exited the SUV, closing the doors quietly. The men crept, hunched over, to the top of the rise. Lying on their bellies in the tall grass, binoculars in hand, they watched the ranch and the front gate.

The noonday sun beat down on the men as they lay patiently, watching. Around one, the gate started opening, they watched intently as a Land Rover pulled out onto the road, only one man in the vehicle. The men decided to let him go. They would find him later. Waiting a few minutes till the Land Rover was out of sight, they climbed back into the SUV and drove through the open gate and up the driveway.

Carlos had failed to persuade Quin to stay and had begrudgingly paid him his cut. Stuffing the money in his bag, Quin took the steps down to the driveway two at a time. Reaching the Land Rover, he threw his bag in the rear seat, never looking back as he drove out of the gate. Carlos watched until Quin turned out onto the road then closed the front doors. He missed seeing the black SUV start up the driveway.

Guns at their sides, the men from the SUV started up the front steps. Vargas's special elite squad were never ones to stand on ceremony and, with one swift kick, the front doors gave way and slammed against the inside wall with a loud bang.

Guns raised, the men stepped through the door into the house, as two women rushed out into the foyer, their eyes wide with terror. The men fired and the women dropped like bags of sand to the floor. Bright red spots spread and instantly stained their clothes. Red puddles formed on the floor and ran down the cracks separating the tiles, forming a bloody abstract design in its wake.

Carlos jumped when he heard the gunfire. He grabbed his gun from the desk and cautiously moved to the door. Seeing Maria and Juanita laying on the floor their eyes wide open and glazed with death, Carlos watched the men, reflected in the mirror at the end of the hall, as they moved forward. He backed up into the study his mind filled with fear, the blood pounding in his ears.

Who are these men?

He realized there was no way out of the room he was hiding in. It was the only room in the house with no windows. He closed his eyes, knowing he had nowhere to go. A cold sweat covered his body—he was trapped.

Ricardo had heard the commotion, grabbed his gun, and crept down the hall to the stairs. Carefully, he peeked through the railing. Below he saw three men, guns ready, walking across the foyer toward the study. Maria and Juanita lay lifeless on the foyer floor in a spreading crimson pool. Ricardo took a few steps down the stairs and fired at the men, hitting the one closest to him in the leg. The man fell, turned, and fired at Ricardo. The bullet missed him by inches. Ricardo ducked and fired again, but missed. The other two men turned and fired. Ricardo lost his footing and tumbled down the stairs. A hail of bullets from an automatic sub-machine gun made a dotted line on the wall behind him as he rolled down the stairs.

Carlos moved to the door again as he watched the scene play out in the mirror. His heart trying to beat its way out of his chest, he stepped around the door and fired blindly at the men. Carlos grazed one of the men in the shoulder. The two men standing turned back-to-back, one firing at Ricardo the other at Carlos. The man on the floor crawled over to the stairway and put two bullets between Ricardo's eyes before he had a chance to regain his footing. His body shuddered and went limp, a shocked expression on his face.

The two men standing turned and walked toward the study. Carlos could see them closing in as he watched in the mirror. His back against the bookcase, he could retreat no farther. Sweat poured down his face. His breath coming in short gasps.

The men walked through the door spraying the room with bullets. Six bullets stitched across Carlos' chest.

¡Dios Mío! This cannot be happening, Carlos thought looking down at his chest in disbelief.

A gurgling sound escaped his lips, blood bubbling

from his mouth and the holes in his chest as he collapsed to his knees and fell forward on his face.

The two men helped the third up. He put his arms on their shoulders and hobbled out. The SUV drove off. They decided not to seek out the Land Rover.

The murders were reported on the evening news. The authorities did not have any suspects.

✺

The migraine had finally eased, and Brad was feeling like he might live after all. Tylenol and a dark bedroom had helped. He had no idea what Angelo and Nicho had been up to. A long hot shower made him feel human again.

Hearing voices, Brad walked toward the sound. The voices were coming from Angelo's television. Nicho and Angelo were sitting on the edge of the couch, staring at the news reporter as he described the gruesome murders at a local residence. The names were being withheld pending notification of relatives.

"What's going on?" Brad asked, dropping down into Angelo's chair.

"From what I can tell, I think someone has killed Carlos and some other guy as well as the housekeeper and the maid," Angelo said, still staring at the screen. "They are not releasing any names, but they showed a shot of the residence and I am pretty sure it was Armando's ranch house."

"Who besides us wanted him dead?" Brad questioned, not expecting an answer.

"Who knows?" Nicho shrugged. He could think of one in particular but did not voice his opinion. He would call Vargas later.

☙❧

The phone vibrated in Luis's pocket. Sitting astride his horse, it took him a couple of minutes to fish it out. "*Sí*," he said, juggling the phone, barely saving it from tumbling to the ground.

"It is done," the man said, flatly. "It made the news, but they have no idea who to look for."

"Excellent!" Luis said, "Pack up and come home. I will call Angelo."

"We will put the SUV in storage and notify the hangar to have the plane on standby. Do you want us to bring Nicho back, too?" the man asked.

"No, I will make arrangements for him." Luis pulled the reins and turned the horse toward the barn.

Shoving the phone back in his jeans pocket, he urged the horse into a full gallop, thinking as he rode that he could not bring Nicho home just yet. He needed him to make sure that, if there were an investigation, it led away from Brad and ORCA, and that Brad went back down to the dome, none the wiser. Other things still needed to be taken care of, too.

Luis had been keeping an eye on the ORCA situation since he had been informed about the attempted sabotage and the board takeover. Luis had been a silent partner on ORCA's board for years and, to keep it that way, there could not be a public investigation into the attempted takeover. Asad Damji the head of ORCA, was trying to contain the situation and, so far, he had kept it internal. Luis had not let Brad know of his involvement with OR-CA—it could cause complications. The less Brad knew about that, the better. Luis also could not let him know his involvement in Carlos's demise. Brad's hands were clean and Luis intended to keep it that way.

The horse snorted and pranced sideways as Luis

dismounted, handing the reins to the stable boy. Knocking the dust off his jeans with his hat, he walked to the house, intending to call Angelo, and then Nicho to tell them what he wanted to be done.

The house was cool inside, a pleasant change from the heat of the afternoon. Luis rang for Jose to refill the ice bucket and poured himself a Scotch, downing it without ice. Filling the glass half full, he waited for Jose to bring the ice for this one.

Leaning back in his chair, Luis decided what he would have Nicho do. He already knew he would have Angelo take care of any loose ends. Angelo was an expert at that.

Luis would have Nicho wait until Brad had returned to the dome and then check in at the ORCA office. He trusted Nicho to give him an accurate assessment of what was happening. He wanted Nicho to review the audio and video that had been collected on Lilly. He had been monitoring her for months, ever since he found out her connection to Javier and the Eastern Alliance and that someone in the EA was behind the attempted takeover of the ORCA Board. Then it was discovered, through the surveillance equipment in Lilly's office, that the same someone was also behind the attempted sabotage, bribing Armando to carry out their plans. Fortunately for ORCA, Armando had botched the sabotage attempt. Lilly, on the other hand, was a different story. She appeared to be quite dedicated to the takeover. From the surveillance equipment in her office, conversations overheard indicated that the EA had promised her Brad's position when the takeover was complete and her brother Javier a place on the EA board.

Luis refreshed his drink and thought about the last ORCA Board meeting where he had been tipped off that there was an EA infiltrator on the ORCA board who would try to manipulate the votes to replace the current board chairman with another suspected EA-backed member. Luis informed Asad of the situation, and he dealt with the infiltrator swiftly. Luis was also thankful that the board had listened to him and not given Lilly complete control of the dome when they had sent Brad to Dallas. However, he was disappointed they had refused to listen when he told them that sending Brad to Dallas that close to the opening, was, not only bad timing, but a bad idea as well, and he had been proven right.

However, maybe it was meant to be. If Brad had not gone to Dallas, he would not have met Darcey, and I would not have found out she was Saleem's daughter.

It was strange how fate had worked its magic, pulling the threads of their lives together in an intricately patterned tapestry of relationships. Lives that would not have found each other, without fate's intervention. It was fate that wove the lives of Brad and Darcey together with Luis and Aicha in this inescapable design.

CHAPTER 15

Anticipation

Brad finally made it back from Lima. He had stayed an extra day, hoping to find out exactly what had happened to Carlos, but there had been no further news broadcasts with any new information from the authorities.

Nicho had dropped him off at the dock before heading back to the ORCA offices to call Luis.

Brad called Darcey from the topside dock to tell her he was on his way.

"I should be there by seven or seven thirty," he told her, already anticipating the feel of her in his arms. He didn't care if she didn't remember everything about him. He was not going to wait any longer to hold her, to touch her, to kiss her, to make love to her. These past few days had been pure hell being away from her. The only thing he had to feel fortunate about was she was safe and Nicho had left for Morocco.

"Okay, I'll order something for dinner. What sounds good to you?" Darcey asked, feeling the tingle beginning to surge through her body as the tones of his velvet voice caressed her ear.

"Doesn't matter to me. You pick something," Brad said softly. He could hear her short intake of breath. Darcey was feeling the pull too. He smiled to himself. The pull was so strong he could almost feel her body next to him.

"Fine," she teased, "you'll have to eat whatever I order." She giggled. She couldn't help it and it was becoming harder to breathe. What hunger pangs she might have had were now replaced with desire. Brad's voice had obliterated everything, except the euphoria it created in her. She didn't know if he would want something to eat. But just in case, she called the Baja and ordered what Brad had said had been their favorite fast food on Saturdays—two hamburgers with everything, fries, and two strawberry milkshakes. She checked the time—two hours and forty-three minutes until she would be in his arms.

What did I tell you? It would come back if you didn't force it. That little voice that had so annoyed her was a welcome intrusion now.

Yes, you were right. I have begun to remember things. Not everything, but the important things like Brad and how much we mean to each other. And, yes, I remember how you pestered me when I first met Brad and how you tried to reason with me about chasing after him. A heavy sigh echoed somewhere in her mind. She smiled to herself.

❧❧❧

Brad barely waited for the captain to open the hatch before he leaped from the sub onto the dock and bounded through the doors to the shuttle bay. Jumping into the shuttle, he pushed the accelerator to the floor, but he knew it wouldn't go any faster than fifteen miles an hour, no matter how hard he pushed. That would have to do. It was faster than walking.

It took about twenty minutes to reach his quarters. The closer he got, the higher his anticipation grew. Butterflies exploded in his stomach. The palms of his hands were sweating like a teenager on his first date. He didn't take the time to park his shuttle in the shuttle bay, but slammed to a halt in front of his door and jumped off. He took a deep breath, trying to calm down just a little before he slid his card, opening the door.

A soft whir sounded as the door slid open. Darcey was standing just inside the door, the irises of her hazel eyes dark with passion. Her perfect lips were slightly open in anticipation. Two steps and Brad swept Darcey up in his arms. Her arms wound around his neck as his lips descended on hers. Her mouth opened and welcomed him in.

A catcall whistle from a passing shuttle in the corridor brought them back to the present.

"Guess I'd better close the door," Brad breathed in her ear, sending goose bumps all over her body.

"Ummm, I suppose you should," she said, as she circled his ear with the tip of her finger. She reluctantly backed away so he could close the door and gave him a wicked little grin. "I'll wait right here."

The fire began to burn through her body, unlike any she'd ever known. She had never burned this hot, not even for the first time she and Brad had come together. She watched his body as he walked toward her, his desire also reflected in his smoldering emerald eyes. She was lost.

Brad shut the door and turned around, watching Darcey as he walked toward her. His body had a mind of its own as he devoured her with his eyes. Never had he wanted or needed anyone like he wanted and needed her. Darcey was his world, his reason for existing. She was what made his world keep spinning. Brad reached for her, and time stood still. Their world spun wildly out of control through the universe.

"I've missed you," he said, nuzzling her ear as he gathered her up and carried her to the bedroom.

Darcey's heart was flying. "I missed you, too, although I didn't remember how much until today," she murmured against his lips. "My memory, parts of it anyway, are coming back and, all of sudden this afternoon— I knew you. I knew us. I knew I couldn't—can't live without you." Small pieces of Darcey's memory had been pushing through the gray haze in her mind, especially those memories of Brad and Dallas. Memories she shared with Brad, the first night he got back from Lima.

She put her hands on either side of his face and drew him to her. He held her tight against his body. The heat between them rose to volcanic proportions, erupting in a blaze of fireworks. They were hungry, but not for food.

Long forgotten, the hamburgers and fries grew cold, and the milkshakes melted.

☙❧☙

The air vibrated, charged with anticipation, as the dome shifted into overdrive, preparing for the official opening. Everything slipped into place. The shops in the retail plaza busily stocked their shelves. The cinema and bowling alley had been full every night since they opened. The entertainment had been enjoyed by almost everyone in the dome, except Lilly. Darcey hadn't seen her much lately. She supposed Lilly had plenty to do getting everything ready for the opening, not that Darcey really cared. She still felt like something just didn't add up about Lilly, but she couldn't put her finger on it.

The hydroponic gardens were a hive of activity as Matt and his crew monitored the first planting cycle, anticipating the first harvest. In the next couple of days, the first cycle would be harvested and the plantings of the second cycle would be nearing their final phase. The first harvest from that first cycle would be used by the chefs in the Bajo el Mar Café for the dishes they would prepare to serve the guests at the grand opening.

Since his return, Brad had been working with Ty and the Three Stooges, as Darcey liked to call them, making sure all systems were up and ready.

Since the virus, Armando's botched attempt at sabotage, and his murder had been closed, filed, and put to bed, things had been running smoothly. It was just a feeling Brad had confided in Darcey, but he worried that things were running too smoothly. He didn't like being pessimistic, but he couldn't help feeling a little paranoid about it. The threat of something going wrong at the last minute still hung out there.

She hadn't seen much of Marti the last few days. Marti and Ty were becoming a real item, and Scott had been pestering Marti to talk Brad into bringing Ashley and a couple of her other friends down for the opening. Darcey had told Brad she thought it would be a wonderful idea, especially since the guys hadn't had any real "girl company" since they arrived on the dome.

CHAPTER 16

The Dead of Night

The hour hand ticked on the three. The alarm shrilled through the blackness of Lilly's bedroom. Fumbling around, she found the off button and pushed it. She was already awake with anticipation of what she had planned for the day. The alarm was merely a formality, in case she had actually fallen asleep. Lying there, staring into the darkness, hugging herself, she thought about how she was going to fulfill her ultimate goal—stop the completion of the dome.

Matt had confided in her that he had decided to drop trying to find out what had happened to his hydroponic ID card until after the opening. He could use a card from one of the other team workers. That had suited Lilly just fine because there would not be an opening. There would not be any hydroponic gardens, at least not under Matt's supervision—she would see to that personally.

She opened her front door and peeked out before stepping out into silent the corridor. The odds someone would be traveling the corridor at this time in the morning was remote, but one could never be too careful. Sliding onto the shuttle's seat, she flipped the switch and drove off down the corridor humming to herself as she went.

Pulling up in front of the storage bay's cargo doors, Lilly opened them and drove the shuttle inside and out of sight of anyone's inquisitive eyes. Continuing past the rows of equipment and supply pallets, she made her way to the back of the storage bay and pulled to a halt in front of a pallet stacked with shrink-wrapped, gray, plastic drums used for the hydroponic gardens. Jumping out of the shuttle, Lilly skipped around to the back of the pallet where she reached down and patted the small container sitting on the floor containing the precious liquid she had so carefully concocted.

Lilly was so excited, she had goose bumps and could hardly contain herself.

This is what I've been so patiently planning for the past two weeks, she thought, clapping her hands. *No,* she corrected herself, placing her forefinger on the side of her face, *I've been planning this since the EA promised me complete control of the dome.*

No one had seen Lilly slipping in and out of the storage bay over the last two weeks. Not that she needed to be secretive. She had every right to be in the storage bay any time she wanted, she reasoned. No one would question her about being there, but it was much more exhilarating to play the part of a corporate spy. She relished the adrenalin rush she got each time she snuck out of her office and stealthily made her way down to the storage bay.

Her most exciting venture, however, happened when she went to the operations room in search of Matt. She had 'accidently' noticed a supply requisition form on Matt's desk that he had already signed but had not filled out yet. Ty and Hot Dog looked up when Lilly had come through the door. She had smiled sweetly at them. A brief nod was the only acknowledgment either man had given before they returned to checking the control panels. They had been a little less than friendly over the past couple of weeks, she reflected. But it did not matter anymore what they thought of her. They, too, would be gone in a couple of weeks.

"Is Matt here?" Lilly asked, innocently, already knowing she had seen him on his way to the hydroponic gardens.

"Naw," Hot Dog said, not looking up from his palmtop. "He left a few minutes ago for the hydro."

"Thank you," she said, walking toward Matt's desk carefully watching the men. "He was going to leave me some papers. I will just check on his desk."

Lilly placed the papers she had in her hand on top of the requisition form and pretended to look at the papers on Matt's desk.

"I do not see them here. I will try later when he gets back." Lilly gathered up her papers with the requisition form on the bottom and walked out the door. Ty and Hot Dog never looked up.

A wicked giggle escaped Lilly's lips. Inwardly, she gloated about her good fortune on the walk back to her office. She had wanted to get Matt's signature on a requisition form but had not quite figured out how to do it. She supposed she could have forged Matt's signature and no one would have been the wiser. Those stupid clerks in the office topside never take the time to check out anything, she thought, disgusted. They simply look at the items requested and fill the request. They did not even take the time to see if the forms are signed.

In reality, it would not have been difficult to get the things she needed, but this was better—now nothing would lead back to her.

Good fortune has indeed smiled on me today.

Now, Lilly loaded the small container onto the shuttle and drove up to the cargo doors. She checked the corridor before opening the big doors. Jumping back into the shuttle, she drove out slowly so as not to spill any of the gray liquid in the container. Unfortunately, she could not find a lid that would fit the opening of this particular container.

A quick check of her watch indicated it was three minutes till four. Still plenty of time before the day workers would start arriving at six.

No more attempts at sabotage had happened since Armando had been murdered, so Matt had eased up on the security. He canceled the overnight watch and had installed security cameras instead. Cameras, to the delight of Lilly, that he had unwittingly shown her the exact places where they had been installed. Now, she knew just how to avoid them.

This is going to be so much fun, she thought gleefully.

Giggling, she pulled Matt's ID card out of her pocket and slid it through the slot. Closing her eyes and inhaling deeply, she let the adrenaline course through her as the door opened. Before stepping inside, she rubbed her hands together in anticipation of this final step of making the dome hers. Carefully, she lifted the container with its deadly poison and carried it toward the solution tanks, conscious of the cameras' blind spots.

Carefully she placed the container on the floor and opened the lid to the feeder trough. The trough supported all of the solution tanks and would carry the poison throughout the gardens. Delighted, she saw the trough had been filled, ready to go when the pumps were turned on in the morning, pumping all of her lovely poison through the tanks and right into the plants.

Lilly giggled as a shiver of excitement ran through her. The giggle burst into an out loud laugh as she picked up the container and carefully tipped it so the gray liquid flowed smoothly into the trough. There was not enough of the gray poison to change the color of the clear orange nutrient solution, so no one would ever know what had happened. She beamed, elated, as the last drop of the poison hit the surface of the nutrient solution and blended in.

There—it is done!

Lilly could not wait to gloat to Javier about her success and tell the Eastern Alliance she had shut the dome down. She, Lilly Montego, who had succeeded where all of those in the EA had failed. She, who had planned, schemed, and kept ORCA in the dark, even after the mess Armando had created. She, who had hidden right under their noses and duped Brad Daniels into trusting her with the total operation of the dome. She who, single-handedly, had now killed all hopes of ORCA opening the dome on time and handed it to the EA on a silver platter.

Those delicious thoughts danced through Lilly's mind as she walked back to the shuttle, grinning. Closing the hydroponics door, she set the container on the shuttle seat beside her. The artificial daylight was just beginning to come up as she stopped by the Bajo el Mar Café for a celebratory cup of tea.

Lilly smiled at the cashier.

That is really weird, the cashier thought. The cashier observed that this was the second time in three weeks she had seen Lilly smile. It wasn't a friendly smile. It was cold with a touch of evil, and it gave the cashier cold chills.

Pausing at the door, Lilly turned and looked back, her eyes roving over the room, observing the day shift workers who were eating breakfast. Her eyes stopped at the cashier. She smiled again.

Enjoy yourselves now because none of you will be here next month, Lilly thought. Everything had worked exactly how she had planned and now she had one final thing to take care of.

CHAPTER 17

Morning of Enlightenment

Brad lay there watching Darcey, enjoying the even rise and fall of her perfect breasts. Darcey was his, all his. She would never belong to anyone else. Their connection was too strong. He had known this from the first moment he saw her. It was as if his soul had been searching for her for centuries and had found her at last. At that moment, he knew that nothing would ever keep them apart again.

He watched her stir and her eyes fluttered open. She yawned, stretched her arms up over her head, wiggling her fingers, and turned to see Brad watching her with passion rising in his eyes. Grinning that heart-stopping grin, he rose up on one elbow and ran his fingers down her arm, releasing the heat of their connection through her body. She gave a short intake of breath as she reached for him, her body already responding to his touch. At that moment, she knew she was his, she had always been his, would always be his. She knew nothing would ever keep them apart.

She couldn't help smiling and mentally hugging herself as the thrill of last night and this morning played over again in her mind. She felt alive again for the first time in a very long time. Things long forgotten were surfacing through the fog in her memory. Even the sad things, the embarrassing things, the naughty things were all welcome awakenings. Even her little voice of reason was welcomed back, although it had been missing these past couple of days. Maybe it was because Darcey felt safe and loved knowing Brad was here.

The phone rang and Darcey went to get it, but Brad had already picked up.

"Brad, here," he said, grinning at her, and making her heart skip a beat. "Yeah, I can be there in five." A frown replaced the grin.

"What's up?" she asked, wondering just what could be so upsetting that it would replace that beautiful grin with a frown.

"I don't know. Matt and Ty want to see me right away. Something to do with the hydro gardens."

Brad was still frowning as he kissed her on the forehead. "I'll grab something at the Bajo. Call you as soon as I know what's going on."

This is not good, she thought, frowning as she watched the door close.

It's too close to the opening for something to go wrong now. Brad had been worrying that something was going to happen to keep the dome from opening on time. He had said his gut was never wrong and that worried her.

Brad had made Darcey an extra ID card for his quarters so she could come and go as she pleased. She was beginning to wonder why they just didn't move into one. Life would be much simpler, although there would be the problem of closet space. Her extensive wardrobe, courtesy of Luis Vargas, left no room for anything of Brad's.

Laughing to herself, she sorted through the hangars full of designer clothes for something to wear.

Just like any woman—a closet full of clothes and nothing to wear. She laughed out loud at the irony of it all. She finally settled on her favorite pair of Dior slacks and a silk pullover top.

The aroma of the freshly brewed coffee that she had put on before dressing greeted her in the kitchen. Filling the travel mug Brad had brought her back from Lima, she picked up her grocery list, the ID cards, and put them in her pocket. Glancing at the counter, she saw the pager Brad had given her when she first arrived. She debated about taking it with her, but she was just going to the supply store and knew her way around without getting lost, so she left it on the counter.

ᥱᦐᥱᦐ

Lilly had gone back to her quarters to change and was now on her way to her office. She decided to stop for another cup of tea and maybe treat herself to a pastry. Her stomach was telling her she needed to eat something. But she was just not hungry. The adrenaline was still running rampant through her system, and she loved every minute of it.

Her hand grabbed the handle of her tea mug as she decided it was time to take care of the last thing that was standing in her way to complete happiness. The one thing that had been a thorn in her side these past few months. The one thing that would give her even more pleasure than the poison she had put in the tanks. She sat down in her chair and reached for the phone, punching in Darcey's number.

The phone rang and finally went to voice mail. Lilly

left her a brief message that she would like to drop by for a visit and could she call her back at her earliest convenience.

Lilly slammed the phone down, furious that Darcey was not home. She sat, tapping her fingers on the desk. She needed to calm down. This mood had been coming on for a couple of days, but she had ignored it. This last little bit of aggravation had pushed her too close to the edge. Reaching down, Lilly opened her secret drawer and pulled out the little silver metal box.

Pulling the chain from around her neck, Lilly took the little key and unlocked the box.

This is too soon.

She should not need another dose for weeks yet, but she had let the stress of the last few days override the usual calm and self-control that the dose gave her. If this kept up, she would have to contact the EA for more. They had been keeping her supplied over the last four years. It was part of her package deal along with a healthy yearly million-dollar paycheck, that went directly into her Swiss bank account, for keeping the EA informed on all of ORCA's internal workings. But once Darcey had been taken care of, Lilly would not have any more stress. It would be smooth sailing and blue skies. She leaned back in the chair, closing her eyes, letting dose course through her veins. Peace settled over her.

The phone shrilled, jolting Lilly back to reality. Startled, she panicked and knocked the receiver off, sending it rattling to the floor along with a file folder she had pulled out of the secret drawer to study later. The papers inside fluttered out and floated to the floor.

Lilly grabbed the cord and pulled the receiver back and then hastily collected the papers, stuffing them back in the folder. She shoved it into the top drawer of her desk, making a mental note to put the folder back in the secret drawer later. "Hello, Lilly here, how may I help you?" she said a little breathless, but in her usual calm business voice that had returned.

"Hi, Lilly, this is Darcey. I got your message," she said, wondering why, after all, this time, Lilly had suddenly wanted to visit. Lilly had hardly said two words to her after Brad left for Lima and certainly nothing since he'd returned.

You'd better be careful of this one, reason cautioned, pushing all her alarm bells. *This one is up to no good.*

Yes, I think you're right. I'll be careful.

Maybe you should call Marti to come over?

No, I think it will be all right. Brad trusts her.

Yes, I know, but do you?

I trust Brad's judgment. I will be okay.

"I was wondering if we could visit. I know I have not been as helpful as Bard wanted me to be in helping you adjust," Lilly purred, into the phone.

"Sure, we could visit," Darcey said hesitantly. "Where did you have in mind? You could come to my place this evening if you want." She really didn't want to visit with Lilly, but she would feel safer if it was at her place.

"Actually, I was hoping we could meet this morning, and your quarters would be fine. Say, around ten thirty?" Lilly said, putting a pseudo friendly smile into her voice.

"Well, yes, I guess that would be okay," Darcey replied, still not sure she wanted to do this, but she could think of no plausible reason not to.

The tiny voice poked her again. *Be careful.*

"Fine," Lilly said, "I'll see you at ten thirty, your quarters." She hung up, tapping the receiver with her finger, thinking that was easier than she thought it would be. She had already arranged what she planned to do several days ago. Just a few final details to tidy up.

Lilly put everything neatly away in the little silver box, locked it, and put it back in the secret drawer along with the file folder she retrieved from the top desk drawer. She checked her watch. She had an hour before going to see Darcey. An hour she was sure would tick slowly by, but in the meantime, she still had to order the pastries.

The minute's seemed to drag by as Lilly waited in her quarters after she had prepared the pastries for Darcey. Lilly injected enough propofol into the pastries to knock Darcey out. Lilly's plan depended on getting Darcey to the location she had set up, and she was positive Darcey would not come without a fight.

CHAPTER 18

Discovered

Okay, guys. What's the big emergency?" Brad asked, walking into the operations room where Ty and the guys were gathered around Matt's computer.

"Ya gotta take a look at this, boss man," Ty said, pointing at the computer screen. "We caught this on the surveillance cameras in the hydro last night."

Brad walked to the desk and looked at the screen over Matt's shoulder. The video showed the inside of the hydroponic area. All looked in order as the surveillance cameras rotated from one to the other. Then when the camera covering the tank area came on, there was Lilly. They watched as she opened the feeder trough and poured something into it. They watched her laughing as she did it.

"What th—" Brad said, running his hand through his hair. "Am I seeing what I think I'm seeing?" he asked, in disbelief.

Backing up, he turned around and paced the floor.

That can't be right, he thought. *Not Lilly. I trusted her. I would have bet my life on her loyalty.*

"'Fraid so, boss," Matt said. "I've been over to check it out and took a sample. It's at the lab being analyzed as we speak. We should know something in an hour."

"I hate to think what might have happened if we hadn't seen this." Ty said. "We were scheduled to turn the pumps on this morning, and whatever she put in the trough would have been pumped into all the tanks," he said, turning around and looking at Brad.

"Has anybody seen Lilly this morning?" Brad asked, walking over to the door and looking down the corridor toward her office. It was dark.

"Naw, we haven't seen her, but I'll ask around and see if any of the crew has," Hot Dog said. "I'll head over to the Bajo and start there. Lilly always comes in for her cup of tea every morning."

"Thanks, I'll check her office, even though it's dark. There might be something to give us a clue of what's going on." Brad shook his head as he walked to the door. He couldn't believe this. Lilly, who he thought, had always had his back and trusted with his life—*no this can't be right*. Lilly was the one who discovered Armando's fiasco. She was the one who insisted he be the one to take care of the problem. Brad couldn't believe that she did this. Something must have happened. She was being forced to do this. No, he would not believe any of this until he heard it from her.

Lilly's office door was locked, but Brad had a master key for all offices and departments. He opened the door and switched on the light. The overheads filled the office with the harsh glare of fluorescent light and revealed nothing amiss. Brad went to check her desk. Items on the desktop were neatly stacked and arranged as usual. Everything seemed to be in order, except, he noticed, she had failed to wash and put her tea mug away. Something she never failed to do. Everything else was where it should be.

Brad put his hands on the desktop and leaned forward, supporting himself with his arms, trying to figure out what to do next. He ran his eyes over the top of her desk again. It was neat and in order as usual. The one thing that was not was the tea mug.

None of this makes any sense, he thought.

As he straightened up, something white sticking out from under the desk caught Brad's eye. Bending down, he pulled out what appeared to be a list of names and phone numbers printed on an Eastern Alliance letterhead.

Now, why would she have this? he asked himself, as he scanned down the list of names.

A few names he recognized as either ORCA board members or investors in the Dome Project. One name, in particular, stood out—Javier Montego—Lilly's brother. Also, on the list was Armando's lawyer, Eduardo Perez. Brad's knees went limp and he sat down hard in Lilly's chair as he read through the list.

He still couldn't believe it, even though he was holding possible damning proof in his hand. No, he still wasn't going to believe it. He knew Lilly would have a perfectly plausible explanation for having this information. It could be in connection with the research he had asked her to do, to investigate the sabotage. Brad still had to hear it from her.

He got up slowly, still in denial, and walked out down the corridor to the operations room. The list in hand, he walked over to where the guys were talking. Matt held up a piece of paper—the report was back from the lab. As they suspected, the sample had proved to be a mixture of chemicals and herbicides designed to instantly destroy the plants.

Brad was not ready to hear that. He still believed Lilly was being coerced into doing this. Unconsciously, he wadded it up.

"Look, boss," Ty said, putting his hand on Brad's shoulder, "I don't know how much more proof you need. This gal's tryin' to shut us down."

"I know what it looks like, but I've got to hear it from her," Brad said, staring at the wadded piece of paper in his fist. "I've known her for over five years. Lilly's never done anything to cause me to distrust her, and I'm not going to start now. Not until I've heard her explanation." He tossed the wadded up list on Matt's desk.

"Sorry, man, but that's what it looks like from where I sit," Matt said. "I trusted her too. I unwittingly gave her all the information she needed to make that solution. What saved us was that I installed that new camera in the tank area just yesterday, and I didn't have the opportunity to tell her about it. Plus, I'm convinced now she is the one who took my hydro ID card. How else could she have gotten in there?"

"Yeah, I know." Scott placed his hand on Matt's shoulder. "Looks like we all got fooled. Hot Dog, did you find out anything at the Bajo?"

"As a matter of fact I did. The cashier said she came in real early this mornin' and got a cup of tea, all smilin' like the cat that swallowed the canary. Then she came back for a pastry 'round her usual time and then 'round ten she ordered more pastries and a bouquet of fresh flowers. Said she picked 'em up shortly after that. The cashier said she was actin' real strange, even for Lilly."

"The cashier didn't happen to mention where Lilly might be headin' did she?" Scott asked.

"Naw, she said she just kept smilin' and told her to put the pastries on her tab."

"Well, that does us no good," Brad said, pacing back

and forth. "Matt, I want you and your guys to drain the tanks. Siphon out the feeder tank first, and then drain and flush all of the tanks. Do you have enough solution prepared to refill the tanks? We should only lose a day on this." He stopped and looked at Matt, who was already on the phone calling his men to come in.

"Yes, we have enough on hand from the reserve for the refill." Scott stepped forward. "But we'll have to order more to restock the reserve. I'll call and order that right now. It should be down by this afternoon."

Brad still paced, trying to make sense of everything that had happened. Try as he might, it all made no sense.

Matt put the phone down and said his guys would at the hydro and ready to get to work within the next hour.

Looking at his watch, Brad saw it was almost eleven-thirty. "I'll meet you over there. I'm going to call Darcey."

He picked up the phone and called her number. He couldn't shake a dark foreboding feeling that he couldn't put his finger on, but knew in the pit of his stomach that something bad was on the horizon.

CHAPTER 19

Attempted Murder

At exactly ten twenty-five, Lilly left her quarters, knowing it would take a little over five minutes to drive to Darcey's quarters from hers. She pulled the shuttle to a stop in front of Darcey's door.

Darcey heard a light tap on the door.

That must be Lilly. She went to open the door. *Now, I wished I had asked Marti to be here, too.*

"Hi. Welcome. Please come in." Darcey stepped aside for Lilly to enter.

Lilly held a bakery box in her right hand, a small bouquet of flowers in her left. She held the bouquet out for Darcey to take then stepped past her and placed the box on the bar.

"Thank you. These are stunning. I'll find a vase for them." Darcey sniffed the roses as she made her way to the kitchen. *I would have never thought of Lilly as one to bring flowers. She just doesn't seem the type.*

Darcey watched out of the corner of her eye as Lilly looked around with a slight frown on her face. Lilly turned and walked over to the bar. A cold smile had replaced the frown. "I've brought some pastries. Do you have plates? Maybe some tea?" Lilly asked, almost friendly but the words turned sour in her mouth. A nasty little smile played on her lips as she turned away from Darcey. *All of this should have been mine and it will be,* Lilly thought greedily. *Just a few more weeks, I will take these quarters for myself.*

Darcey's alarm bells began ringing. A feeling of foreboding welled up in the pit of her stomach. Now, she really wished she had called Marti, but it was too late.

Reason punched her in the gut. *When are you going to start listening to me?*

"Sure." Darcey pulled a couple of plates from the cabinet, along with forks and napkins. She placed them on the counter for Lilly to pick up. "I'll put some water on for the tea," she said. Darcey turned on the tap to fill the teakettle. "So, what did you want to visit about?" she asked, hoping she didn't sound as nervous as she felt. Just being this close to Lilly made her skin crawl.

Lilly fidgeted with the forks before answering. "Oh, nothing, in particular," she said. Looking up from the forks, she gave Darcey a cold smile. "I just feel bad that I have not been able to help you settle in and see to the things Brad asked me to do for you."

A chill ran up Darcey's spine. A slight tremble caused her to fumble opening the box of tea bags. "You shouldn't worry about that. Looking after me would have taken you away from your duties, and Ty and Marti and the guys have been a real big help," Darcey said, hoping Lilly hadn't noticed the fumble. Trying to sound more confident, she turned to face Lilly. "They have taken me most everywhere and introduced me around. I think the only people I haven't met are the people in the office topside."

"Well, you are not missing much there," Lilly said sarcastically and laughed a cold, bone-chilling laugh.

The shrill whistle of the teakettle caused Darcey to jump. Her eyes flew to Lilly, who had walked into the living area. She hadn't noticed Darcey jump.

Placing the cups and saucers on the bar, Darcey dropped a tea bag into each cup and poured hot water over the bags. The water turned a translucent brown as it released the richness of the tea.

"Cream, sugar?"

"No, just tea, thank you."

Darcey picked up the cup and saucer and placed it on the bar in front of Lilly who had placed one pastry on each plate. She slid one in Darcey's direction.

Darcey picked up her cup, saucer, and plate. She walked around the bar over to the table. "Why don't we sit at the table? It's much more comfortable," she said.

Lilly frowned but followed.

"This is a new pastry the chefs at the Bajo are trying out. I think they will be serving them at the opening. I got us an advance tasting." Lilly said, almost giddy as she cut off a piece and put it in her mouth. "Mmmmm. Delicious. Give it a try," she prompted, pointing her fork at Darcey's plate. She had treated a special one just for Darcey. Lilly could hardly contain herself as she watched Darcey cut off a piece and place it in her mouth.

"Yes, it is delicious. I can't quite make out the flavor, but it's delicious." Darcey said, taking a second bite. It was delicious, but there was a flavor she couldn't quite put her finger on. Then she noticed Lilly was watching her closely, and that made her more nervous. She took another bite, still trying to name the elusive flavor.

Lilly watched as Darcey took another bite and another. Lilly enjoyed her pastry with relish. She could hardly wait for the propofol to take effect.

"This is really delicious," Darcey said, trying focus on Lilly's face that kept moving. "I don't feel so well. I think I neeee—" Darkness descended.

Lilly jumped up and caught Darcey before she toppled out of the chair.

"Cannot have you hurting yourself until I have had a chance to do it first," Lilly said out loud, latching on to Darcey's arm with her claw-like fingers.

Lilly quickly moved the plate with the pastry out of the way and laid Darcey's head on the table, her arms, dangling lifelessly from her shoulders.

Darcey's ID card was lying on the bar and Lilly used it to open the front door. She had come prepared. Unloading the wheelchair from the back of the shuttle, she congratulated herself on this stroke of genius. The new shipment for the medical wing had arrived yesterday, and among the items were wheelchairs. It had been easy to take one. No one ever questioned her, as Lilly often transported items in her shuttle, so taking the wheelchair had been a snap.

With Darcey loaded in the wheelchair, Lilly rolled her into the corridor and closed the door, stuffing Darcey's ID in her pocket. She pulled Darcey from the wheelchair and pushed her limp body as far as she could up and onto the floor in the back of the shuttle.

Humming, Lilly skipped around to the other side, stepped up in the shuttle, and grabbed Darcey's arms, giving her one final jerk to finish pulling her in. The wheelchair rolled a short distance down the corridor as the shuttle took off.

It took over twenty minutes to reach the place where Lilly had everything prepared. She had picked the sanitation waste station of dome number four. Although it was still under construction and would be the last one completed, the sanitation station in each dome had been operational as soon as it had been anchored to the ocean floor. All the waste from each dome was collected, filtered, and treated. Most of the waste could be recycled and used in the dome. That which could not be used was processed and neutralized before it went to the dumping port and released into the ocean waters.

Lilly pulled the shuttle into the open area close to the dumping port's inside access door. It would just be a matter of unlocking the access door and shoving Darcey down the chute. Lilly giggled. She had measured the chute. Darcey would fit nicely and flush with ease out the port door.

Humming to herself, Lilly jumped out of the shuttle and hurried into the station's operating room, coming to an abrupt halt just inside the door.

"¡*Maldito*! This is not like the one I have been studying in preparation for this," she grumbled out loud, as she studied the plethora of buttons and switches on the shiny new console panel. "This system looks completely different. It must be one of the new ones Maintenance has been talking about using to replace the old ones."

Lilly stepped forward and ran her hand across the console. "This is only a minor setback," she said. "It will just take a little longer to figure out, but it can be done. And it will be done." She was not going to be denied the pleasure of disposing of Darcey.

She started humming again, pushing the buttons and pulling switches. She knew one of them had to release the lock on the port door.

CHAPTER 20

The Rescue

Darcey's phone went to voice mail. Brad hung up and called her number again. It should not be going to voicemail. Voicemail again.

The knot in the pit of his stomach grew bigger. He hollered over his shoulder, as he ran out the door, "I'm going to find Darcey. She's not answering, and she should be. I'm worried."

"Hang on, boss," Ty said, grabbing his hat. "I'll go with you. I'll give Marti a call and let her know what's up. She's just down the corridor and closest to Darcey's quarters."

"Thanks. Does Marti have a card to Darcey's quarters?"

"Yes, I believe so."

Brad pushed the accelerator all the way to the floor, knowing it wouldn't go any faster than fifteen miles an hour, but it made him feel he was doing everything he could. He couldn't let anything happen to Darcey. His heart constricting as he thought of what might happen to her, he jumped out of the shuttle before it came to a halt and rushed through the open door. Marti paced just inside.

"Darcey's not here," Marti said, panicked, "but someone has been." She pointed to the two plates and cups on the table.

Brad quickly accessed the situation. The bakery box was from the Bajo el Mar Café. He flipped up the lid and there was still one pastry inside. He noticed the tea bags lying on the side of the saucers. It was a safe bet that the other person had been Lilly.

Darcey would not have made tea unless the visitor requested it, and the only one that jumped to mind was Lilly.

This can't be right, Brad thought, running his hand through his hair. He still couldn't believe that Lilly was behind it all.

"Let's face it, boss, you gotta let go. You know Lilly is behind this, too," Ty said, standing next to Marti, his arm around her shoulders.

Brad studied Ty for a second then looked at Marti.

"I know Darcey wouldn't have gone without a fight, and there's not a sign of a struggle. She must have been drugged. That's the only explanation." Brad paced, running his hand through his hair. "Marti, don't throw out that tea. Put it in a sealable container and put those pastries back in the box," he directed. "Please take them to the lab and tell them I want a rush on the results. Tell them to look for anything—poison, drugs, everything— tell them to run the whole gamut. I want the results as soon as they have something!" he barked at Marti, the enormity of the situation underscoring his words.

Marti jumped and began looking for a container for the tea. "Sure thing,"

"Where do we go from here?" Brad wondered aloud

as he ran his hand through his hair in frustration, then he noticed Darcey's pager lying on the bar. Damn.

"Brad, look out here," Ty called, from the corridor. "What's a wheelchair doing here?" He pushed it up to the door.

"Lilly must have used it to move Darcey from the room to a shuttle," Brad mused. "Looks like she has been planning this for a while."

Where would she take Darcey? What did she have planned? Whatever it was, he was sure it wasn't good. He began to realize there could be no other answer—it was Lilly.

"Call the guys and get as many workers as you can muster up. Have them come here," Brad instructed Ty, who was already on the phone before Brad had finished the sentence. "Now, where would be the logical place for Lilly to take Darcey if she wanted to get rid of her?" Brad asked. The thought sent cold chills through his body.

"Some place where she would be sure no one would bother her. Maybe a place that is still under construction? Who has the work logs?" Ty asked, putting his phone back in his pocket.

"The work logs would be in Lilly's office. She has access to all of the construction information and does all of the ordering for the departments." Brad slammed his fist on the table. Damn. "I'm going back to her office. You stay here and coordinate the men when they get here. Divide them up into search teams. I should be back in about fifteen minutes." He bounded out the door and into the shuttle, flooring the accelerator again.

Opening Lilly's office door, Brad turned on the overheads, and two long strides brought him to the filing cabinets. He wasn't exactly sure how Lilly would have it filed. She did not file things the way other people did. Lilly had her own system, most likely designed to keep people coming back to her for the files they needed after they gave up trying to find them themselves.

Searching through several drawers with no luck, Brad decided to try the computer.

I should have thought of that first, he admonished himself angrily. Lilly would have entered the information there first, and then, made hardcopies to file.

Brad found the construction files and scanned through them, looking for completion dates. He discovered that dome number four was the only one that had not been worked on as of yesterday's date. Ten minutes later, he was back at Darcey's quarters where Ty had the guys divided up into search teams just waiting for Brad.

Brad shouted from the shuttle as he drove by. "Darcey's in dome number four."

The guys scrambled to the shuttles and followed Brad down the corridor. Brad knew it was going to take at least fifteen minutes, maybe more, to reach dome number four and then try to figure out just where Lilly would have taken Darcey.

Where would be the best place to start? Where could Lilly easily dispose of a body? That thought caused his heart to sink.

If Lilly wanted to dispose of Darcey's body, the easiest place for her to do that would be the sanitation station, he decided. Anxiety took over and his heart raced as he imagined what Lilly could have in mind for Darcey.

Brad grabbed his pager/walkie-talkie and opened a channel to Ty. "I think I know where to look for them. The sanitation station on number four. There is a dumping port there that can be accessed from the inside," he told Ty. "Tell the men that's where we're headed. Send some to come in from each direction so we can cut her off just in case she tries to escape."

"Will do, boss." Ty notified the others and they split up, going around the ring in opposite directions.

∽∾∽

The "Unlocked" light for the dumping port access door finally lit up. Lilly laughed and clapped her hands.

Yessss! She thought gleefully. *Now, to get that damn woman.*

She spun around and stepped out of the operation room. She did a little dance humming merrily as she made her way to the shuttle.

"Nooooo!" she screamed as she starred at the empty back seat.

The sound reverberated through the room and echoed down the corridor. Lilly scrambled into the shuttle, mumbling unintelligibly to herself. She slammed her foot on the accelerator and headed out the doorway. Not sure, which way Darcey would have gone, she went on instinct and headed to the right. Lilly did not think Darcey could have gotten far. She was on foot.

At the connecting corridor, Lilly paused. Darcey would have probably figured out that she was in the center ring and had to make it to the outer ring to find the connecting tunnel to the main dome, so Lilly turned to the right again.

∽∾∽

The sharp stabbing pain in Darcey's side was getting worse. She had to slow down and catch her breath. She hadn't run this much since high school. She stopped and rested her hands on her knees, breathing hard.

I can't stay here long. Surely, that connecting tunnel is close.

Pulling herself up, she started a steady jog down the corridor. Then she heard it. That soft, electric motor hum coming up behind her. She turned and saw Lilly in the shuttle bearing down on her. Darcey had nowhere to hide. She took off running again but knew it was useless. Still, she kept going—pushing herself harder.

Lilly got closer and closer, then aiming the shuttle, ran into the back of Darcey, sending her sprawling onto the corridor floor. Lilly pulled the shuttle up beside Darcey. An evil grin spread across her face. "Thought you could get away from me, did you? Well, you cannot." Lilly backed the shuttle up and rammed into Darcey again.

Lilly laughed as Darcey cried out in pain. Her leg throbbed from where the shuttle had hit it. She didn't think it was broken. She wasn't sure about her arm where the fender of the shuttle had caught it. The lump forming on the side of her head hurt like hell. Darcey tried to get up, but she couldn't get any leverage with her good arm. She saw Lilly get out of the shuttle. Lilly's face had turned into an evil mask as she walked toward Darcey. That was the last thing Darcey remembered.

Lilly reached for the wrench in the toolbox under the shuttle's seat. Grabbing it, she leaped out of the shuttle and walked over to where Darcey was struggling to get up. Lilly raised her arm and hit Darcey on the head with the wrench. Darcey slumped to the floor.

Grinning, Lilly stood back and placed her hands on her hips, the wrench still clutched in her right hand. "Serves you right. Now I have to load you up all over again," she grumbled.

Grabbing Darcey's arm with her free hand, Lilly dragged Darcey's limp body to the shuttle. The wrench clanged on the floor of the corridor as she tossed it aside and stepped up into the shuttle. Lilly pulled Darcey by the arms halfway into the shuttle then jumped out and pushed her legs and feet in. Darcey lay in a tangled mess on the shuttle's floor.

Humming, Lilly jumped back in the shuttle, turned it around, and headed back to the sanitation station. Seeing the port door, she gauged the distance she would need to stop the shuttle in order to have easy access to the dumping port door. She pulled up alongside it. Jumping out, she opened the access door and turned back to get Darcey.

She looked at the distance she would have to maneuver Darcey to shove her down the chute and realized she had misjudged the distance. She was too far away to move Darcey easily. She had to be closer.

No use in pulling a muscle, she decided. Lilly backed the shuttle up and maneuvered it closer to the door. That should do it.

She snatched up one of Darcey's legs and began pulling her out of the shuttle. She almost had Darcey all of the way out when she heard a sound out in the corridor.

Have to hurry, Lilly thought. She yanked harder on Darcey's leg. The final jerk dislodged Darcey, and she slid out of the shuttle, her head bouncing off its edge and then hitting the hard surface of the floor as she landed.

Lilly continued pulling on Darcey's leg, grunting as she gave it one final jerk to move Darcey closer to the door. She stepped around to lift Darcey under the arms and grunted as she pulled her up to the chute. She readjusted her hold for better leverage in order to drape Darcey's head and shoulders over the edge of the chute. She struggled with Darcey's dead weight that made it difficult to get Darcey into the position she wanted. Finally, she had Darcey's head and shoulders draped over the edge of the chute.

Just get the legs, Lilly thought, huffing, out of breath. *Get the legs and all of this will be over.*

Lilly heard another shuttle coming closer. Panicked, she worked faster to finish the task.

Just one more push and it will all be over, just one more push and it will all be over, she repeated, in her head, panting now. *I have to get this done now, and all will be okay again. I. Have. To. Do. This. I. Have. To. Do. This.*

Now, in a frenzy, Lilly blindly pushed on Darcey's unconscious body, inching it farther into the chute.

Brad was the first through the doorway. He headed straight for Lilly's shuttle. His heart stopped as he saw Darcey's body draped over the edge of the chute and Lilly frantically pushing on her. Furiously, he aimed his shuttle at the back of Lilly's and rammed it, sending it forward, out of the way.

Totally oblivious to what was happening around her, Lilly continued trying to get Darcey into the chute, all the while mumbling incoherently to herself.

Brad was out of his shuttle in a flash. He grabbed Lilly by the arm and jerked her away from Darcey. He heaved Lilly, sending her sprawling across the concrete floor several feet before coming to a stop. All the while, Brad held onto Darcey with his other hand to keep her from slipping over the edge and down the chute. His heart pounded wildly.

He lifted Darcey's limp body off the chute's edge and placed her gently on the floor, out of the way. Caressing her cheek he looked at the bruises already turning a deep shade of purple. Anger welled up inside of him.

Leaning over, he whispered in her ear, "I love you. You're safe now."

Brad's hands balled into fists as he stalked across the floor toward Lilly, who had pulled herself up and was heading back toward Darcey, her eyes glazed in fury.

"No. You. Don't!" He grabbed for her again, but Lilly jerked free and ran toward the dumping port door.

Brad reached for Lilly again but missed, as she side-stepped him. She was mumbling nonsense under her breath as she ran. Ty was closer now, and he tried to grab her, too, but she sidestepped him, also.

Lilly paused slightly and looked in Ty's direction. Her eyes were glazed orbs. She turned her gaze toward the dumping port door and sprinted off.

What started as a low chant turned into an explosive, deranged narrative. "I have to reach the chute. If I reach the chute, it will be all over, and I will have everything I ever wanted. I will be the hero. I will be the one who brought ORCA down. Everyone will look up to me. I will get rid of all of the useless cockroaches who are ruining my dome. Yes, my dome. I am in charge. Everyone will look up to me. Me. Everyone will do as I say," she screeched.

Lilly rushed madly forward, determined to reach the access door. She slowed only slightly as her body came in contact with the outer rim of the chute. Her arm stretched out and she slammed the palm of her hand into the flush button just before she dove headfirst down the chute. The auto-lock function kicked in as soon as the button was pushed. That triggered the port door to slam shut and lock behind Lilly.

Ty grabbed the handle on the door, but it had locked tight. He watched, powerless to save Lilly, as the chute filled with water. Once the chute had filled with the ice-cold seawater, the outer door opened triggering the vacuum to turn on. With a whooshing sound, the vacuum sucked the water out, taking Lilly with it. Brad rushed up, just in time to see the last of the water leave the chute and outer door shut. Both men stood there, starring through the window into the empty chute, unable to believe what just happened.

⌘

A blazing pain ran around in her head. Darcey reached up, touched the spot, winced, and moaned. She had a goose egg the size of a lime forming on the back of her head. Her arms and legs hurt. She didn't know how much until she tried to get up off the concrete floor. Unable to focus her eyes, Darcey thought she saw Brad running toward her, but couldn't be sure. Her sight was fading in and out. It hurt too much to move so she just lay there, moaning.

Brad knelt down beside Darcey. Thank God, she's safe. "Stay still," he said, softly. "We'll get you out of here." He looked up to see Matt and Ty rushing over. "I've called for the medics to come. They should be here in a few minutes," Brad said, taking off his jacket and rolling it up. Gently, he lifted Darcey's head and slipped the jacket under it. He held her hand, his heart pounding as he worried if she could have another concussion and more memory loss.

"I'm so sorry," he said, lifting her hand to his lips and kissing the palm. "I had no idea."

In spite of the pain, his kiss on the palm of her hand did crazy things to her. Her heart went into overdrive. The heat was rising in her body, and she wanted him. Her eyes closed. *This thing, this connection between us is real,* she thought through the haze of pain. *I am a part of him. He is a part of me. Together we are a whole.*

Brad watched as the passion lit her eyes before she closed them. He could feel it too, then as his eyes wandered over her battered and bruised body, a sharp pain stabbed his heart.

What would he have done if something worse had happened to her? He didn't even want to think about it. It hurt too much. Brad was sure he could not live without her. Darcey was a part of him. She made him complete. The vision of her when he first saw her floated through his memory. She was the oasis in the barren desert that his soul had been wandering through. Darcey was the essence that gave his soul life.

Anger welled up. Lilly was gone. There was nothing more he could do to her, but the ones who had set all of this in motion were still out there, and he was going to take them down. He had the list he had found in Lilly's office. He would start with that.

The medic's shuttle arrived. The two medics gave Darcey a quick once over and determined that nothing was broken, but thought she should be checked for a concussion—the lump on the back of her head looked bad. The two medics carefully lifted Darcey onto the gurney and carried her to the shuttle.

Brad stood and watched as the shuttle left. He would have gone with Darcey to the infirmary, but there were things that had to be taken care of here immediately. The one thing the dome did not have yet was a permanent security department.

Corporate had not deemed it necessary until the dome was officially open. The corporate headquarters would have to be notified, and they would call in the authorities. Brad decided he would notify Asad later.

"I'll need you all to make written reports on this," Brad said, to the men. "The authorities will want a written account of this, and you'll also have to give an oral statement. Just tell everything that you saw and did." He raked his fingers through his hair and kicked the tire of the shuttle. "Damn!"

Ty walked over and placed his hand on Brad's arm.

"Take it easy, boss man. This will all work out. We'll get whoever is behind this."

Brad turned and looked at him. "Yeah, and I know just where to start. Come on."

The list. Brad had to get back to the main operations room. He had tossed the list on Matt's desk when he rushed out looking for Darcey. He couldn't let anything happen to that list.

Reaching the operations room, Brad went directly to Matt's desk. He shuffled through the papers and various items on the desktop. No list. He checked the floor around the desk. No list there either. He paused trying to remember exactly what had done with the list. He remembered wadding it up before he tossed it on Matt's desk. Maybe someone had thought it was trash. The trashcan was empty.

"Hey! When did they pick up the trash?" Brad yelled, startling everyone in the room.

"'Bout an hour ago," Scott answered. "Want me to go chase 'em down? They should still be on their rounds."

"Yeah, let's go."

Brad was already out the door and had the shuttle in gear and moving when Scott jumped in.

Scott looked at Brad. "What's the rush?"

"I found a list of names in Lilly's office this morning, and I brought it back with me to the operations room. I was frustrated, so I wadded it up and then tossed it on Matt's desk. I'm sure that list has the name of the corporate contact that Lilly and Armando dealt with. I have to get that list. It is the key to all of this."

"Whoa! I had no idea. I picked it up off Matt's desk. I thought it was trash. Sorry, boss."

Brad laughed. "That's okay, but you'll be the one sorting through the trash to find it."

"Aw, com' on, boss. How was I to know it was important, huh?"

"Fine, I'll help."

They found the custodian's shuttle with the trailer of trash bags sitting at the back entrance of the Bajo el Mar Café. Brad jumped out and pulled the first bag off. Scott grabbed another. They wasted no time ripping the bags open and sorting through them.

The contents of six bags lay in disarray on the corridor floor before Scott jumped up and threw a wadded piece of paper at him. "That it?"

"Yes! Let's get all of this picked up before the guy comes back."

They put the last bag back on the trailer just as the custodian walked out of the Bajo el Mar Café's door. "What's goin' here?" he asked, gruffly.

Brad stood up.

"Oh, Mr. Daniels. I'm sorry I didn't know it was you. Is there anything I can help with?"

"No, I've found what I was looking for, but thanks anyway."

Brad handed the list to Scott and asked him to look over it and see if he recognized any of the names.

"Naw, none of these look familiar," Scott said.

"Oh, well, it was worth a try." Brad knew Scott and the others had come onboard after the virus had been found, so it was a long shot at best that he would have known anyone on the list.

Brad dropped Scott off at the operations room before he returned to his office. He watched the rich amber Scotch fill his glass. One big gulp almost emptied the glass.

I really needed that.

Refilling the glass, he walked over to the desk, sat down, and pulled the wrinkled list out of his pocket.

Carefully, he smoothed out the paper on his desk. The first thing he needed to do was to make a copy and put the original somewhere safe. Once the original was safe and locked away, Brad took the copy and sat down at the desk, scrutinizing all of the names and phone numbers. Besides Javier's name, one phone number looked familiar. If he was right, it was the phone number to Mon Rêve—Luis Vargas's ranch.

Brad took a big swallow of the Scotch as he stared at that number in disbelief. Anger began to boil inside him.

Can it be that Vargas has been a part of it all along?

Brad didn't want to believe that but there his phone number was in black and white. That at least meant Luis must know something about what was going on.

Apparently more than he was willing to share with me. I'm not going to jump to any conclusions, but I had trusted Lilly and look how that turned out.

He thought he knew Vargas. But did he? He only knew what Vargas had been willing to tell him. Brad remembered his college professor who had told him many times he was too trusting, always looking for the good in people. Instead, he had tried to impress on Brad that he should be more suspicious of people and their ulterior motives.

Maybe my professor was right. Right now, I certainly feel like he was.

Brad finished his Scotch and checked the time. The doctor should have finished the tests and Darcey would be back in her room by now. He couldn't wait any longer. This would have to wait till later. Brad folded the list up and shoved it in the back pocket of his jeans.

CHAPTER 21

Recovery

The doctor handed Darcey's chart to the nurse. "I believe a couple of pain pills and rest is all she needs," he explained. "The MRI showed nothing. I do want her to stay overnight for observation, though."

The nurse pushed Darcey's wheelchair out of the door and back to her room where Marti waited. Marti hovered around Darcey's bed as the nurse helped her into it. She reached for the glass but the nurse already had it in hand and filled the glass with water. The nurse tipped up a tiny plastic cup and two Extra-Strength Tylenol tablets tumbled into Darcey's hand.

Handing Darcey the glass of water, the nurse smiled. "The doctor said you are to rest. Take these, and I'll be back later to check on you." The nurse included Marti in her smile as she left the room.

Darcey hurt from head to toe, especially her head. She carefully turned it to the side to stay off the big goose egg throbbing on the back.

Marti had been pacing the floor, waiting for Darcey.

She knew she could take care of Darcey just as well as any nurse, maybe even better. So, as soon as the nurse left, she wasted no time starting to fuss over Darcey.

"I'm fine, Marti. Really I am. Just some bruises and a big lump on my head, but otherwise I'm okay."

Darcey laughed, as Marti gently pulled the pillow from behind her head and proceeded to fluff it, even though it didn't need it. She put it back, carefully avoiding the lump.

"Now isn't that better?" Marti smiled, looking around for something else to do for her.

"Marti! Stop! I'm fine. You don't have to worry about me. Lilly's gone. I don't have anything else to worry about. You need to go find Ty and fuss over him."

In spite of her head throbbing, Darcey laughed at the exasperated look on Marti's face.

"You never let me fuss over you, you know that— well you used to." Marti paused and pointed her forefinger at Darcey. "Anyway, I have you right where I want you and you are going to lay there and take it."

They both began laughing until tears rolled down their cheeks.

"Okay, gals, what's so funny?" Brad asked, stopping in the doorway before entering.

"Oh, nothing. Just Marti can't keep from mother-henning me." Darcey laughed again. "She's worrying me to death. I told her to go fuss over Ty. I bet he could use some of that awesome fussing—if you get my drift." Darcey winked at Brad.

Marti stuck her tongue out at Darcey as she sashayed out the door.

Brad jumped back out of Marti's way as she went out. Marti stuck her tongue out at Brad, too.

"What did I do?" he shouted, down the hall after her.

Marti turned and waved, giving Brad a toothy grin. "Later." With that, she disappeared around the corner.

"Come here," Darcey whispered.

She would have raised her arm, but right now, it hurt too much. All she wanted was to touch him, to feel his skin. More than anything else, she wanted him to kiss her. At that moment, that was about all she could do, but it would be enough.

Brad looked at her, lying in the bed, bruised, with no makeup, her copper-colored hair askew. She was beautiful. His heart turned over. The need to touch her, to kiss her was overwhelming. Brad gently placed his lips on hers, and the fires were ignited, racing through his body. Darcey purred under the soft assault of Brad's kisses. Suddenly he pulled away, breathing heavy.

He watched as Darcey's eyes flew open. Disbelief registered in her hazel eyes. "Why?"

It took all of his self-control not to gather her up and take her right then. "I can't do this now," he breathed, his voice heavy with passion. "I won't be able to stop if we keep going. And let's face it, you're in no shape to do what I have in mind."

Brad grinned that heart-stopping grin, taking a step back from the bed. Darcey grinned slyly, her eyes sparkling mischievously. "I know we can't really do what we both want to do, but I can't see where a little more kissing can hurt. Come on, whatta ya say?"

She ran the tip of her tongue provocatively over her lips.

Brad laughed. "We're a sorry pair." He bent over and kissed her, careful not to let himself go. It wasn't as satisfying as it could have been, but it would do for now.

"I love you, you know," he whispered, in her ear, "so very much."

"I know," she breathed slowly. Her fingers, that had

been entwined in Brad's hair, slowly slipped away. Her eyes closed as the Extra-Strength Tylenol did its job.

Brad stayed until he was sure Darcey was asleep before he slipped out and went back to his office. He wanted to call Luis to see if he had any insight into the things that had transpired over the last couple of days, especially the meaning of the list he had found and why Luis's phone number was on it. He suspected Luis had his finger somewhere on the pulse of everything that went on in ORCA. Although, Luis had never actually said he was connected to ORCA, Brad had been reading between the lines, noticing little slips by Luis in some of their conversations. Whether by design or unintentionally, he didn't know, those little slips gave him cause to wonder.

Brad glanced at his watch. It would be late, but not that late by Morocco standards. Right now, he didn't care if he disturbed Luis's evening or not. He needed answers. Pouring himself a Scotch, he sat down and reached for the phone.

The phone rang twice, three times—

"*Si*, Luis here."

"Luis, Brad here. We need to talk."

Over the next half an hour, Brad relayed the events that had happened over the last few days. As Luis listened, he began to realize that his hope of keeping Brad in the dark about his involvement with ORCA was quickly evaporating, especially since Brad had found the list in Lilly's office, a list that Lilly should not have had access to. Well, if he must reveal all, it should be done in person, not over the phone.

Luis waited until Brad had finished. "Yes. You are right. We do need to talk. I will send my jet to pick you up in the morning." He had many things to think about and decide how to handle the situation. There were preparations to be made.

"Have your pilot call me when he lands. I will be ready to leave by the time he has finished his check and refueling."

"Yes, I will. See you tomorrow." Luis rang off, his elbow resting on his desk, his head resting in his hand as he stared at the framed photo of Darcey on his desktop.

This is what Luis dreaded because it would mean exposing his involvement with ORCA and possibly the Eastern Alliance. His loyalty lay with ORCA and that was all Brad needed to know. There was no reason for Brad to know about his connection with the EA. It was purely to advance his "other" business interests.

In hindsight, Luis realized he should have kept a closer eye on Javier. One of his oldest friends, a member of the EA board, had called to inform him about Javier's plan to sabotage the Bio Dome Project. Luis's friend was hoping to get his influence to derail Javier before he did something that would jeopardize the Bio Dome Project as well as exposing him to the EA Board as one of the largest investors in the project. Unfortunately, by the time Luis's friend had worked up the nerve to contact Luis, it was too late. Javier already had his hooks in Armando and the plan had been set in motion.

According to Luis's friend, Javier had been approached by the EA and offered ten million dollars and a place on the EA Board if he would find a way to cripple the Bio-Dome Project before ORCA could reach the opening deadline. Javier had put together a plan and presented it to an eager EA Board. The board approved the plan, but it was not unanimous, nor was it without many changes to his original plan. Several more sensible members of the board had tried to put a stop to it, but, unfortunately, they were only a small part. The majority of the board was eager to embrace Javier's plan with open arms.

Although Javier tried to keep it secret that he was

Lilly's brother by having little or no contact with her, the news reached Luis. As soon as he confirmed their relationship, he sent members from his elite force to keep an eye on them both. Luis passed his suspicions on to Asad.

Since the Bio Dome Project began, Asad's security people had insisted there be surveillance equipment installed in all offices at all ORCA's locations to protect against corporate espionage. The bio dome was too important to take any chances. The Lima office not only had surveillance equipment topside, but they were also to be installed in the dome as soon as it was feasible. The equipment for the Lima office was scheduled to be installed the week the Bio Dome Project began. Unfortunately, that particular work order had mysteriously disappeared from the maintenance schedule.

It was only when Luis had informed Asad of the relationship between Javier and Lilly, and after he had requested the surveillance tapes be pulled for his review, that it was discovered the equipment had never been installed. Asad immediately instructed his security team to find the equipment and secretly connect it during the overnight hours when the office would be closed. He hoped that, by doing this, it would keep whoever had pulled the original work order ignorant of the fact that the equipment was now live.

Fortunately for the time being, Asad had been able to keep the turmoil at the Lima office and the dome internal. It was important that what had transpired not make it out into the public domain. Drawing unnecessary attention to ORCA's top-secret project would not be prudent. Asad had his suspicions that the EA was at the bottom of the sabotage attempt.

Luis was also thankful that the situation had not been made public. He could not afford to have his connection to the EA be known. It would damage his position on the

ORCA board, as many of the members had no idea of Luis's "other business."

Since Armando's murder, Javier had been keeping a low profile. No one had seen him for weeks. This worried Luis. He was waiting for Nicho's report on what he had found out after reviewing the last of the surveillance tapes. Nicho would be calling in the morning and what Luis would reveal to Brad would depend on what Nicho found out. Luis had too many stains on his soul. He did not want any of them rubbing off on Brad or Darcey. Besides, he had yet to tell Aicha about her granddaughter. He felt that the time was not yet right. Aicha had seen the photographs, yet she had not questioned him again about the results of the DNA test. Maybe she did not want to know and that worried him, too. How could she not want to know about Saleem's daughter?

CHAPTER 22

A Revelation

The nurse pushed open the door, letting the light from the hall stream in. It hit Brad in the face, waking him from a fitful sleep. He had spent the night in the recliner in Darcey's room after returning from his phone call with Luis.

Brad stood and stretched, twisting his torso from side to side. His back popped. A small stab of pain caused him to wince, but it relieved some of the kinks that had taken up residence overnight.

The nurse gave him only a cursory glance, as she busied herself taking Darcey's vitals. Darcey was awake and grinning at Brad as she watched him stretch, trying to straighten out his six-foot-seven-inch frame.

Darcey patiently waited until the nurse had left. "You look terrible." She laughed as the door to her room closed behind the nurse. Grinning sexily, she winked at him. "Come here and give me a good morning kiss. Your feeble effort last night left a lot to be desired,"

Brad sat down on the side of the bed, picked up her

hand, and kissed the palm. "Aw shucks, ma'am, I was just doin' my best not to hurt you."

Darcey jerked her hand back, shoved it under the blanket, and pouted at him. "Don't do that unless you plan to follow through,"

Brad grinned, slipping his hand under the blanket, reaching for hers. "Well, you're mighty feisty this morning. You must be feeling better,"

He closed his hand over her delicate one and pulled it out. Placing his thumb on her wrist, he felt her heart beating wildly.

Her hand was tingling where he held it, making small, soft circles on the back with his thumb, sending her heart into overdrive. "Yes, I am. What do you plan to do about it?" she teased.

"Well, you will have to wait until I get back from Morocco. I need to talk to Luis about all of this. It seems he has some information that could help me find out who is behind this whole situation." Brad paused lightly brushing her fingers with his lips. "I'm leaving this morning and should be back hopefully in a couple of days. I'll let you know."

His eyes darkened as he put the palm of her hand to his lips and kissed it. He watched the pupils of her eyes dilate to big round saucers. Brad could feel his desire rising. He laid her hand down.

Don't start something you can't finish, he admonished himself.

A heavy sigh escaped Brad's lips as he leaned over and kissed her forehead. Gently, he caressed her cheek with the back of his hand before turning and walking out the door.

Darcey lay there watching as he left. She already missed him.

⌘⌘

Hastily, Brad tossed some jeans and shirts in his bag, then, he debated whether to pack a suit. Even though he was only going to be gone a couple of days.

Might as well, he decided. *With Luis, I never know what he might have planned.*

Brad picked up his passport on the way out the door and stuffed it in his jacket pocket. A check with the chief at the docking bay informed him the sub should surface by seven, in plenty of time to make his seven-thirty departure time.

Back at his office, Brad called topside and notified them about Lilly. He told ORCA's main office director Leo Jordan on the phone that he would give a full statement to the authorities when he returned from Morocco. In the meantime, Ty, Matt, Scott, and Hot Dog, along with all of the workers who had helped, would have written statements and would be available to the authorities if needed. Brad cautioned Leo that Asad wanted all of it kept under wraps after the authorities had finished their investigation, and absolutely no media interviews. The official word from ORCA would be "No Comment."

Brad stopped by the operations room on his way to the docking bay to let Ty know the authorities had been notified and to expect them sometime today to talk with everyone.

"Be sure to keep an eye on Darcey for me," Brad told Ty.

"Won't be a problem. Marti has already taken over." Ty laughed and winked at Brad. "That gal wants to take care of everybody, and she does a mighty fine job of it, especially taking care of me."

"Then you'd better not let that one get away," Brad said over his shoulder as he headed out the door.

He had a short wait before he could board the sub. The trip to the surface was uneventful. He was still trying to figure out what went wrong with Lilly when he boarded the jet to Morocco.

Never in his wildest dreams would he have imagined anything like what he had witnessed in dome number four. It was bizarre—no—it was beyond bizarre. Lilly acted like she was on something, but he had never known her to use anything stronger than tea, maybe herbal tea once in a while, but nothing harder. Maybe Luis could shed some light on this and all of the other things that had been happening.

<div style="text-align:center">~~~</div>

Luis strode down the hallway, his boots thudding on the stone floor on his way to his office. Jose had buzzed the stables on the intercom to tell Luis that Nicho had called and would be calling back in fifteen minutes. Luis had just entered his office when the phone rang.

"*Buenas Dias*, Nicho. You have news for me?" Luis tossed his hat on the sofa and shouted for Jose to bring some coffee. "Sorry, you were saying?"

"Yes, I have gone through all of the tapes. It appears that Lilly was more involved than you thought. On one of the last tapes from Lilly's office, Javier and Lilly argued, and they were not cautious about what they said. Either they did not know the office was bugged or they just did not care. Regardless, it was a heated argument about Armando and the tech guys hired to take care of the virus. Lilly said Javier was an ass for hiring Armando. Javier told her he had no choice. The EA board had directed him to hire Armando as well as the technicians. Unfortunately, Javier did not mention who his contact on the EA board might be. Of course, all of this means nothing now that Lilly is dead and everything is secure again." Nicho paused waiting for Luis to respond.

"Yes, I suppose that is so," Luis said thoughtfully and motioned for Jose to set the coffee service on the credenza. "But it still does not answer who on the EA board might be behind it. How much damage did she do to the hydroponics system? Brad did not elaborate on that."

"None that I could find out. They apparently caught it in time before any damage could be done."

"That is good."

Jose poured Luis a cup of coffee and left.

"*Gracias*, Jose."

"The blow up happened before Armando's murder, and it does not appear that she has been in contact with Javier since. I suspect it was Javier who killed him. Lilly has had no contact with the EA since then either. In a couple of the last tapes, I observed her using some substance that she shot into her arm. For as long as you have had her under surveillance that has never happened before. I have no idea what it could have been," Nicho reported. "And on the very last tape, the day Lilly tried to murder Darcey, she is heard arranging to meet with Darcey that morning. There is nothing on the tape after that except for Brad searching through her files."

"Well, there is no use in worrying about it now. Lilly is gone and cannot be prosecuted. Javier is still around and can be charged. However, I am not sure what can be done to the EA board member or members who had their hands in this. We have no names and there is no hard evidence that any of the board were involved. We only have proof that Javier instigated it all."

Pausing, Luis thought for a few minutes. "Go get him and bring him here."

Luis sat staring out the window, watching the horses

in the paddock. His mind was weighing the options. Nicho's report gave Luis no reason to tell Brad about his involvement in Carlos's death or with the EA. He only needed to tell him what he knew about Lilly, Javier, his involvement with ORCA, and his knowledge of Armando's murder.

"Gracias, Nicho for your report." Luis turned around and refilled his cup. "I will personally take care of Javier once you get him here. There is no need to be gentle."

☙❧☙

Vargas's limo waited on the tarmac as Brad deplaned. Brad settled back for the forty-five-minute drive to the ranch. He poured himself a drink and relaxed against the soft leather seats of the limo. He was looking forward to seeing Luis again, in spite of everything.

Jose smiled as he held the doors open for Brad. "*Bienvenido*, Señor Daniels. It's good to see you again."

"Thank you, Jose, good to see you, too." Brad walked on into the foyer, his boot steps echoing down the hallway. "Is Señor Vargas in his office?"

"Si. Señor Vargas said you should go right in." Jose gave a slight bow and closed the doors.

Brad's footfalls preceded him down the hallway, giving Luis advance notice he had arrived.

Luis stepped out into the hallway to greet him. "Brad, my boy." Luis reached out his hand to him and pulled him into an embrace. "It is wonderful to see you. I hope you had a good trip."

"Yes, and it's good to see you again." Brad took Luis's hand and welcomed his embrace.

"Come in. How about a nightcap?" Luis put his hand on Brad's back and directed him into his office.

"Yes, that would be fine."

"Tell me, how is Darcey? You must tell me all about the incident with Lilly." Luis poured two drinks and handed one to Brad, noticing how exhausted he looked and the dark circles under his eyes.

A few days relaxing here will do him good, Luis thought.

"Darcey is fine. Just a few bruises, nothing serious." Brad looked at his drink, remembering her bruised body as the medics loaded her on the gurney. "She's handling it pretty well, considering she was almost killed. Darcey will be back in her quarters today. Her friend Marti will be keeping an eye on her…" His voice trailed off as he thought how close she had really come to death. The sickening feeling in the pit of his stomach started up again.

Luis sat down in the chair next to Brad's. "That is fine, I am most happy to hear that."

They chatted for a while, getting the obligatory topics out of the way. But before the conversation could turn to the real reason why Brad had come to Morocco, Luis said, "Now, my boy, we have lots to talk about, but not tonight. We will take this up in the morning. I will have Jose show you to your room."

Brad, seeing that Luis had closed the conversation for the evening, finished his drink. Luis stood, walked across the floor, and signaled for Jose, who must have been standing just outside because he immediately appeared as soon as Luis pulled the brocade sash beside the door.

"Show Señor Brad to his room, *por favor*," Luis said to Jose. Luis turned back to Brad, "See you in the morning. Sleep well." He walked out past Jose and down the hall.

Brad sat his empty glass on the desk. "Well, Jose, lead the way." He grinned at Jose as he followed his stiff back down the hall and up the main staircase. *Some things never change,* he thought.

"This will be your room, Señor Brad." Jose opened the doors for Brad to enter. "Will you need anything else?"

"No, thank you, Jose. Good night."

"*Buenas noches.*"

⁀ᴐᴇ⁀

Fresh country air greeted Brad as he stepped out on the balcony of his bedroom. He inhaled deeply. Brad loved the smell. It was exhilarating. The sun was just breaking over the horizon, silhouetting the distant mountains. Already the heat waves were rising from the ground. It will be hot today, he thought as he watched the horses milling around in the paddock. Brad saw Luis's horse among them.

Hmmm, so he is already back from his morning ride, he thought. *Breakfast is probably being served in the dining room. I certainly could us a cup of coffee right now.*

As he stepped back into the cool interior of the room, thoughts of Darcey flooded his mind. Brad checked the time. Darcey would still be up. Breakfast could wait. Sitting down on the edge of the bed, he reached for his phone and called Darcey.

"Hello."

Brad heard the soft melodic tones of her voice. He closed his eyes and relished the sound, but his inner voice poked him. *Something's wrong.*

"Hey, how are you feeling?" Brad asked, his ears alert in anticipation of her response.

"I was feeling just fine until the authorities came asking questions about how I knew Lilly and Armando, what did I know about Armando's murder, was I the woman in the wreck who was kidnapped, did I know anything about the murders at Armando's ranch," she said, in one big frustrated breath. "Thank goodness Marti was here. I know I couldn't have handled it by myself. They didn't believe me that I couldn't remember anything about Armando and the wreck." She drew a ragged breath, on the verge of tears, remembering all the nasty implied accusations. "Marti saw how they were upsetting me and called Ty. He came to my rescue and made them leave. To say they weren't pleased is an understatement. They will return as soon as you get back." She heaved another heavy sigh and closed her eyes. *Will this nightmare ever end?* she asked herself.

Her head began to throb. A tear slipped out of the corner of her eye and escaped down her cheek. Life was so much simpler at Señor Vargas's, she remembered.

Hey! No pity party allowed. You are stronger than that, her little voice chided her.

Oh, Brad, why can't you be here? She immediately felt selfish for even thinking that. Brad was in Morocco, trying to get to the bottom of the mess Lilly had created and keep the project on schedule. He was just doing his job. She sniffed again.

"I'm so sorry, babe. Don't worry anymore about it. I will take care of it. They won't bother you again," he promised.

Running his hand through his hair, he stood up and walked to the balcony doors. The vista before him faded as he tried to digest what she had just told him.

Brad couldn't believe this. Why was this happening now? Why would they think she had anything to do with the murders at Armando's when she couldn't even remember him? Maybe it was just that they thought she knew him, so figured she would have some information. Still, it made no sense. Darcey was in the dome when the murders occurred. Maybe Luis might have an answer.

Brad rubbed his hand across his eyes. It was obvious Darcey needed a change of scenery before she had a complete breakdown—he had a plan. "I have the perfect solution to all this chaos. I'm going to have Marti and Ty take you topside for a little shopping spree, credit card included. Besides, you haven't seen real sunlight for weeks," he said enthusiastically. He hoped it would boost her spirits and wished he could be there, protecting her from all of this.

"That would be nice," Darcey said, sniffing and smiling at the same time. "It would be wonderful to see real sunlight again."

The artificial sunlight in the dome was as close as it could get to the real stuff, but it's still not the same. And shopping? She had no idea how long it had been since she had been shopping—*Do I even like shopping?* That part of her memory had not revealed itself yet.

"Super! I'll make the arrangements. You won't have a thing to worry about, except deciding what to wear and where you want to go," he told her. "You go and get some rest. By the time you get up in the morning, all plans will be in place." Brad paused and said, his voice full of passion, "I love you. I miss you. You have no idea how much I hate being here, and not being able to protect you from all of this." He sensed the heat of their connection burning in him and could almost feel her.

"I know. I love you, too," she purred, holding the phone close to her mouth as if it would bring her closer to him. She felt the heat pulsing through her, closed her eyes, and let it envelope her.

Brad hung up, called Ty, and arranged for the shopping trip. He also asked him to watch out for the authorities and make sure they left Darcey alone.

Brad then called the ORCA's corporate lawyer and

informed him about how the authorities had harassed Darcey. The lawyer assured him that he would handle it, and Darcey would not be bothered again.

CHAPTER 23

Shopping

Darcey had no idea if she liked shopping as she flipped through the hangers draped with designer clothes. All of these clothes were given to her so she had no idea if they were actually things she would have bought for herself.

"Hurry up, girl, times a wastin'. We have some serious shopping to do," Marti hollered as she lounged on the sofa behind the headboard of the bed.

Darcey stuck her head around the closet door and pulled a face at Marti. "Did I really like shopping?" she asked, pulling on a pair of navy Dior slacks. She had discovered something about herself—she much preferred slacks to dresses.

"Yes, you do." Marti walked over to the closet and leaned against the door frame. "Back home, your closet is full of clothes, but it's mostly jeans and tees. You really are very casual. I remember the tough time I had coaxing you to buy a dress for the prom. You wanted to wear your Wranglers." Marti laughed. "Your Uncle Jack footed the bill for the dress. You took it back the next day and got a refund then, bought six pair of Wranglers." Laughing, Marti walked to the closet and selected a cream and navy print silk blouse and handed it to Darcey. "Here wear this. It will look good with those slacks."

Darcey smiled and took the blouse. Holding it up to her, she looked at her reflection in the mirror. "Yes, I think you're right. Will you hand me those sandals and I'll be ready to go?" Darcey asked, buttoning up the blouse. Slipping on the sandals, she gave herself a quick look in the mirror and grabbed Marti by the arm. "Let's go! What are you waiting for?" she said with a giggle and pulled Marty with her out the door.

A soccer match was playing on the flat screen TV. The home team scored the winning goal and the roar of the crowd drowned out the announcer as Ty and Scott jumped off the sofa and high-fived each other. Marti and Darcey looked at each other and burst out laughing.

"Okay, guys, let's go," Marti said, wrapping her arms around Ty's waist and giving him a squeeze.

Pulling her arms from around his waist, Ty planted a kiss on her forehead and led her out the door. Laughing, Scott and Darcey followed them.

ↀↀↀ

The captain lifted the hatch. The sun flooded through the opening and pooled on the sub's floor. Darcey grabbed a rung of the ladder and started up, feeling the warmth on her skin. Stepping out on the dock, she inhaled. The air tasted of salt and she remembered another sea voyage—Quin. She shook her head and walked down the gangway.

That was a hundred years ago.

Ty had arranged for a limo, so they piled in and

headed for the Larcomar Shopping Center. Marti had checked on the Internet for the best places to shop. There were several, but she thought this one looked the best.

Hours later, eight tired feet climbed into the waiting limo as the frustrated driver tried to fit their numerous bags and boxes in the trunk. The driver said something in Spanish under his breath as he slid in behind the steering wheel.

Darcey was exhausted and she laid her head on Marti's shoulder.

"That was fun, but I'm beat." She sighed and kicked off her sandals, pulled her feet up on the seat, and wiggled her toes just to make sure they still worked. "My feet will never be the same."

Everyone laughed.

Ty reached over and pushed the button, dropping a panel and revealing the bar behind. "I'll play bartender. What does everyone want?" he asked, as he examined the numerous bottles of alcohol and soft drinks.

Almost in unison, everyone gave Ty their choice. And, with the skill of a seasoned bartender, he prepared each request exactly as ordered.

"Where did you learn to do that?" Marti asked, looking at him over the rim of her glass.

"I haven't always been a geek you know. I had to work my way through college and bartending came easy to me." Ty grinned. "If they ever get rid of computers, I have a job to fall back on." He laughed and downed his drink then clicked the intercom button, signaling the driver.

"*Si, señor?*" the driver asked.

"Take us to the ORCA office, *por favor*," Ty told the driver and released the button. "I have to collect some paperwork for Matt, and I thought it would be fun for Darcey to see ORCA's corporate offices as well."

Darcey thought that would be fun, too. She had been wondering what topside, as everyone called it, looked like.

Ten minutes later, they pulled up in front of the building where the ORCA offices were located.

"We will probably be a little while," Ty told the driver, "Why don't you take a break and be back here…say…in an hour?" Ty handed him some money, then followed Marti, Darcey, and Scott through the front doors.

Ty grabbed Marti's hand and led the way through the reception area over to the elevators.

"ORCA's offices are on the fifth floor," he said, holding the elevator door open so they could enter.

The door closed, and Marti pushed the five button.

Darcey leaned back against the elevator wall and wished that it were a bed. She was soooo tired and had barely gotten her sandals back on. Her feet had swelled just enough that they were a real tight fit, and now they hurt even worse than before she took them off.

Maybe this tour won't involve too much walking. Maybe they could push me in one of the office chairs, she pondered.

Darcey's little pity party was interrupted when the elevator doors opened and Ty ushered everyone off. She stepped out of the elevator into an open area filled with cream-colored leather chairs, potted plants, and a huge semi-circle, marble topped reception counter that some-how looked familiar. It was like *déjà vu.*

Have I been here with Armando and don't remem-ber?

She didn't remember Armando, so she guessed it was possible, but somehow she didn't think so.

As Darcey contemplated why this looked familiar, a door at the end of the hall opened. She looked over and blinked. She was staring into the handsome face of Nicho.

Nicho! Nicho! She repeated over and over in her mind. Her heart fluttered, and a slow smile spread across her face.

Darcey took a small step forward, then, started running. She slammed into Nicho and wrapped her arms around his neck.

"Oh, Nicho! I can't believe it is actually you," she cried, out of breath, still holding tight to his neck. "I thought I would never see you again." She squeezed her eyes and buried her face in the side of his neck.

Nicho braced for Darcey's impact as he saw her running toward him. He was not sure he could handle the feel of her in his arms again. It had taken all of his resolve, these past several weeks, trying not to compare every woman he met with her.

As she flew into his arms, her arms locking around his neck, he hesitated only a second before wrapping her up in his arms and pulling her close. He closed his eyes and buried his face in her hair, her fragrance making him slightly lightheaded.

Someone cleared their throat.

Nicho opened his eyes and saw three pair of eyes staring at him and Darcey. He unwound her arms from around his neck and pushed her slightly away looking over her head at the three people watching. "I believe we have an audience," he whispered to her, his eyes never leaving the three people across the room.

"Oh!" Darcey had completely forgotten about Marti and the guys in her joy of seeing Nicho again. Blushing, she turned around to meet three stunned faces and cleared her throat, "I'm sorry. This is Nicho. He was my protector at Señor Vargas's. Nicho kept me sane and made my life there bearable." She knew she was blushing, but she couldn't stop. Her heart was light, and she even forgot her feet were hurting.

Marti was the first to reach them. She gave Darcey that "we're going to talk about this later" look, as she extended her hand toward Nicho. "Hi, I'm Marti Campbell."

Marti smiled sweetly at Nicho, but Darcey could tell she was in for some tough grilling when Marti glanced in her direction as she shook Nicho's hand.

"Yes," Darcey jumped in quickly, "Marti is my best friend and has been helping me recover my memory." She glared at Marti and turned to introduce the guys. "This is Ty Horton and Scott Taylor. They work in the dome with Brad."

"Nice meeting you all." Nicho shook hands with the guys and stepped back next to Darcey. It was all he could do to keep from putting his arm around her waist. The not-too-friendly vibes he got from those three let him know that his protective mode was still alive and well.

"Ah...eh...Ty why don't you take Marti and Scott and go pick up that paperwork for Matt? I'd like to visit with Nicho and catch up on what's been happening at Señor Vargas's," Darcey strongly suggested to them, looking directly at Marti. Darcey's blush had finally receded and she had almost returned to normal.

Marti took the cue but was not happy about it. "Come on, Ty, let's go get that stuff for Matt. You too, Scott," she said, as it looked like that Scott was planning on hanging around. Marti gave a glaring parting glance in Darcey's direction as she followed the guys through the door.

Darcey glared back at Marti as they disappeared through the door at the end of the hall then turned to see Nicho staring intently at her. "Oh, I've missed you," she said, placing her hand on his arm. She felt the muscles in his arm tighten and drew her hand back. "What are you doing here? How long are you staying? Are you going down to the dome?" Darcey bombarded him with questions, uncertain about his reaction to her touch.

"I am here on an errand for Señor Vargas. I will be leaving in the morning back to Morocco, and, no, I have no plans to go down to the dome," Nicho answered as quickly. He had to get away from her as soon as he could. Just being near her was painful.

If she touched him again, he would be lost. There would be no stopping him from taking her in his arms and that was something he did not want to do. He respected Brad too much. Their time together in Lima showed him Brad was a good man worthy of her.

Darcey sensed he was uncomfortable, and she couldn't understand why. Nicho was acting like he couldn't wait to get away from her. She needed an answer. "What's with you?" She glared accusingly at him, her hands on her hips. "Aren't you glad to see me or was I such a burden that you really did mean you were glad to get rid of me?"

Nicho looked into her hazel eyes that were shooting daggers at him and sighed. "Yes, I am glad to see you, and, no, you were not a burden." He sighed again then took her arm and led her down the hall into an empty office.

He shut the door and turned around. Darcey was just a few feet in front of him. In two steps, Nicho was right next to her. He only wanted to talk in private, but seeing her standing there he knew, he wanted more than talk. Reaching out, Nicho pulled her hard into his arms, smothering her face with kisses, finally finding her lips, and all the pent-up passion he had for her came flowing into the kiss. He would feel guilty about it later.

He felt her stiffen and then relax as he deepened the

kiss. Her arms wound around his neck, her hands played in his hair, and then she returned his kiss heartbeat for heartbeat. He pulled her tighter against his body. She felt so right in his arms.

Coming to her senses, Darcey pushed hard on his chest, pushing him away. "Nicho, please. We have to stop." She looked up into his face. His eyes were still dark with passion. "Why?"

"I am sorry. I do not know what came over me." Nicho pulled away and let his arms drop. Turning, he raked his fingers through his hair and walked to the window, his back to her. She heard him draw a ragged breath before he turned around but didn't look at her. "I should not have done that. Brad deserves better than that from me." He ran his hand across his brow and sighed. "The night of the Gala he asked me if you were in love with me and I told him no. But he never directly asked me if I were in love with you." Nicho raised his eyes and looked into Darcey's.

She could see the pain. "Y—you love me?" She stared at Nicho. "Why did you never tell me?" she breathed.

Nicho walked over and stopped a few feet away from Darcey. He looked her in the eye and held his hands out, palms up toward her. "You were not mine to love. You belonged to Vargas. I was to protect you, not to fall in love with you. But I had no control over it. The moment I saw you, I knew you would be trouble for me. I knew, even then, that I was falling for you, but would not admit it to myself until I saw you kicking and crying draped over Brad's shoulder as he carried you out the door. And, then, it was too late."

He gave a half-hearted smile and turned back toward the window. "I did not know how you felt about me. You never gave me any indication you felt more than friendship, your dinner companion, so I never let you know." He leaned forward, bracing himself with his arms against the windowsill. "I did not want to destroy what we had by pushing you into something. You had made very clear from the start that you did not want to be treated like a 'piece of meat,' I believe is how you put it."

Darcey's heart hurt for him. She owed so much to Nicho. He saved her. He kept her from falling to pieces. He was her rock. But she didn't feel that way about him. She may have when she was in Morocco, she didn't know, but not now. "I'm sorry, Nicho," she said, softly. She walked to where he was by the window and put her hand on his arm. She felt him stiffen. "I have always had feelings for you, but as a good friend. A very good friend." She saw the realization in his eyes that she would never feel for him the way he did for her.

He felt her hand on his arm. He looked into her eyes and saw that what he wanted most was not to be. It would be hard, but he would try to make it work, just being friends. Yes, he would always be her friend, but that did not stop him from wanting more.

It will be easier to handle when I am back in Morocco, he assured himself.

Darcey looked at the delicate watch encircling her wrist that Brad had given her. They had been in the office for almost half an hour. She figured Marti would be worried and, at this very minute, probably tearing the place apart looking for her.

"We'd better go." She smiled at Nicho and he gave her a small sad sideways grin.

"Yes, they will be looking for you. I am sure they think I have kidnapped you again. Your friends seem very protective of you," he said, opening the door and standing aside for her to pass through.

"Yes, they are. Brad gave them a directive to keep me safe while he is in Morocco."

"Morocco? Brad is in Morocco?" he asked, raising an eyebrow. "I will be there tomorrow. I will tell him you are being well taken care of."

Nicho closed the door and followed her into the reception area where he saw her friends were waiting. Pacing was more like it. He laughed to himself. Her friends would have made quick work of him if he had tried to harm her.

"Well, it's about time!" Marti scolded Darcey, with her hands on her hips and her left foot tapping the floor. "We've been waiting for almost an hour." Marti glared at her, through narrowed eyes.

"No, you haven't." Darcey laughed. "It's barely been thirty minutes."

Marti tried to still look mad, but a smile was creeping up the corners of her mouth. "Well, it seems like it."

"Okay, looks like everybody's here, so let's get going. The sub leaves in forty minutes." Ty looked at everyone and then his eyes settled on Nicho. "I guess I should say it's been nice meeting you, but I'm not sure it has." Brad had told him enough about Darcey's situation to know this guy had been a part of it.

Darcey raised an eyebrow at Ty and he turned and walked out with Marti and Scott. She looked back at Nicho and smiled. "I am so glad we met again. I have thought of you often, especially when I am feeling down and struggling to remember things about my past. I would think of how you kept me sane and how much just standing beside you made me feel safe, and I knew I would get through everything."

Nicho watched as Darcey's friends walked out, thinking they probably would have nothing good to say about him to Brad. He probably deserved it. The guilt of his actions settled like a rock in the pit of his stomach. Nicho turned back and saw that Darcey had extended her hand. He gently took it in his. It felt delicate and warm. Nicho pulled her toward him and gave her a hug as a friend. He would be glad to be back in Morocco and away from her. He needed time to heal.

His hug held none of the passion his previous embrace had. It was just as well because she couldn't return his feelings. This is how it would be from now on.

"I will not say goodbye, just until we meet again," he said, releasing her. The sad little smile was back and she felt sad, too.

It was a long, silent drive to the dock.

CHAPTER 24

Morocco

The kitchen staff was lining the buffet with the main course breakfast items when Brad walked into the dining room. Luis had just filled his cup with tea for the third time and was eyeing the delicious spread on the buffet.

"Brad! You are just in time," Luis said, greeting him. "Grab your plate and get started. I believe there are still some pastries left."

They ate in silence for a while, each wondering how to bring up the subject that neither particularly wanted to discuss.

"I suppose you have lots of questions for me," Luis finally said, taking a drink of the heavily sweetened green tea. "Let us finish breakfast and go to my office where I will answer everything that I can."

"Thank you, Luis." Brad laid his fork down and looked at Luis, then dropped his eyes and studied his plate. "Yes, I have questions."

The meal was finished in silence, Luis wondering

how Brad would take what he was going to say, and Brad wondering if he could believe what Luis would say.

Luis instructed Jose to bring coffee to his office as he followed Brad out of the dining room. Luis could only speculate on the questions Brad would have for him and hoped they would be ones he could answer truthfully.

Jose quietly brought the coffee service in and sat it on the credenza. He gave a slight bow and walked to the door, pulling it closed as he backed out.

Luis and Brad talked till it was well on noon. Luis had been able to answer Brad's questions without deviating from the truth. For that he was relieved. The thought of being untruthful to Brad, who he now considered family, was unthinkable.

Thankfully, the subject of Carlos only came up in passing as Brad thanked Luis for sending Nicho and Angelo to help him even the playing field although their services had not been needed. Brad was sorry, though, that he had been deprived of the pleasure of avenging Darcey's honor himself.

The only question left was who was the person or persons behind the attempted takeover and sabotage at ORCA. For that, Luis had no answer to give Brad. He had always presumed that it was Javier, who had orchestrated everything, but from what he had learned from Nicho, other parties on the EA board were involved as well.

Initially, all of the information that had filtered back to Luis said Javier was the one. The information came from a reliable source, so he had no reason to doubt it until now. His informant had never mentioned Lilly. It could be that they didn't know about her relationship with Javier or that she was involved, too. However, he thought that highly unlikely—if they knew about Javier, they would have known about Lilly. Javier had dropped off the grid after Armando's murder. If he was orchestrating it, why had he suddenly done a disappearing act right before the finish? It would appear that he was leaving it all up to Lilly to make it "fait accompli." Fortunately, Lilly would not make it happen, either.

News traveled fast, and Luis's old friend on the EA board called just a few hours after Brad had called with the news of Lilly's suicide. According to his friend, the board members were furious over the millions of dollars that had been lost on the deal and were frantically looking for Javier for an explanation. But, as of last night, he was nowhere to be found.

Who had informed the EA about Lilly so quickly? ORCA's head office was keeping it internal. The only other people who knew about it were the authorities. The EA could have an informant in either place. However, Luis felt sure it was not at ORCA, so that left the possibility of someone in the authorities. However, there was nothing he could do about that now. His influence did not stretch into the inner workings of the authorities. He had purposely avoided any contact with them, knowing that they most likely knew about his "business enterprises." Still, they had left him alone. But he was sure that, if he had tried to make a "friend" on the inside, it would have given them the opportunity to delve their sticky fingers in for a piece of his business.

Luis's friend had called back, right before Brad arrived last night, saying the board had received a message issuing a stand down on the mission. No one on the board knew who had sent the message. The message had been delivered by special messenger, and there had been much grumbling among the board members, especially the ones who had been backing Javier.

Luis was glad it was over, but he still did not know who was behind it. However, he would not rest until he knew. If they tried once, what was to keep them from try-ing again? It could be putting a lot of people in danger if another attempt were made to damage the inner workings of the dome.

Luis would put all of his resources on it, especially Nicho. Nicho had a knack for finding out things other people could not.

Jose gently tapped on the door before opening it to announce lunch was ready and ask if they would be din-ing in here or the dining room.

Luis looked at Brad, "Do you have more questions?"

Brad stood and stretched. "No, I think we have cov-ered everything we can for now."

"Fine. Then we will proceed to the dining room," Luis told Jose.

"*Si*, Señor Luis. I will tell the kitchen." Jose gave a slight bow and backed out of the room, closing the doors as he left.

"Nicho will be arriving this afternoon," Luis told Brad, walking to the dining room.

"I will be glad to see him again," Brad replied. "I like to think we sort of bonded over the Carlos thing. I wasn't too happy with him for the way he kept Darcey away from me at the Gala. But I realized he was only protecting her, and for that I am grateful."

Luis gave him a broad smile and a slap on the back as they entered the dining room. "Some time ask him about Darcey locking herself in the bathroom the day she arrived."

"Locked herself in the bathroom? Darcey hasn't told me much about her time here." Brad paused. "I haven't pushed her. I figured she would talk about it when she's ready." He sat down at the table and grinned at Luis with a twinkle in his eye. "But I'm sure going to ask Nicho about that."

420

Nicho boarded the jet for Morocco at eight. He would call Luis with his report after they were in the air, but was not sure how Luis would react to the information.

After his stupid lapse of good judgment with Darcey, Nicho had spent the rest of the day tracking down Javier. He started with the office call logs and discovered that several of the calls made to Armando and Lilly had actually come from a phone in the building. The last time a call came from that phone had been the day Armando was murdered. Checking phone locations, he found the office with the phone, but it was unoccupied and had been for over a year. No one in or around the area could remember seeing Javier or anyone else using that office.

Picking the call logs back up, he checked the outgoing calls from both Lilly and Armando. Calls from both were made to an unlisted number in Miraflores. Nicho reached voice mail when he called the number. He decided it was time to call in a favor from an acquaintance who worked for the phone company. One quick call and twenty minutes later he had the address.

Pulling up the tree-lined drive of the address his acquaintance had given him, Nicho noticed the mailbox was overflowing. Envelopes and periodicals covered the porch under the mailbox. Exiting the car, he followed the stone walkway that led around to the side of the house. He saw the garage door open, and a red Mercedes convertible parked inside.

This does not look good, he thought, his hand moving to the gun he had tucked in his waistband.

Continuing around on the stone walkway, he unlatched and opened the wrought iron gate to the backyard. Cautiously, he surveyed the area before stepping up on the stone patio. He paused before he moved slowly over to the French doors that led to the interior of the home. He tried the handle. It was locked. Then he peered through the glass into what looked like a study.

Nicho backed away quickly and headed for the front of the house, calling the authorities as he walked back to his car, having seen that Javier was lying in the middle of the floor, his throat cut. Nicho had no idea how long Javier had been dead, but it had to have been at least a couple of days for the edges of the blood pool to start drying out. Nicho definitely did not want to be here when the authorities arrived.

If Javier had been the mastermind behind the takeover and sabotage, who had killed him? Why had he been killed? Someone taking care of loose ends? Maybe, Nicho pondered. *That seems the most logical conclusion. This runs deeper than Luis had thought.*

An hour into the flight, Nicho put the call into Luis.

CHAPTER 25

Preparations

Brad's flight back to Lima was uneventful. Although he was disappointed that the question of who was behind everything could not be answered, Brad was sure Luis would not rest until he knew. And, with the opening of the dome on the horizon, Brad had to let that take top priority for now.

Ty and the guys had been working nonstop to get everything ready while Brad was in Morocco. Now, with the opening just a few days away, the RSVPs, from the invitations that had been sent out weeks earlier, were pouring in. From international dignitaries, world news media, to heads of state, all were confirming they would be there. Housekeeping and maintenance were working day and night preparing the quarters for the one hundred seventy guests who would be arriving.

The first crop from the hydroponic gardens had been successfully harvested by Matt and his crew and delivered to the chefs who were busy preparing the dishes that would be served at the opening. Brad had asked Darcey to go to the kitchens and consult with the chefs and to do some sample tasting. She found all of the dishes a delight to the palette and rivaled the meals that had been served at the Bel Ami Gala dinners. It was obvious that ORCA had spared no expense in employing top chefs from around the world for the dome.

With Lilly gone, that meant Brad had to coordinate the logistics for transporting everyone to the dome. He looked around for the data Lilly was supposed to have compiled but found nothing. A search of her computer turned up nothing relating to the opening, except a cancelation notice she had prepared but never sent to the sub company, canceling the fleet of subs ORCA was buying for the opening. Brad finalized the delivery date with the sub company then had Lilly's office sealed until after the opening was over so he could go through it with a fine-toothed comb. There were still unanswered questions concerning the last few days of Lilly's life.

It gave Darcey chills every time she had to pass Lilly's darkened office. She tried to avoid going that way as much as possible. With all of the work going on around Darcey, she felt totally useless. She wanted to help more than the few, yet delicious, tastings she had been doing. Brad assured her what she was doing was very important to the success of the opening. The variety of the food served would show that the hydroponic gardens were capable of producing food and sustaining a population of more than a thousand souls. This made Darcey feel better, but she still wanted to do more.

She still had not regained her full memory. Even though Marti kept telling her she was a successful graphic designer, Darcey didn't have a clue what it was she actually did. So she didn't feel like she could draw on that resource to help. Ty sensed her frustration and had given her a few odd errands to do, running paperwork back and forth between offices and job sites. Ty said Darcey was doing him a real big favor, and it saved him lots of time. Time he needed to spend making sure everything would be running smooth for the opening. Still, it didn't feel like she was doing enough. Brad reassured her again, for the umpteenth time, that what she was doing was contributing to the success of the opening. Even though they were little things that she had been charged to do, Darcey gave them all a hundred and ten percent effort.

She had talked Brad into sending the ORCA jet to fly down Ashley, Melanie, and Wendy in for the opening. Darcey suggested that Marti go on the jet to Dallas to pick up the girls so she could explain about the dome before they arrived. She thought about accompanying Marti, but just couldn't bear the thought of spending more time away from Brad. The few days he had been gone to Morocco to see Luis had been terrible. Having to deal with the authorities had been the worst. Thank goodness for Marti and Ty. She had no idea what Brad had told the authorities, but they never bothered her again.

Darcey hated the feeling of helplessness that seemed to surround her. Somewhere deep inside she knew she once stood on her own two feet with no help from anyone.

Yes, you did and you will again. The time is just not right yet. Be patient, her inner voice told her.

I don't know if I can.

Yes, you can. Remember—trust yourself.

Marti was back with the girls, now, and Darcey enjoyed getting them settled in the quarters that had been prepared for them. It was good visiting with the girls again, although the memory of them still remained out in the gray fringes of her mind. She felt awkward when they were doing a "remember when" and she couldn't remember, but they didn't seem to notice. Darcey realized they were truly her friends and wanted to help her as much as Marti did. She welcomed them with open arms.

❦

The response to the opening had been tremendous and, with one hundred seventy confirmed reservations, the logistics of getting everyone down safely depended on the expert captains and crews of the new ORCA subs. Brad called a meeting of all of the sub captains to coordinate the trips. Each captain had his schedule and list of passengers he would be responsible for. The trips were scheduled to begin two days before the official opening date.

The morning before the first guests were to arrive, Brad commandeered the girls to handle the decorations in the main plaza where all festivities would be happening. This appeared to be right up Ashley's alley, as she quickly took over and started coordinating everything and everyone. Darcey was amazed, watching her, and then she remembered Marti telling her Ashley was the party planner for their little group back home. In no time, Ashley had the plaza transformed into an elegant setting for the dome's opening festivities.

Watching from across the plaza, Brad folded his arms and leaned against the corridor wall, his eyes never leaving Darcey as she and the girls laughed and joked changing the main plaza into a wonderland setting. Brad could feel the electricity flowing between Darcey and himself, although she had not acknowledged his presence. She was beginning to look more like her old self. His Darcey was coming back. He watched as the new Darcey—feisty and vulnerable—begin to blend with the old Darcey—self-assured and confident. Brad had noticed the difference, in spite of the run in with the authorities, just in the few days he had been away to Morocco. Now, with Ashley and Marti here, the change was even more noticeable to him.

Even though Darcey had not seen Brad arrive, she knew he was there. A warm glow flowed through her body and she knew his eyes were on her. She looked up and smiled and she could feel the electricity pulsate between them.

"Well, looks like you gals have everything under control here," Brad said as he walked up. "Marti why don't you ask Ty to round up the guys and we'll all meet over in the park in dome number two. I'm cooking."

He grinned a toothy grin and everyone laughed.

Ashley jumped down from her perch on one of the tables. "Sounds like fun. What's on the menu?"

"Well, I thought I would take advantage of one of the grills that have been installed in the park there," Brad told her, pulling Darcey next to him. "They have to be tested and I thought we could do it with a bar-b-que. My grilling skills are world-renowned, you know," he finished smugly.

"What's this about world-renowned grilling skills?" Scott asked, sauntering over and leaning on the edge of a table next to Ashley.

Ashley fluttered her eyelashes at Scott. "We're going to bar-b-que over at the park in dome number two."

Another match in the making, Brad thought, as he gave Darcey a little squeeze and planted a kiss on her cheek.

"That sounds like a plan," Scott said. "When do we start?"

"Well, if you gals will get the food, Scott and I will round up the guys and head over to number two and check things out," Brad said. He pulled Darcey around in front of him and kissed her soundly on the lips.

"Now, now. There will be plenty of time for that later." Marti giggled and playfully slapped Brad on the arm before she started putting the unused decorations on a rolling cart.

"Right," Darcey said, pushing away from Brad and giving him a shove in the direction of Scott. "You guys go do the macho stuff and we'll get the food."

They were all laughing as they parted.

Ashley turned and walked backward out ahead of Darcey, Wendy, and Marti. "This is going to be lots of fun," she said, turning around as the others caught up to her.

Matt had asked Melanie to accompany him to check on the hydro gardens. The others stopped at the hydro and informed Matt of the plans then grabbed Melanie to go with them to the Dome Supply Store.

By the time the girls arrived, the guys had the grill going and the beer iced down. The girls made quick work of laying out the food, preparing the steaks, and setting the table before they also sat down with beers. The steaks sizzled as Brad slapped them on the glowing grill.

❧❧❧

The meal over and things cleaned up, the rest had wandered away in pairs, leaving Brad and Darcey alone in the park. Sitting on the grass, she leaned back against Brad, snuggled into his hard chest, and watched as the artificial daylight shifted into the twilight that would soon give way to night. Soft night sounds played in the background. Looking up, Darcey watched as the special effect evening stars made their appearance on the dome's ceiling. The grillwork lampposts came on and cast soft circles of light around the picnic area.

"If I didn't know we are actually five miles under the ocean, I would swear we are outdoors on a warm summer evening. It's beautiful here," she whispered, afraid if she spoke any louder the spell would be broken. "Who would believe you could build something so wonderful under the ocean? You are truly a genius," she said, snuggling farther back as Brad's arms closed tightly around her.

"It was my dream and, if it hadn't been for ORCA, it would have never been realized," he whispered, in her ear. "And, in a few hours the whole world will know about it."

CHAPTER 26

Showtime

The alarm blared, jolting Darcey out of a dream that was quickly becoming a nightmare. She rolled over, still breathing in gasps, her heart racing. Brad reached across her and shut the alarm off. He caressed the side of her face with his hand and breathed in her ear, "It's all right. I'm here. You don't have to be afraid anymore."

Her heart settled down.

Rising up, he kissed the tip of her nose and jumped out of bed. "Time to get up. Today is the day…" he shouted over his shoulder. The bathroom door shut and she missed the rest of what he was saying.

Still exhausted from last night's cocktail party, Darcey sat up on the side of the bed and waited to see if the room was going to spin or stay still. Nothing moved, so she stood up and made her way to the kitchen. She needed coffee—lots of it.

Ashley's plan and flawless execution of the cocktail party for the guests had been a hit. Brad had asked

Darcey to hostess the event, and she found she really enjoyed it. The confidence she felt interacting with the guests seemed a natural part of her life.

Possibly a part of my job with the ad agency, she wondered.

When all of this was over, she would have time to research who she was before her nightmare had begun. The struggle between who she was now and who she was then no longer worried her. Her little voice said she could be both and now she believed she could.

Yes, just as I told you, you will know when the time is right.

A resounding round of applause broke out as Brad and Darcey entered the Bajo Café where the guests were enjoying the first full meal prepared from the hydroponic gardens. Brad took her hand and they walked to the front of the dining room where a podium had been readied for the announcements of the plans for the day.

Brad gave a brief speech, welcoming and thanking everyone for attending the official opening of the dome. He introduced the section heads, who, each in turn, gave a brief description of their section. Finally, Brad explained that the number each guest had received as they entered would correspond to one of the tours on the schedule sheet that could be found in the center of each table. Lastly, he introduced the chefs who received a standing ovation from everyone in the room.

Scanning the guests, trying to remember faces and names of those who she had met last night at the party, Darcey's eyes kept coming back to an older woman in the back of the room, who kept watching her, almost to the point of outright staring. It made Darcey feel uncomfortable. She didn't remember seeing her at the party the previous evening. She would ask Brad if he had any idea who she was.

In the confusion of the guests finding their groups according to their numbers, Darcey lost track of the woman. Each section head greeted their group and the escorted tours began.

Brad finished speaking with the chefs, shaking hands with each one, as Darcey walked over and stood beside him. He wrapped his arm around her waist, watching the chefs disappear behind the kitchen doors, then turned and smiled at her, giving her a small squeeze. "That went well."

"Yes, very well," she said, thinking about the woman. "Did you notice the older woman who sat in the back? The one sitting by herself? She kept staring at me. It kind of gave me the creeps."

"No, I didn't. What did she look like?" Brad asked as they walked out of the Bajo, heading for their shuttle.

"The woman had on an embroidered black, two-piece Kaftan. She looked to be maybe in her seventies or eighties. Not sure. A scarf partially hid her face."

"No, I don't remember seeing her, but I'll keep an eye out for her while I'm visiting the tours," Brad said stopping the shuttle in the main plaza.

Darcey hopped out, noticing that Marti and the girls were already there. They were preparing the plaza for the noon meal.

"Okay. I'll see you later," Darcey said, leaning in to give Brad a kiss. That little uneasiness in the pit of her stomach fluttered again. She ignored it. There was too much to do and she didn't give it another thought.

Working quickly, the girls had the plaza transformed from the party atmosphere of the night before into an elegant setting for a garden luncheon. The tours were scheduled to break for lunch around eleven-thirty giving the guests time to work their way back to the plaza by noon.

The chefs and the kitchen staff had everything prepared when the guests started to arrive. The elongated 'S' shaped buffet table featured an ice sculpture at each end of the table and one in the middle. In between, were an array of delicacies from each guest's country, and all had been prepared from the produce grown in the hydro gardens.

Giving the buffet table one last look before Darcey assumed her role as hostess, she mentioned the woman to Marti and the girls, and they volunteered to help look for her, too. Darcey was hoping that one of them could get close enough to read her nametag without making contact.

The guests began filing in, and Darcey kept her eye out for the woman as she greeted them. She spotted the woman when she came in with a group of seven. The woman stayed on the outer edge of the group away from Darcey so she had no opportunity to read the nametag. Darcey didn't have time to study the woman but tried to watch where her group was seated. She only hoped that Marti had seen her, too. The last of the guests had been through the buffet line and were seated before Darcey had a chance to talk with Marti.

"Did you see her?" Darcey asked, walking up to Marti as she filled her plate.

"Yes, she is with the group from Morocco," Marti said, turning slightly to indicate where the group was seated.

Morocco? That was interesting. Bard had not mentioned anything about someone from Morocco coming. Darcey wondered if Vargas was here also. However, she had not seen him.

She picked up a plate and followed Marti down the

buffet table. When the table curved, she could see the woman without looking over her shoulder. The woman was staring at Darcey. She smiled, acknowledging the woman's stare. The woman looked quickly away and started conversing with the person next to her. It was obvious the woman had not intended for Darcey to catch her watching. That little twinge of foreboding came up in her stomach again.

Marti elbowed Darcey. "There's a table just behind the table where she is sitting that's empty. Let's mosey over that way."

Ashley, Melanie, and Wendy were already headed in that direction. Darcey followed Marti as she skirted around the dining area to avoid walking through the rows of tables. Darcey kept watch on the woman out of the corner of her eye as they made their way to the empty table. She had the distinct feeling the woman was doing the same, although she never looked directly at Darcey again.

"Did any of you get a chance to read her nametag?" Darcey asked, placing her half-full plate on the table before sitting down.

"Yes," Wendy said, casually looking in the woman's direction. "Her name is Aicha Kaddur. She is with the Morco Investments and Securities Company group. I believe they are an investor in the project."

"Thanks, Wendy. Who has the list of the guests?" Darcey asked.

"I do," Ashley said, flipping open the folder she had placed in the middle of the table. "Here is the list."

Darcey quickly scanned the list looking for the group's name. She found it and there were seven names listed as invited members, but Aicha Kaddur was not among them. That was odd since no one was to be admitted without an invitation. Darcey looked through the other groups and the names in each group. The woman's name was not on the official list anywhere. The knot in Darcey's stomach tightened.

"Excuse me, I've got to find Brad," she said, picking up the folder.

Breathe. Don't panic. Find Brad and let him explain. You don't know what this means yet, her inner voice cautioned.

I know, but you said to trust my instincts and right now they want to push the panic button, and I don't know why.

Find Brad. He will know.

Darcey slipped out, making sure the woman did not see her. At least she hoped the woman hadn't. She went directly to Brad's office. He had said he would be there until the luncheon was over letting the section heads take care of the guests.

The door was open, but he wasn't there. Darcey paced back and forth, waiting. Surely, he wouldn't be gone long. She sat down. Fidgeting in the chair, she decided pacing back and forth would be better, and she needed something to do. She got up. She had made three circles around Brad's office when he walked through the door.

"What's up?" he asked, walking up to her taking hold of her arms.

She pulled away. "That woman. The one I told you about at breakfast. Her name is not on the list," she said, near panic and shaking the list at him.

"Whoa, slow down," Brad said, grabbing her hand with the list. He gently took it from her. "Here sit down and tell me what this is all about."

"That woman. I found out her name and she's *not* on the list," she said, with emphasis on "not.'"

"What's her name? I'm sure you just overlooked it.

You know no one is here unless they had an invitation," he said, sitting down behind the desk.

Brad could feel her anxiety rising and knew he had to calm her down before she reached full-blown panic mode. He had been keeping an eye out for the woman but hadn't seen her yet. He had three more groups to visit with this afternoon. Most likely she would be in one of those.

"Her name is Aicha Kaddur. She's from Morocco and she's not on the list." Darcey stared at Brad wondering how he could sit there so calmly. There was something not right about this woman being here. She could feel it. Surely, he could feel it too.

Brad's face betrayed nothing. He couldn't let her see how much that name upset him. And she was right. Aicha was not on the list. Brad had not issued an invitation to her, so how did she get one? Then it hit him—Luis. That was the only way. Luis had connections.

"I will look into this. I'm sure there is a reasonable explanation," he said softly, coming around the desk. He reached his arms out to her. He had to make her feel safe again.

With his arms open, Darcey all but flew into his embrace. He wrapped them around her and she felt safe. Darcey buried her face in the curve of his neck. She didn't know why, but she knew there was something very wrong with this woman being here.

CHAPTER 27

Aicha Kaddur

Brad walked Darcey back to the plaza. She discretely pointed out the woman and went back to finish her meal with the girls. She felt much better now. She really felt foolish and was sure she had blown it all out of proportion, although that foreboding twinge was still there.

Brad visited with some of the guests, working his way toward the table where the woman sat. As he approached the table, the woman excused herself and walked off in the opposite direction. Brad reached the table, introduced himself, and politely asked their names. After introductions, Brad asked who the señora was that left just before he arrived. No one at the table had any idea who the woman was. They said she had just joined their group before the tour this morning, saying she was by herself and asking could she join them. No one seemed to remember her mentioning her name although she did have a nametag and possibly presumed that was enough of an introduction.

Perhaps Darcey had a right to be worried. Brad did not like the direction this was taking. He had to talk to Luis.

Brad stopped at a few more tables before making his way back to his office to call Luis. The man had some explaining to do. For the life of him, Brad couldn't figure out what would possess Luis to send Aicha here. Glancing at his watch, he decided to wait an hour before calling him. The last two times he had called he had gotten Luis out of bed. Probably shouldn't try for a third, he mused, chuckling to himself.

Brad picked up the guest list lying on the desk and thumbed through it. What group had Darcey said she was with…Morco something? He ran his finger down the list. There it is, Morco Investments and Securities Company. Darcey is right. Aicha's name is not there.

Unfortunately, none of the seven names listed rang a bell. Luis had not mentioned any of these people. Brad flipped back through the list of names, checking to see if maybe she had been listed under some other company. He recognized many of the names.

Although he had not met them, he basically knew who they were. Corporate had made up the guest list. Maybe he should call the office topside and see if they could shed some light on this before he called Luis. Brad rang the main office extension and asked to speak with Aarón Cruz, the new Lima office director. Cruz would have been the one who would have made up the guest list.

"¡*Hola*! Aarón here," Cruz answered.

"Brad Daniels here. I have a question about the guest list, if you have a minute," Brad inquired.

"Certainly. What is it you wish to know," Cruz replied.

"Well, we have a lady here who is not on the guest

list, and I am wondering how this could have happened," Brad said, leaning back in his chair.

"I'm not sure. What is the lady's name?"

"Señora Aicha Kaddur," Brad said.

There was silence on the end. Cruz cleared his throat. "Ah—hem—yes. I am sorry I do not have an answer for you, at the moment. I will get back to you. Please excuse me." Then he hung up, the dial tone buzzing in Brad's ear.

That was strange.

The heck with waiting for Luis to get up, Brad was calling.

The phone rang once, twice. "*Si*, Luis here," a sleepy voice mumbled into the phone.

"Brad here. Sorry for the early hour, but I have a situation here, and I hope you are the one who can help me out."

"What is it with you, Brad? Can you not call at a decent hour?" Luis grumbled.

Brad smiled at Luis's discomfort. "Sorry, I tried to wait, but things have been developing fast here and I need some answers."

"Okay, okay, I am up. What is this situation that demands my immediate attention?" Luis asked, throwing back the sheet and swinging his legs over the side of the bed as he sat up.

"Aicha Kaddur."

"What?" Luis was now wide-awake.

"Aicha Kaddur is here."

"That is impossible. How did she get an invitation?" Luis demanded.

"I don't know. I was hoping you could tell me."

"Well, I did not get it for her. They sent me the list for approval, and her name was not on it. If it had been, I would have taken it off," he declared.

"Then who would have arranged it for her? Have you spoken to her about Darcey? Do I need to be worried about this?" Brad asked as a twinge of foreboding hit his stomach.

"I have not seen or spoken to Aicha since I asked for her DNA for the test. Aicha did not even call me back to find out the results. She did not seem interested if Darcey was Saleem's daughter. I suppose I should have been suspicious when she did not call back. But I was so elated with the news it never crossed my mind," Luis said, as if thinking out loud. "No, I have no idea who could have arranged an invitation for her, but I will find out. Yes, I would keep an eye on Darcey. I do not think she would do anything to harm her, but it will not hurt to be cautious."

"All right, I'll tell my people to keep a close eye on the woman and Darcey. Also, just before I called you, I called Aarón Cruz in the office here to check on Aicha. When I asked how she got an invitation he said he couldn't answer that and hung up on me. Any idea what that was all about?"

"No. Let me do some calling, and I will get back to you. Other than that, how is the opening going?" Luis had managed to slip into his robe and ring for Jose to bring his morning tea.

"It's fantastic. We're finishing up the section tours this afternoon, for which I need to get going. I have three more groups to see. Tonight will be the ball, and then trips to the surface will begin in the morning. Call me as soon as you know something." Brad hung up and joined the group passing his office on the way to the operations room.

He followed the group into the room. Ty had just started talking about the functions of the panels when Brad noticed the woman standing off to the side. He moved around to get closer and, as he moved, so did she. The woman waited until he was almost to her before she walked into the middle of the group and out the other side, close to the door. By the time Brad had made his way to the door, she had already disappeared.

Brad took out his cell and called Darcey. She answered on the first ring.

"Where are you?" he asked, a little breathless.

"I'm helping get things ready for the ball tonight. Why?" That knot in her stomach grew tighter, listening to Brad.

"Where are the girls?" he asked

"They're right here. We're all working to get things ready. What's going on? You're beginning to scare me," she said. She could feel his agitation through the phone.

"I've talked with Luis and he thinks you should be with someone at all times until this is over. Luis doesn't know what this woman wants, but he thinks it best for you to be cautious. I want you to have one of the girls with you every place you go. Do you understand?" His voice left no doubt that it was an order, not a request.

"Yes, I understand and I will," she said, her hands beginning to shake, the knot in her stomach tightening almost to the point of nausea.

Darcey sat down at the table closest to her. Her knees felt as if they would give way any second. Marti noticed something was wrong and rushed over, giving her that "are-you-okay" look.

Darcey nodded her head and tried to smile. "I'll be okay," she told Brad. "Marti is here. You know she won't let anything happen to me." She winked and smiled at Marti, trying to give the appearance of confidence. She guessed she didn't do such a convincing job since Marti looked more worried than before.

"I love you," Brad breathed into the phone.

"I love you, too," Darcey said, and they hung up at the same time.

"Now, just what is all of this about?" Marti demanded, standing in front of with Darcey hands on her hips.

"Brad has talked with his friend, and he thinks I should be cautious, at least until all of this is over. Brad wants one of you to be with me at all times. I hate imposing on you all, but I'm worried. I have no idea why she is interested in me. I've never seen her in my life. This woman was not supposed to have an invitation, and no one knows who gave it to her," Darcey said, putting her head in her hands and leaning her elbows on the tabletop.

"Now don't you worry, girlfriend, we'll take care of you," Marti said, rubbing her back as she motioned for the others to come over.

Darcey explained once more what was going on and what Brad wanted them to do. They were all eager to help.

CHAPTER 28

Getting Ready for the Ball

Well, girls, we've got to get a move on or we won't have this place ready for tonight," Darcey said, forcing herself to her feet. She still felt shaken but was not going to let it keep her from making the ball a success. *Damn the torpedoes. Full speed ahead!* she thought.

That was something she had been telling herself since the nightmare began when she needed all her will to tackle a difficult situation. It definitely seemed most appropriate for this situation.

"Right," Ashley chimed in. "We've got a lot to do, but if we work together, it won't take long. I've enlisted help from some of Matt's guys and a few from maintenance to help with the heavy stuff. They should be here in just a few minutes."

Ashley headed off to the storage bay with Melanie to get the table linens. The helpers arrived just as Darcey and Marti went to the kitchen to get the timeline on the delivery of the courses. Wendy started directing the helpers as Darcey and Marti walked down the corridor.

Tonight's dinner would be a black tie, sit-down affair, served by the kitchen staff. Marti double-checked the menu while Darcey confirmed with the chefs the order of the courses. A sample place setting had been laid out on one of the worktables for their review. Darcey thought it was exceptional and congratulated the chef on the choice of dinnerware. However, she asked them to replace the wine glasses with a simpler one so it wouldn't overpower the China. Marti agreed.

Arriving back at the plaza, they were amazed at the amount of work that had been accomplished just in the short time they had been gone. The tables and chairs were all arranged and the linens were being added. The rolling carts from the kitchen with the place settings arrived only minutes later, and Ashley directed some of the workers on how the settings should be arranged on the tables.

The fresh floral centerpieces would be placed an hour before the guest were due to arrive. The stage and dance floor were completed, the sound system and lighting had been set. Marti and Darcey watched as the orchestra members filed in and began arranging the chairs on the stage for a practice session. Darcey checked the time. It was going on four when they all stood back and surveyed their handiwork.

Cocktails were being served around seven, and dinner would be served just after eight. They had around three hours to get ready and since Brad wanted someone with her at all times, Darcey had a brilliant idea. She invited the girls back to her quarters to go shopping in her closet for their dresses to wear tonight. They were all about the same size and Darcey had lots of designer gowns. The girls were excited and talked nonstop on the way back to Darcey's quarters. Giggling and laughing, they headed straight for the closet. Darcey showed them the gowns and the jewelry they could use for tonight and, the shoes they could wear—if they fit—but no one could have her favorite black strappy heels.

Thank goodness, her bathroom had both a huge tub and a shower. This would be the first time all of the things that Vargas had given her would be used. It was "girl party time."

Darcey stood in the doorway, leaning against the frame, and watched as the girls sorted through the gowns. Smiling and musing to herself—I have friends—these are my friends. Then, as if a switch had been flipped, the fog lifted and her memories came flooding back. It was like a movie playing in her mind. She thought your life only flashed before your eyes when you were on the verge of dying, but, now, she was experiencing her life in Technicolor! It was wonderful—her parents, Uncle Jack, Marti, Sweetwater, girl's night out, college, high school, her job, her apartment, and Brad—every little detail about Brad. Her heart took wings and she had goose bumps of joy.

"I'm back!" she shouted, and the girls all spun around staring wide-eyed at her. "I'm back! I'm back!" she kept repeating, jumping up and down and twirling around, laughing and crying at the same time. "I remember everything! I know who I am! I know who you all are! I'm back!"

They all rushed over to hug her, all talking at once. Darcey was laughing and crying. She felt as if a ten-ton weight had been lifted from her soul. She knew who she was. They all collapsed on the floor in the middle of the closet, hugging each other, laughing and crying.

"This is wonderful!" Marti jumped up and pulled Darcey with her. "I knew you would remember." She wrapped her arms around Darcey, gave her a big-sister-bear-hug, and then turned around. "Okay, girls, enough of this. We have a ball to get ready for."

Laughing and talking, they finished dressing. It was just an hour before the first guests would start arriving when they walked out the door of Darcey's quarters. Running her card through the slot, she noticed some scratches on the device but didn't think too much about it. She made a mental note to tell Brad about it, though.

On the way to the plaza, Darcey let her life memories play in her mind as she mentally hugged herself. She could hardly wait to tell Brad.

I'm complete again. I know who I am, she thought joyously.

I told you it would happen when the time was right, her inner voice said.

Yes, yes, yes. I'm me again!

"We're here," Marti said, shaking Darcey's arm.

Darcey's eyes fluttered open. They must have slipped shut while she was remembering. "Yes, sorry. I was remembering the night I met Brad." She smiled and winked at Marti. "And you had to go and mess it up." She laughed, stepping out of the shuttle careful not to step on the hem of her dress.

"Well, excuse me." Marti grinned. "You have the rest of your life to remember that. Right now, you have a ball to put on. Come on, girl. Get a move on." She laughed, as she walked across the corridor and entered the plaza.

Darcey followed, grinning. Maintenance was putting out the last of the centerpieces on the tables and setting potted palms around the outer edge of the dance floor. Darcey walked over, stepped onto the floor, and twirled around, sending the skirt of her gown billowing out. She felt like someone who had just won the lottery. She had complete happiness again.

Across the corridor, an unseen pair of eyes watched from the shadows.

CHAPTER 29

A Proposal

The waiters stood ready with their trays laden with drinks and hors' de oeuvres, as the first of the guests began to arrive. Darcey stood vigil by the designated entrance, greeting the guests as they entered.

She looked up to see Brad heading her way across the plaza. Her heart skipped a beat as she openly admired her handsome, sexy man in his tux. A big lopsided grin spread across Brad's face as he saw her. She blushed and almost missed greeting the Spanish ambassador and his wife.

Brad watched the blush flush her face, making her even more beautiful. For a moment, he forgot just how uncomfortable he was in his tux. He put his arm around Darcey's waist and gave her a squeeze, brushing his lips across her cheek. "You look beautiful," he breathed in her ear. "How long do we have to stay at this thing?"

"As long as necessary. You're the host. It won't look good if the host leaves his own party." She giggled, then, quickly regained her composure as she welcomed a reporter from Globe International. "You have to quit that. I'll never make it through the evening if you keep that up. Go find some dignitary to talk to," she said, laughing as she elbowed him in the ribs.

"If that's the way you feel, I'm outta here."

Brad grinned that grin again and her heart did a little flip as he walked away.

He was having serious thoughts about grabbing Darcey and running away to the farthest part of the dome. But he couldn't. He was the "man of the hour." ORCA had given him the opportunity to make his dream come true, and he was going to enjoy every minute of it. The best part was now he had someone to share his dream with—Darcey. He was no longer alone. He had found his other half. He was now whole.

෧෩෧

The gong sounded, signaling everyone dinner was about to be served. Brad found Darcey and escorted her to the head table. She was seated next to an ORCA board member she had not met. Brad introduced them before sitting down.

"Nice to meet you, Señorita Callahan," he said. "Are you enjoying your stay in the dome?"

"Yes, very much. It's so unbelievable that all of this has been built on the ocean floor," Darcey said, noticing his smile didn't reach his eyes.

"Yes, it is. Brad is an engineering genius. We are lucky to have him," he said, looking past her to Brad. "We have great plans for him," he said, looking back at her, and she felt that twinge in the pit of her stomach again.

Darcey was about to answer him when the man seated next to him commanded his attention, and he turned away. She had a feeling he was just conversing with her because Brad had introduced them. Which was just as well, he made her uncomfortable and reminded her of some of the men at the Gala. Thank goodness, he ignored her for the rest of the dinner.

A dark, rich after-dinner coffee was being served when the head of ORCA Asad Damji, stood up at the podium and turned on the microphone. After a brief speech, he introduced Brad, who received a standing ovation as he came to the microphone.

Brad had worked for days on the speech—writing and rewriting it. He still wasn't satisfied with it, but time had run out, good or bad, he had to go with what he had. The closer to the end of his speech he got, the more nervous he became. Perspiration broke out on his forehead.

This is crazy, he thought. *Calm yourself down or you'll never get the words out,* he admonished himself. "…and, I want to thank ORCA again for giving me this opportunity to realize my dream. Now, I have another dream, but, I don't think ORCA can fulfill this one for me. For this dream, I will need the help of this beautiful young lady here." He reached his hand out to Darcey.

Darcey looked at Brad, wondering just what was going on. She placed her hand in his and stood up, giving him a nervous smile.

As Brad was helping Darcey stand, he reached his other hand into his jacket pocket and pulled out a small velvet box.

"Darcey Callahan, I need your help in fulfilling my second dream." He dropped her hand and opened the velvet box, revealing a gorgeous pear-shaped diamond surrounded by ten flawless ruby baguettes. A small gasp circulated through the audience as Brad took Darcey's left hand.

"When I met you, I knew I'd found my match. You

complete me. Take my love, multiply it by infinity, and you still have just a glimpse of how much I love you. From the depths of my soul that has been in love with you for an eternity, Darcey Callahan will you do me the honor of becoming Mrs. Brad Daniels?" He held his breath as he looked into her beautiful hazel eyes for the answer he saw there waiting to be said out loud to the world.

"Yes, oh my gosh! Yes!" Darcey almost screamed and jumped into his arms. She completely forgot there were two hundred pairs of eyes watching. Then it hit her, and she buried her face in Brad's white shirt. She could feel herself blushing, a blush that covered her entire body. She was vaguely aware of the applause as she raised her head and looked into Brad's emerald green eyes. He was grinning his lopsided grin as he reached for her left hand and slipped the ring on her ring finger.

The orchestra started playing a rendition of "This Guy's In Love With You," as Brad lifted her hand and kissed the palm before turning to the audience and raising their linked hands. The applause increased and everyone stood whistling and shouting "Bravo!"

She couldn't stop smiling. Her heart was overflowing with love. Earlier, she had thought she had found complete happiness again, but now she truly knew the meaning of happiness. They stood there holding hands and looking into each other eyes, completely oblivious to what was going on around them.

"I love you forever," she whispered, just before he claimed her lips. She had no idea how long the kiss lasted. The next thing she heard was Marti forcing a cough.

"Ah, guys?" Marti coughed again. "The workers are waiting to put this stuff away so the dancing can begin."

"Oh, my." Darcey blushed again and looked around. Some of the guests were still watching them, but most had moved away to the tables surrounding the dance floor. "I guess we'd better move." Laughing nervously, she looked at Marti, who was trying to look at her new piece of jewelry.

"Here, don't break your neck." Darcey laughed and held her hand out for Marty to admire her new engagement ring.

"It's beautiful," Marti said, hugging Darcey. "I am so excited for you. I just love a happy ending."

Brad walked up behind them and pulled Darcey back against him, nuzzling her neck and sending goose bumps all over her. "Shall we dance?" he asked, taking her hand and looking at her ring as he led her to the dance floor.

She settled in his arms like she had the first night they met at the Sweetwater. She knew she was home. The phone in his inside jacket pocket vibrated and she jumped.

"Damn!" he said, under his breath.

"That's okay. Go take it. It might be important," Darcey told him. "I'll go find one of the girls and sit with them till you get back."

"No. You're coming with me," he said, taking her hand. He led her off the dance floor. "I'm not letting you out of my sight tonight."

They stepped out into the corridor and stopped. Brad pulled the phone out of his pocket and looked at the caller ID. It was Luis.

"Brad here," he answered. "What did you find out?"

"No names, but I did find out the invitation was issued by the Eastern Alliance."

"The Eastern Alliance?"

"Yes. My contact said someone on the EA board initiated the invitation. He was unable to find out just who it was, but that the invitation had been requested specially for her. On the other thing with Cruz, he has not returned my calls either. I am not sure what to make of it. Cruz is new to ORCA, and I did not have a chance to personally vet him before they hired him. I have my suspicions about who vouched for hiring him, but as of yet I do not have enough proof to act on it," Luis finished, waiting for Brad to answer.

"Thank you for looking into it. I have tried to talk with her, but she evades me. I suppose I could call on my guys to search her out and detain her. But I don't want to cause a scene with the head of ORCA here and all of the guests," Brad said.

"So, Asad made it? I wondered if he would come. Asad is not one for social gatherings, so he must think very highly of you for him to attend,"

"Yes, I wondered about that. In fact, it went very well," Brad said, pulling Darcey close to his side. "On a happier note, I have some fantastic news. I have asked Darcey to marry me and she has accepted."

"What wonderful news!" Luis exclaimed. Excitement evident in his voice. "Have you set a date yet? Where will the wedding be? You must come here for the wedding, I insist."

"Whoa, slow down. Darcey just said yes twenty minutes ago." Brad laughed and gave Darcey a squeeze. "We'll talk it over and get back to you."

"So you just asked her tonight?"

Brad laughed and kissed Darcey on her forehead. "Yes, I proposed to her in front of the whole gathering. I think she was a little overwhelmed with it all."

"Well, you talk her into coming here for the wedding. I will make all of the arrangements. Darcey will want for nothing," Luis said, already making plans.

"Well, I will do my best, but no guarantees." Brad laughed. "Thanks, Luis. I've got to get back to my guests. I'll call you later." Brad put the phone back into his pocket and pulled Darcey into his arms. "Luis wants us to have the wedding at his ranch." He felt her stiffen.

"I don't know," she said, quietly. She didn't know how she felt about what had happened there. Now that she knew who she was, it threw a different perspective on everything. She wondered if she would be able to look at everything that happened there objectively. Nothing physically harming, or for that matter mentally, had happened to her. She was treated with respect and protected by Nicho. She had not been subjected to any of the horrors the other women had experienced before coming to Vargas's. All in all, she had been very fortunate, and for that she thanked God. "I don't know," she repeated again. "Let me think about it." She looked up at his emerald eyes, filled with love and passion. Brad put his finger under her chin and tilted her head back, kissing her neck under her jawbone, and then her lips.

"Ahem. 'scuse me, boss," Matt said, looking a little embarrassed. "Mr. Damji is lookin' for you. An' congrats on the engagement." He hurried back to the plaza.

Darcey could see Melanie standing just inside the corridor that opened into the plaza.

"We'd better go find Asad. I'm sure he will want to meet you." Brad took her hand and they walked back into the plaza where they saw Asad walking toward them.

"I want to extend my congratulations to you both," Asad said, extending his hand to Brad. He acknowledged Darcey with a slight bow and a gracious smile.

Darcey lowered her eyes and returned his smile. She wasn't exactly sure what the protocol was for this.

Brad shook his hand. "Thank you."

"I am retiring for the evening, but I want to meet with you in the morning before I leave. Will eight o'clock work for you?"

"Yes, that will be fine. My office. At eight? Would

you like me to have breakfast brought to my office as well?"

"No, just some strong tea will be fine." Asad turned once more and looked in Darcey's direction before leaving.

She wondered what that was all about. Maybe it had something to do with what that horrid man sitting beside her at dinner had mentioned. Brad took her by the hand and led her through the crowd to the dance floor.

"We have a dance to finish," he said twirling her around and pulling her into the circle of his arms.

CHAPTER 30

Morning

On the spur of the moment, Ashley had planned a small engagement celebration back at Brad's quarters after the ball. She had Ty commandeer several bottles of champagne and Marti boxed up some hors' de oeuvres from the kitchen for the little celebration. It was after two before Brad and Darcey turned out the lights and fell into each other arms.

Brad had set the alarm for six and he was up and dressed by six-forty-five. Darcey smelled the coffee and decided she had better get up, too.

"Mornin' sleepyhead," Brad said. "I was going to let you sleep in while I went to see Damji," He poured Darcey a cup of coffee. She scooted up onto one of the bar stools and reached for the cup. The light over the bar bounced off the diamond on her left hand. She stared at the ring. It was real. She hadn't dreamed it.

Brad watched her as she examined the ring. He had had it made special for her while he was in Morocco. It suited her.

"It's beautiful," she said, holding her hand out in front of her. She moved her hand back and forth watching as the diamond and rubies caught the light and sparkled. "I love you," she whispered, looking at him.

Brad moved around the counter and stood behind her. He spun her stool around to face him. Taking her face in his hands, he kissed her.

"Yes, I love you, too," he whispered, in her ear. Brad pulled her off the stool and held her close. She knew she was his and he was hers, now and forever, however long that might be.

⌘

Brad was in his office by seven thirty. The kitchen staff had delivered a pot of hot tea and one of coffee and a basket of scones. Brad poured a cup of coffee and wolfed down one of the scones to quiet his stomach's protesting that he hadn't eaten.

Asad arrived at eight on the dot and held out his hand. *"Buenos días."*

"Yes, it is," Brad said, smiling. They shook hands. "Tea?"

"Sí, por favor."

Asad took his cup of tea and sat down in the chair in front of Brad's desk. He looked around the room, and then back at Brad. "I have come to offer you a position at our Dubai office. I have a project in mind, and I believe you are the one who can make it happen." Asad watched Brad a moment before he proceeded. "This project will encompass some of what you have done here, but on a larger scale. I am not at liberty to give you specifics as of yet, but if you are interested, we will welcome you to come to Dubai and discuss this further." He paused, waiting for Brad to respond.

"I'm intrigued, to say the least, but this project has at least two more years before it is complete," Brad replied.

"Yes, we know, but that is not something that requires you here to accomplish," Asad said, setting his cup of tea on the desk. "You have an excellent staff who can complete this project. Of course, should there be any reason your presence should be required, you would be able to return."

"When do you foresee this project beginning?" Brad asked.

"We would like to start work on it in the next few months. I encourage you to come to Dubai." Asad smiled at Bard. "I do not know how soon you plan to be married, but Dubai is an excellent place for a honeymoon."

"Let me think this over. How soon do you need to know one way or the other?" Brad asked.

"By the end of the month will be fine. We do not want to rush you, but I believe you should come and learn more of the details before you decide," Asad said, standing up. "Give me a call when you plan to come and I will make arrangements. And, please bring your fiancé." He extended his hand to Brad.

"Yes, I will let you know soon." Brad shook his hand.

Brad watched as Asad's shuttle drove away. This new project sounded intriguing. He couldn't imagine what would be larger than this project, but whatever it was, it was too important to trust anywhere, but the Dubai office to talk about it. Security there was like Fort Knox. Brad would have to talk with Darcey before he made any decision.

He walked to the Bajo el Mar Café where the guests had assembled for a light breakfast and a formal goodbye from Brad. He noticed that Asad was not among them. Asad had probably already left in his own sub. Brad didn't notice the Kaddur woman either and wondered what had happened to her.

He pulled out his phone and called the chief of the sub bay, and asked if anyone other than Asad had left. The chief didn't think so. All of the subs were still docked and waiting for the passengers. Brad described the woman and asked the chief to keep an eye out for her.

As Brad finished his remarks, he noticed Darcey standing at the door ready to say goodbye to the guests. She looked beautiful in her navy and cream print kaftan.

The section heads joined Darcey at the door to say goodbye to the guests also. Brad talked and shook hands as he worked his way to the door. By the time he had reached it, most of the guests had departed. There were a few still visiting as they walked to the waiting shuttles.

The sub bay chief called Bard to report he had seen the woman board one of the subs and it had just left. Brad thanked him. He felt relieved.

"Come, let's go back to our quarters," Brad said, taking Darcey by the hand. "We have some things talk about."

Darcey smiled at Brad as he took her hand. That tingling sensation ran up her arm and she wondered if it would go away in time. She hoped not.

୧୭୧୭

"Okay, what things do we have to talk about?" Darcey asked as she curled up on the sofa, tucking her feet up under her kaftan.

"Well, Asad has another project he wants me to take on. It's something big. Bigger than this project, but I don't know what. Asad wouldn't say, but he wants us to come to Dubai and talk about it. I have till the end of the month to give him my decision after we've talked."

"Oh, that sounds wonderful, but what about the wedding. We have to plan that," she said then paused. "No, we don't. That's selfish of me. We can get married anytime. This is about your job."

"I just have to give my decision by the end of the month. The project won't start for several months," Brad said, sitting down, taking her hands, and kissing them. "We have plenty of time to plan the wedding." He pulled Darcey onto his lap and kissed her. "Speaking of planning a wedding, what do you think about Luis's invitation to have the wedding at the ranch?"

"I don't know. What about my family? How would they get there? And my friends? They can't afford it," she said, sitting up and looking at Brad.

"Not to worry," he said, pulling her back into his arms. Luis said he would take care of everything. He said for you not to worry about anything except setting the date." He laughed, hugging her closer.

"I don't know. I don't like the idea of imposing on him. It's too much," she said.

"Honey, he wouldn't have suggested it unless he wanted to do it. Luis does not suggest something unless he plans to do it. So, just pick a date and let him do everything else."

Darcey felt Brad's hand slip up under her kaftan as he kissed her on the neck. It was getting hard to breathe.

"Are you sure? Really sure?" she asked, her breath coming in short gasps.

"Yes, silly. I'm sure. You will make him the happiest man alive next to me, of course."

"Okay, call him. First what date do you want?" She sat up. She had to clear her head so she could concentrate.

"I don't care. You pick. Any date is okay with me as long as it makes you Mrs. Brad Daniels."

"Okay, let's do September twenty-sixth. It gives us four weeks and we can honeymoon in Dubai and you can give Asad your answer," Darcey said, grinning.

"That sounds like a plan. I'll call Luis." He dialed the phone. "Luis," Brad here. "The wedding date is September twenty-sixth if you still want to have it there."

"Yes, yes, yes. You have made my day!" Luis almost shouted. "When are you coming? There is much to do."

"We have to wrap things up here first. Probably the first of next week. How does that sound?"

"Wonderful! It will give me time to set appointments for fittings for Darcey's gown and her bridesmaids' gowns. Also, there is the food, the cake, the flowers, the guest list, travel arrangements. Oh, so much to do. I will get my ladies right on it. We have not had this much excitement since my fourth daughter's wedding. Tell Darcey, she has given my heart wings."

"Here tell her yourself." Brad handed the phone to Darcey.

"Hello?"

"Yes, Darcey. I cannot tell you how much you have made me happy. You must not worry about a thing. I will take care of it all. I will see you in a week." Luis hung up. She handed the phone back to Brad with a stunned look on her face.

"See I told you. Now, go get the girls and start planning the guest list."

The End?

About the Author

Madge Gressley lives in Missouri with her granddaughter and three dogs (Pixie, Lily, and Milo). An award-winning visual artist for over thirty years, she decided to trade her paintbrush and canvas for paper and pen—but, in this case, computer and keyboard—and started her writing career in 2013. She works from home where she squeezes her writing in between jobs for her graphic design business and letting the dogs in and out—a full-time job in itself.

Gressley is an accomplished, award-winning visual artist. She is a Signature Member of the Missouri Watercolor Society and Best of Missouri Hands Juried Artist. The scope of her artistic talent covers a wide range of media, including acrylic, oil, watercolor, clay, and graphic design. Her work is proudly displayed in the collections of numerous corporate and private collections throughout the United States, Great Britain, and China.

She is also co-owner and graphic designer for Art & Graphic Innovations, LLC, a Missouri based graphic design firm, and owner of MEG Originals Fine Art.

9 781626 947771